Richard Barnes studied medicine at Cambridge and University College Hospital, and pursued a career in teaching and research at Cambridge for many years. He is passionate about theatre, education, and equality of opportunity. He now writes murder mysteries which draw on his experience in both university and secondary education. Richard is married, with four grown-up children who are out there, saving the world.

This book is dedicated to my family, each and every one. To my brothers and my sister who have put up with my many drafts. To my children, who have provided, through their excellence in sport and in life, inspiration for many elements of this book. To their partners, who have added to the richness of our existence, and last but not least, to my own partner in life, Patti, as a fifty-second Anniversary gift.

Richard Barnes

KARMA

AUSTIN MACAULEY PUBLISHERS™

LONDON * CAMBRIDGE * NEW YORK * SHARJAH

A CIP catalogue record for this title is available from the British Library.

ISBN 9781035821693 (Paperback)
ISBN 9781035821716 (ePub e-book)
ISBN 9781035821709 (Audiobook)

www.austinmacauley.co.uk

First Published 2024
Austin Macauley Publishers Ltd®
1 Canada Square
Canary Wharf
London
E14 5AA

I would like to acknowledge the helpful criticism of all those who have read my first two books and encouraged me to improve my style. It is sometimes tough to take, but it is always worth listening.

By the same author

An Ideal Daughter (2022)

Scales of Justice (2023)

Chapter 1

Martha McArthy was fourteen years old. She lived in a smart house on West Blithedale Avenue, a quarter of a mile out of the centre of Mill Valley in Marin County, California. The family home was up among the redwoods. Her parents encouraged her to be independent. She earned money by babysitting for Dr Mark Strauss and his English wife, Sarah, who had two small children, aged five and three. In addition to paying her for babysitting, they allowed her to use their rather splendid swimming pool whenever she liked. It was a good arrangement. Martha's younger brother Vincent, just thirteen, was too young to babysit but he earned money by delivering newspapers, keeping the Strauss's pool clean and hygienic and doing the odd bit of gardening for them. Vincent was also a good athlete, but he was more into team sports. Tall for his age, he was all-state basketball in his age group.

Martha was a very popular girl, full of practical common sense and bursting with good humour. She was also remarkably intelligent and was being encouraged by her school, Marin High School, to think of Cal, Stanford, or an Ivy League as a college choice.

Martha was a middle-distance runner and captain of her school cross-country team. She was already well known throughout California for her potential as a 400 and 800 metre runner, with several state age group victories under her belt. In due course, a sports scholarship seemed a very likely possibility.

On this Saturday evening, Mark and Sarah were home rather later than usual. Martha had put the two children to bed at their regular bedtimes and had fallen asleep in front of the television. That is where the parents found her when they came home, a little shamefacedly, at 1 am.

"I'm so sorry," said Mark. "Let us pay you double for this evening. We were having such a good time, we quite forgot ourselves."

Martha rubbed her eyes sleepily. "That's alright, Dr Strauss," she said. "I'm glad you had a good time."

"Let me walk you home," said Strauss.

"Oh, no bother," said Martha. "It's only fifty yards. I'll call you as soon as I get there."

Mark Strauss was tired and a little drunk. He acquiesced to Martha walking home alone.

Mark and Sarah sat up for another twenty minutes and, when there had been no telephone call, they assumed that Martha had forgotten her promise to call and went off to bed.

Martha started to walk towards her home. It was, indeed, only fifty yards away from the Strauss home but it was pitch black, there being no streetlights on the Canyon Road beyond the city limits. There was not much moon this night, for the moon itself was very new.

Martha did not see the man hiding behind the trunk of the redwood by the gateway of her house. As she walked past him, he stepped out from behind the tree, clamped his hand over her mouth and dragged her into the bushes. He was wearing one of those stocking masks that hide the features.

Still holding his hand over her mouth, he showed her a large jagged edged knife he was holding and said, "If you scream, I will kill you. You will do as I say and then you will not be harmed. If you try to run, I will catch you and kill you. I know you are a very fast runner, but I'm also very fast; I'm faster than you. I'm going to remove my hand in a moment, and you will not make a sound. If you do, I will cut your throat."

The man released his hand and, almost before she realised it, replaced it with some duct tape, which gagged her but left both his hands free.

He tied her hands behind her back, blindfolded her, cut away her clothing, threw her, face down, on the ground and raped her. He raped her twice.

Then he tied her feet together, looped the cord around her neck, and left her there, lying on the ground, and simply walked away.

Martha lay there all night, lonely and frightened. She was unable to see anything, she was unable to free her hands or her feet. He had bound her expertly in such a way that when she tried to reach her feet with her hands, she pulled tight the rope he had looped around her neck. She almost throttled herself but was able to somehow loosen the rope again. She had no option but to lie still until someone found her.

The earth cooled quickly under the clear night sky and, with the classic California fog creeping in from the sea on the far side of the canyon, the night became very cold. There is a saying, falsely attributed to Mark Twain, that the coldest winter he ever spent was the summer in San Francisco. Although this saying is apocryphal, there is a truth that one side of Mill Valley gets the fog and is several degrees colder than the other side, but the cooling effect extends across the canyon to the houses on the far side. This is welcome in the heat of the summer, but on this occasion, and at night, it led to Martha's body temperature dropping dangerously low, so that she became confused and semi-comatose. It was not until the morning, at about 7 am, that the newspaper boy found Martha, naked, cold, and barely conscious, lying on the ground beyond the verge of Canyon Road, not more than fifteen yards from her front gate and safety.

The ambulance and paramedics arrived within minutes. Martha was wrapped in a space blanket and put onto a stretcher. The paramedics had brought with them some hot chocolate drink, very sweet, and they fed this to her in small sips. They put a thermistor device in her ear to monitor her body temperature via the tympanic membrane. Martha's mother, Patti, joined her in the ambulance which, sirens sounding and lights flashing, drove straight to the hospital where she was admitted to a critical care ward.

The police surgeon, an intelligent and sensitive young woman, was immediately involved in the treatment and examination. Alerted by the ambulance crew and police, she was waiting at the hospital when Martha arrived. She conducted the post-rape protocol to the letter. There was semen, and hence DNA, around Martha's pubic area and in the vagina. There was little else to find. The DNA would be able to convict the rapist, without a shadow of doubt on the part of the jury, if the culprit could be apprehended. If the DNA was on the database, that would be a rapid process; if not, it might take years, or it might never happen at all.

The police would check the CCTV in and around the centre of Mill Valley, and, especially, the traffic on West Blithedale Avenue heading up into the redwoods. There are basically two roads in and out of Mill Valley from Highway 101, at least as far as entry to the canyon goes, and they are Miller Avenue and East Blithedale Avenue, which become Corte Madera Avenue and West Blithedale Avenue respectively. Every car entering the city on the night in question would be logged and considered, but it would be a big ask, given the resources issue, to follow up on every car owner in any meaningful sort of way.

The information would probably be put into a database and held against any future similar analysis from the next crime scene. It was frustrating, but that is the reality of crime investigation in the twenty first century.

Martha's temperature on admission was 32.2°C and, using a forced warm air system, they had her temperature back to normal within four hours. Mrs McArthy knew things would be alright when Martha sat up in bed and asked for a stack of pancakes with some bacon and, please, another cup of hot chocolate. There were a lot of people in tears at that point, including some of the medical staff.

The doctors allowed the detectives to interview Martha as soon as she had eaten her way through the stack of pancakes. In fact, Detective Shapiro had to sit there and watch Martha finish her last few mouthfuls as his stomach rumbled, jealously.

'*What an amazing kid,*' he thought to himself. Then he said: "Martha. I'm Detective Lionel Shapiro. Do you mind if I ask you a few questions? Do you feel up to it?"

"Yes sir," said Martha.

"How do you feel?" asked Shapiro.

"Angry," said Martha. "Angry that some coward did this to me. I really hope you get him and lock him up indefinitely. I suppose I'm just glad he didn't kill me."

"I'm very glad too," said Shapiro. "Murder is always a possibility with rapists under these circumstances. Sometimes they just panic and do it. Sometimes they always meant to kill. I'm glad that he stopped short of killing you. But it shows a touch of arrogance on his part. It must mean that he thinks there is nothing you can tell us that will help us catch him. Is there anything? Can you tell me precisely what happened?"

"There is something Mr Shapiro" said Martha. "It is someone who either knows me or knows about me."

"What makes you say that?" asked Shapiro.

"There was something he said when he told me he was going to let go of me. He said, and I'm quoting exactly, 'If you try to run, I will catch you and kill you. I know you are a very fast runner, but I'm also very fast; I'm faster than you.' Either he has seen me run or he's read my times in the newspaper, I have had a lot of publicity through my running. But I think he must be someone who measures his own running speeds because how else would he know he's a quicker runner than me?"

'*Smart kid*,' thought Shapiro.

Martha went through the whole event from start to finish. She explained that she saw his hand and it was white, that he was wearing the stocking mask and she hardly saw him at all because he was always behind her and then he blindfolded her. She said he had a muscular body. She said he was quite tall because, when he was raping her, she could feel his knees digging into the top of her calves; he had raped her from behind.

She described the knife.

"It was one of those jagged edged knives, black and, possibly, orange with something written on the blade near where it inserted into the handle. I suppose the blade was about 4 inches long."

"Thanks, Martha. You're a very brave girl. I'm so sorry this happened to you. We will do our best to get the guy. I fear, otherwise, it may happen to other people. I know this feels a bit like shutting the stable door after the horse has bolted but I have a very good attack alarm here which I would like you to have. I'm reasonably confident you will not be attacked again but you might feel safer with this in your hand. If you just drop it on the ground, it will go off. No need even to press a button or anything like that."

"Thank you, Detective," said Martha. "He's not going to ruin my life, but I do need to make changes, just to feel that bit safer. I'll go to some self-protection classes and learn how to defend myself. I didn't stand a chance last night because it was all so sudden, and I was so unprepared. I still want to babysit and go out at night without fear. Catch him please. He mustn't do this to anyone else. Just one more thing, I'm sure he had a local accent, California."

The police combed the area around where Martha had been found, looking for clues, but there was really nothing they found that could help them make a swift arrest. They had the duct tape that had been removed from her mouth, and that contained a partial print or two, but, like the DNA evidence, without a suspect to match with, the prints were no use. The description of the knife matched a particular type of hunting knife associated with a well-known survival programme on television, Bear Grylls. Lots of these were sold by mail order throughout the States. It was unlikely to be able to narrow the search significantly.

They would check the DNA against the police database, and the fingerprints against all those on file, but this might be a completely novice criminal. One thing Shapiro was confident about, this might be the perpetrator's first offence, but it wouldn't be his last.

Chapter 2

Patti McArthy brought Vincent to see Martha that afternoon. He was upset but he hid it well and was as supportive as a thirteen-year-old could be, under the circumstances.

Mark Strauss was full of remorse. If only he had insisted on walking Martha home. It was only fifty yards; she had walked it dozens of times before. How was he to know that, on this occasion, a rapist would be lying in wait?

Martha was held overnight in hospital, mainly to recover from the hypothermia and exposure. She was released the next morning into the care of her mother, who had stayed overnight with her in a second bed in the same private room. Matthew McArthy, Martha's father, came with Vincent to collect the two women and, as they drove home, they talked about what had happened. Martha made it very clear to everyone that this event was not to become a focus for the family, she wanted to put it behind her and move on. It was not going to define her as a victim.

Shortly after Martha was released from hospital, she went around to see the Strauss family. It was very tough on the Strauss parents. They had so much guilt feeling. But Martha pointed out that she had insisted on walking home alone, that she had done it a hundred times before, and that it was not anyone else's fault that some sick psycho had been lying in wait. She said that she really liked babysitting the children, and she liked using the pool. Lying on her back in the pool, looking up through the fringes of the redwoods at the blue Californian sky was one of the highlights of her life. Please would they continue to ask her to babysit, and please would they try, as she was doing, to put the event out of their minds. It was done, and it was time to move on.

The crunch came about six weeks later when Martha realised that she was pregnant. It was impossible to know who was to blame for not administering the morning-after pill. It seemed somehow to have been forgotten in the rush to deal with the hypothermia and the physical trauma.

The McArthy family were Catholics but they realised that having a baby would destroy their daughter's life. It would rob her of the rest of her childhood, it would damage her dreams of going to Cal, it would stigmatise her in the eyes of so many. They decided to acquiesce to Martha's wish to terminate the pregnancy. The best Ob-Gyn doctor in Marin was Robert Simms. The McCarthys arranged for Martha to see Dr Simms at the medical centre in Sausalito as soon as they realised she was pregnant, and Dr Simms arranged to terminate the pregnancy for her.

It sounds perfectly straight-forward but this was a time of considerable unrest among the Ob-Gyn community, for a bill to legalise abortion on demand was due to be voted on in California in the very near future, and the pro-life lobby was strong. Robert Simms had a mirror on a stick that he used, to look under his car every time he got into it to drive anywhere. He was looking for bombs. He used it even when he went back to his car in the car park after going to a restaurant for a meal with his wife. It had become a way of life.

For Martha, her first ever clash with a dissident pro-life faction came as she arrived at the hospital for her pre-operative assessment. There was a barrage of hatred and vitriolic abuse hurled at her as she entered the clinic. She was called a whore, a murderess, and so many other names that it was impossible for her not to be upset. Dr Simms was wonderful with her. He explained that the protesters outside were there almost every day, that they felt very strongly about their cause, and that he and others ran the gauntlet almost every time they came to work.

He explained the procedure for terminating the pregnancy and both Martha and her parents signed consent forms. Because of her age, she was kept in the hospital overnight and her mother stayed with her in a private room. The following morning, Robert Simms called to check that all was well. He declared her fit to go home. He asked Martha and her mother to call on him to collect a discharge letter when they left the ward.

Robert's son Jonathan, Jonny for short, was sitting in his father's office writing a school assignment. Robert introduced Martha and her mother to his son. The boy looked up, looked down at his book and closed it, and looked up again. He could not take his eyes off Martha. This was not lost on either of the two parents, nor was it lost on Martha. Martha was feeling a little low and, perhaps, short of self-esteem after all that had happened, but it helped her no end

18

to know that this rather nice-looking young man was looking at her with more than a little interest.

"Hello Martha," said Jonny. "I'm afraid I've been a bit busy with one of my class assignments. I'm hoping to go to Cal, so I have to keep on top of my work."

"Me too," said Martha. "I want to be a doctor, so I was thinking Cal for pre-med first and then, maybe Stanford, or UCSF, or even somewhere on the East Coast."

"I know it's terribly rude to ask a lady her age so can I just ask you which grade you're in?" asked Jonny.

"I'm just finishing ninth grade," said Martha.

Jonny beamed a huge smile. "Me too. Maybe we'll be in the same freshman class. Do you do sport or music at all?"

"I run. And I play the piano and the violin, and I love singing," said Martha.

"I'm a cyclist," said Jonny. "I also do triathlon, but swimming is not my strongest event and, although I love running, that's less strong than my cycling. I also love singing, but I'm a lazy piano player and a very lazy violinist."

"Dad," said Jonny, "can Martha come over and have a meal with us sometime? If you'd like to, of course," he added to Martha.

"Could I, Mum?" asked Martha.

"Of course, dear," said Mrs McArthy. "If Dr Simms says it's OK."

Robert Simms thought about this. It is unethical for a doctor to go out with a patient, but this was a new one for him. Was it unethical for a doctor's family member to go out with a patient? This was clearly a date that his son was proposing. It was the first time his son had shown an interest in any young lady and, for Martha, it could be the final element in her healing. '*Don't be an idiot,*' he thought. Then he said: "I think you two youngsters had better exchange cell-phone numbers and fix it between you, don't you, Mrs McArthy?"

And that is what happened, and that is how Jonny and Martha first met.

Chapter 3

A couple of weeks later, the rapist was feeling smug. He had spotted the girl at an athletics meeting down in Palo Alto at the Stanford track. With curly blonde hair, green eyes with flecks of gold, freckles, and a ready smile, she had been impossible to ignore. That she was a brilliant runner and a suitably athletic build was a bonus. He had fantasised about her. He had gone home and googled her, seeking images on his laptop. He had done his homework, found out where she lived and observed her routines. Eventually, he had decided that his best chance of attacking her was after a baby-sitting session at the Strauss's. He really believed he had got away with it. That was why he felt so smug. Six weeks on and he was sure the police did not have a clue. He began to wonder whether this was something he might repeat, if he could find another victim worth taking the risk over.

He turned off the computer and went back into the lounge. His daughter, like her father, an athlete, was sitting there watching the National Geographic channel on television.

"Hi Daddy," said Sarah. "Are you taking me to the meet tomorrow?"

"Yes, Honey. Sure am. I wouldn't miss it for the world. Remind me what time we have to leave?"

"It's a 2 o'clock start for the events so we need to get there around 1:30, to warm up and register. Does that work, Daddy?"

"Sure does, sweetheart," he said. He gave her a very chaste peck on the cheek and, very gently, patted her bottom.

The next day, they packed Sarah's athletics kit into the car, added some drinks and some snacks, and drove off to the San Rafael High School Stadium where the track and field events were taking place. It was a three-way interschool meet between the San Rafael Bulldogs, Mill Valley Jaguars, for whom his daughter was running, and the Novato Hornets from very much upstate.

Sarah went off to the changing rooms and put on her athletics gear. It was too warm to wear a full tracksuit, but she did put on her tracksuit top, which marked her out as a Mill Valley Jaguar Varsity colours holder. It was one of the rules of the meets that each participant should be easily identifiable as belonging to one of the participating teams. Once stripped for action, their team running vests and shorts would mark them out clearly but even during the warmup and around the event they were meant to wear identifying clothing.

Sarah wondered why it was that her father seemed to be so distracted. She kept trying to attract his interest and attention and felt a little bit hurt when he seemed to be ignoring her and her event. She spent some time talking to Martha. Martha was not running today as she was only just back in training following some illness that the girls at Mill Valley High did not actually know about. She had come to the meeting with her new boy-friend Jonny. It was only while Sarah was talking to Martha that Sarah's father came over and showed any interest at all.

The four of them, Jonny, Sarah, Martha, and Mr Jackson, chatted for a while and that might have been that, but Sarah's father was becoming far too cocky and he made a huge mistake.

"Well," he said, "you girls run quite fast. Martha, your best time for 400 metres is 55.4 seconds. I'm faster than you. I bet even Jonny here is faster than you."

Martha's blood ran cold. She saw the knife, again; she heard the voice. The voice said, "I can run faster than you."

She recovered quickly. Surely it could not be Sarah's father who had raped her. Surely not? But it might just have been, and she started noticing, or, maybe just imagining, that he was staring at all the youngsters in their very short shorts and skimpy running vests, and the doubts began to creep in.

Jonny's response covered up the thinking time.

"Mr Jackson, I've no doubt you can run faster than these two, but I'm not sure I can. I might outlast them over 3,000 metres but 55.4 seconds for 400 is probably well beyond me."

"Mr Jackson," said Martha, "can I get you a drink or something?"

Flattered to distraction, Mr Jackson asked for a cup of coffee, and Martha duly went over to the refreshment stand and got three coffees, one for herself, one for Jonny, and one for him.

They chatted, seemingly happily, while they drank their coffees, and, when Mr Jackson had finished his drink, Martha said, very casually: "Let me take that for you. I'm sure you want to get over to watch Sarah run. She should do well in this event. It's the 800 metres and that's easily her best distance."

Jackson handed his cup over to Martha and watched as she walked over to the recycling bin. When she got there, he had already turned away and gone off to watch the start of Sarah's race. He did not see her carefully put his cup into her purse.

The rest of the meet was uneventful but, when they had said their goodbyes and Martha got into Jonny's father's car for the ride back to his house in Belvedere, Martha suddenly burst into tears and Dr Simms had to stop the car.

"What's the matter?" he said.

"I think it was Mr Jackson who raped me," said Martha.

"My God. What makes you think that?" asked Jonny.

"When he said, 'I can run faster than you,' it was exactly what the rapist said to me. And why did he know my exact personal best time?"

"It's a bit of a stretch," said Jonny. "What do you think we should do about it?"

"I've done it," said Martha. "I have his DNA."

"Is that why you put that cup in your purse?" asked Jonny. "I wondered what the heck you were doing."

Back at the Simms house on the Belvedere Heights, Martha telephoned Detective Lionel Shapiro.

"Detective Shapiro," said Martha, "I think I know who raped me."

She explained what had happened and why she thought Jackson was the rapist. She explained that she had a cup with his DNA on it.

Lionel Shapiro explained that they could not directly use the evidence of the cup because there was not a clear chain of custody for the evidence, but he agreed that the cup would be sent for analysis and that, if it came back as a match, it should not prove too difficult to close the case.

"Clever girl," said Shapiro. "I'm coming for the cup now."

The DNA was indeed a match and Jackson was questioned by Shapiro. He started by denying the claim and he began by refusing to take a DNA test formally, but, in the end, he realised it was no use and eventually he confessed. He was duly convicted and sentenced to 10 years in prison, slightly less than the statutory maximum because he had spared the victim from having to appear in court.

And with that sentencing, Martha was able to put the whole incident behind her, but for Sarah, the nightmare of life without her father was only just beginning. Sarah, her mother, and her younger brother sold their house and moved away to Chicago and began to rebuild their lives.

Chapter 4

Growing up in Marin County in the 21st century was not as easy as it had been during the 1980s. The vast expansion of the dot-com economy and the support industries had led to a huge explosion in the population and a total overcrowding of the infrastructure. There was still the amazing climate, the almost continuous and guaranteed sunshine for the vast part of the year and the limited rainfall, concentrated in a few short periods, to keep the area green in the spring and early summer. The downside of that rainfall was that it could be torrential at times and was liable to cause land slips and destruction of those homes built, unwisely or insecurely, on the hillsides of the slopes of the Bay. It was also true that the Bay Area was given to periods of drought, and the anti-drought measures put in place were an all too frequent visitor as climate change began to hit.

Martha and Jonny remained firm friends throughout their high school years. Martha's family were comfortable financially. Martha's father worked as the Manager of a Branch of Wells Fargo Bank in the City and her mother was a senior nurse at the Veterans Hospital overlooking China Beach, just across the Golden Gate bridge from Marin. The commute from West Blithedale Avenue to Wells Fargo went over the bridge, and Robert, Martha's father, always ferried Patti, Martha's mother, to work on his way to the bank. It could be described as one of the truly great commutes if there is ever such a thing as a great commute. The view of the Bay from highway 101 as it approached the bridge, and the view from the bridge itself, never grew tiresome, never lost its magic.

It would take a very disillusioned soul to remain unmoved by the sight of Alcatraz and Angel Island, the bridge itself and the Pacific Ocean, stretching out to the west, towards Hawaii and Asia beyond.

Martha cycled to school from her home in the Blithedale Canyon. It gave her freedom and, sometimes after school, she would join Jonny for a cycle around the Bay or, if Jonny was really in training for his triathlons, up through Muir Woods along the Panoramic Highway to the top of Mount Tamalpais. The return from Mount Tam was downhill all the way, a roller coaster ride, a white-knuckle ride, a ride requiring considerable technical skill if it were to be taken at speed. Jonny would usually take it fast and Martha would have more sense than to try.

They would usually end up at the McArthy home to keep each other company as they completed their class assignments. At least once a week, Jonny would stay over for supper. Both Jonny and Martha had part time jobs. Martha was a waitress at the very popular and rather up-market Italian restaurant in downtown Mill Valley. Her working hours were 4pm until 9pm Saturday and 4pm until 8 pm on Tuesday, which left her much of the day on Saturday, and the whole of Sunday, free at the weekend. Jonny worked in a bicycle shop in Sausalito from 8 am until 7 pm on the Saturday.

He had negotiated with the owner that he could also work in the repair shop on Tuesday evening after school, paralleling the working week that Martha already subscribed to. The first two hours on Saturday were also spent on cycle repair and, indeed, much of Jonny's time at the shop was in the workshop servicing bicycles. It suited him, he was an outstanding cyclist and it was almost an obsession. During the major cycling tours in Europe, he would record and watch every minute of the coverage. He owned an excellent racing bike as well as two very serviceable work-a-day, but still upmarket, bicycles for everyday use. He probably didn't realise it but Martha rather fancied Jonny in Lycra.

He had a mountain bike as well, and, every now and then, would take it for cross country training on the slopes of Mount Tam, and on the paths and wilderness along the Pacific Coast. Martha had a very respectable general purpose road bike on which she accompanied him when they went out together for a training spin, and a standard hybrid cycle that she rode every day to school. If Jonny looked OK in Lycra, Martha looked spectacular!

Sunday was very much a day that the two of them spent together. There might be training runs and schoolwork, but Sunday evening was always dinner at one or other household, or a date out together in the town.

The rape, and the problems it had caused Martha, were soon completely forgotten and by the time they reached the 11th grade, they were very focussed on their applications for university. Jonny had set his sights on University of California at Berkeley for engineering; it rather fitted with his love of cycles and things mechanical. It was always a bit of a coin toss whether Stanford or Berkeley was the best engineering school on the West Coast but for Jonny, Cal— as Berkeley is called by all those who love it dearly—was an ambition for a long time. He had even mentioned it to Martha on the very first occasion they had met. Martha was torn about where to go for pre-med, but when she ran a 50.22 400-metres at a meet on the Stanford track she was offered a full scholarship, and that could not easily be turned down.

"It's not as if Palo Alto is a hundred miles away," said Martha.

Jonny sulked for a bit, but in the end he too realised that it might be good for the pair of them, having been almost joined at the hip for four years, to find some distance and some personal space.

"After all," said Robert Simms, "if it is really meant to be, it will last through college, and you cannot do anything more than just stick together until Martha finishes med school when she reaches the ripe old age of 93, or whatever the age of graduation is now."

Jonny laughed, stopped sulking, and they somehow seemed to become even closer, Martha and he.

Both Martha and Jonny received early acceptance letters for their chosen universities and they proceeded to make the most of the glorious summer that followed their graduation from high school.

Chapter 5

Meanwhile, in Chicago, Sarah Jackson and her fatherless family were struggling to come to terms with the huge change in climate and the completely different culture of their new home. They had moved to Chicago in the August as Sarah entered 10th grade. Sarah's mother, Susan, had reverted to her maiden name, Susan McElroy, and the children had taken their mother's new surname for enrolment in school and for the future. Susan McElroy had divorced her husband at the earliest opportunity and the family had cut all ties with him.

At first, following the move from California, the weather was simply hot and humid, with occasional quite heavy cloud bursts, but as summer turned to autumn, the rain and the cold began to seep into their bones, and, by December, the biting wind off the broad expanse of Lake Michigan was turning the conditions to near Arctic.

Chicago itself is a strange city. Less than 200 years earlier, it had been a small town of fewer than 500 inhabitants, but it is situated between the two great river systems of the East Coast of America, the Mississippi river system, and the Great Lakes. It became the centre of a number of government-sponsored engineering projects involving rail and canal, and, almost before you could blink, it was a huge hub for the handling of cattle and goods from the vast central areas of America. It has little in the way of history. It is very much an immigrant city with a strong Irish presence and influence.

Initially, the Irish settled in Chicago to work on the Illinois and Michigan Canal, in the stock yards, on the railways, in the steel mills and the lumber yards, but they stayed to become heavily involved in the running of the city. It is not beautiful, it is rather a functional city and, without the natural beauty of the urban wilderness interface that is the Bay Area, it is a harsh shock to the senses of those brought up on the West Coast.

Sarah and her family were very unhappy during those first few years in voluntary exile, but they knew that Mr Jackson's crime had left them with little choice. Sarah continued to take part in track and field. It was hard to train in the inclement weather of the Midwest, but Sarah's school had access to the University of Chicago indoor running track. Although it was only a 200m track, it did allow speed work, with a reduced risk of pulling muscles, and it had good shower facilities and changing areas to make the experience more pleasant.

By the spring of her junior year, Sarah was posting 400-metre and 800-metre times comparable to those posted by Martha, and she was attracting the attention of athletics coaches from many of the top schools. The University of Chicago is an NCAA Division III school for athletics and so is not able to offer scholarships for sport. Sarah and her mother weighed up the situation and decided that there would be no problem with Sarah applying to West Coast Schools, specifically Cal and Stanford, under her new name. There might be a few people who recognised her, but not many, and Marin is West Bay, while Cal is East Bay, and Stanford is down South in Palo Alto. The quality of education and the potential quality of life was worth the gamble.

How strange it was then, that, like Martha, Sarah took an athletics scholarship at Stanford, for track and field, and, like Martha, and Jonny, Sarah had an early entry offer. Susan and Sarah's younger brother Timothy, Tim to his friends, had moved back to the Bay area. Susan had received a generous settlement at the divorce when the house in Marin had been sold and, with further support from Susan's parents, they had bought a house in the East Bay. They found a three-bedroom detached house on Ocean View Drive in Rockridge, which may, once, have had an ocean view, but now did not.

In the late summer of Sarah's senior year at high school, the family relocated back to California, and Sarah, Martha and Jonny got ready to start their undergraduate careers.

Chapter 6

A few months later, in December, in Cambridge, England, a very sad event was taking place. The Master of St Joseph's College, Sir Anthony Jones, had died. He was a much-loved man who would be sorely missed. He had overseen a resurgence in the fortunes of the college, both financially and academically, and he had left, not only the college, but the world a better place for his having been there. He understood the moral imperative as it applied to university education, and he instilled in everyone around him the same sense of values.

He created a values-led society, within the walls of St Joseph's, that produced more than a generation of people going out into the world, to spread that influence in all walks of life. His authority came, partly from the sharpness of his mind, his intellectual genius, and partly from the sense of inclusivity that he generated; the genuine interest that he took in everyone around him, from the humblest to the most exalted.

It had been a shock to everyone when Sir Anthony had calmly announced that he was suffering from late-stage cancer which had spread to an irrecoverable extent. He died within three weeks of that announcement.

The funeral arrangements were in line with tradition. The funeral service took place in the college chapel, presided over by the Dean of Chapel, and, following the ceremony, the coffin was carried, in procession, out of the chapel and across the pristine grass of Main Court, around the college grounds on the York stone paths between the ancient cobbles, and out to the front gates, where the hearse was waiting to take the coffin to the crematorium for a private ceremony.

On this occasion, the ground was lightly dusted with snow, it was bitterly cold. The Fellows, in their academic dress, lined up in pairs behind the coffin as the pall bearers placed it upon their shoulders. The old Master's closest two colleagues walked beside the coffin. It was dark, late afternoon in the middle of winter. The lights above the doorways were already shining with an eerie orange glow and the reflection from the sandstone walls created a halo around each of the staircase lights. The sky was heavy with cloud, and the cloud was heavy with snow.

The procession walked slowly, and, as it walked, the snow began to fall, lightly at first, and then more heavily. The little beacons of light around the courtyard added to the sense of ghostly presence, as if the souls of all those who had been honoured in this way, since the foundation, were watching over the procession. The staff of the college, feeling as bereaved as the Fellows themselves, stood silently around the Main Court. Some, those closest to the Master, those who had looked after his rooms or cooked for him as part of their duties, they were in tears. The deep gloom of the occasion was made worse by the dourness of the day. The snow was falling so heavily now that the coffin could not be seen from one side of the court to the other. It seemed as if the gods were reminding people that life and light were gifts that might be withdrawn at any time.

The coffin arrived at the gates as the hearse drew up onto the pavement outside. The porters went out into the road, to stop the local traffic while the coffin was placed in the hearse. The immediate family were whisked away in a second car as part of the cortege. The Fellows withdrew to the dining hall for cakes and tea and to talk about the future.

Colleges are cruel places where memories are short lived. For twelve years, the Master had been the central figure in St Joseph's. In three years' time, not a single undergraduate would remember him. The record would show that he had been there, that he had been important, but the present would show that he was no longer there, and no longer important. The pragmatists among the Fellows, what Cornford described, in his Microcosmographia Academica, as the Adullamites, anxious to maintain the flow of money, and the Young Men in a Hurry, anxious to get something done and change things, were already talking about the next Mastership election. Some of the older members of the Fellowship had ambition for the role of Master, other older members were simply sad and reflecting upon their own mortality.

The following Monday was the final meeting of the governing body of the college for the Michaelmas term. The meeting began with two minutes silence for remembrance of the late Master. It was chaired by the Vice-Master, a scholarly and kindly man, a seismologist, who had come late to Cambridge having lived and worked for many years in China. He had known Mao from the very foundation of the People's Republic and Mao's assumption of the role of Chairman. He had strong socialist principles, and a generosity towards all humankind. He was too old to stand for the Mastership himself, and he would be responsible for conducting the business of the search and then election of the new Master.

In normal times, a Mastership election is a somewhat protracted affair. The statutes of a college, the set of legally binding rules under which a college is governed, have been carefully crafted, through trial and error, to ensure that the election is handled in a manner that gives plenty of time for reflection at each stage of the process. It is also crafted in such a way as to minimise the risk of factions forming, of alienation of some segment of the fellowship. It is not always successful, but it works more often than it fails in its intention. The election itself requires more than a simple majority of the fellowship to vote in favour of the successful candidate, and that is where the final safety valve lies. In the end, a Master will usually be elected by a very large majority.

This election was accelerated. An Acting Master was appointed as a custodian of the role, someone to preside over the committees and functions that the Master was required to lead on. An advertisement was placed asking interested parties to apply. A search committee was set up to seek recommendations from Fellows and distinguished alumni and to make preliminary enquiries to find out if any of the names put forward would, indeed, be interested in having their candidacy considered. Distinguished clergy, politicians, diplomats, and academics were among the names put forward. Many of those named had no interest in a largely titular post at a Cambridge college but others did show an interest. A short list was drawn up.

The election meeting, at the end of the Lent term, was the most contentious in the college's history. There were three names before the electors. One was a spymaster; one was a senior politician; one was a very distinguished academic. The first scrutiny of the votes found the college split three ways. The intellectual purists wanted one of their own, the Regius Professor. The rest of the fellowship was evenly split between the two other candidates, who each had serious merits. As was the measured practice of the procedure, the meeting was adjourned for a week, to allow time for reflection.

The meeting was reconvened the following Monday. In the meantime, terrorist activity in London had created seeds of doubt in the minds of many who had previously voted for the spymaster. It was clear that electing that person

31

would lead to a significant increase in the security arrangements around the college. The everyday life of the college would be affected, even entering, or leaving, the college would become an issue. The spymaster would be a target, and the college was not yet ready for that. The votes of the spymaster lined up behind the senior politician and, at the third scrutiny, the politician was elected Master. The pattern for the next few years was set. He was flamboyant, very high profile and still politically very active. The college would be dragged, willingly, or unwillingly, into the limelight.

It was ironic that the need for security for the new Master was no less significant than it would have been for the spymaster. Security cameras were installed in the Master's Lodge, so that the Master could see who was at the door, before answering it. There were alarms and cameras placed everywhere that intruders might seek to gain access. Most of the Fellows and staff were unaware of these new security measures. So were the students. The members of St Joseph's were probably the most scrutinised group of people anywhere in the British Isles.

The senior tutor, Adrian Armstrong, had worked under the previous Master for the past seven years and had with the Master, piloted the college through to its position of academic excellence. There had been great synergy of values and ambitions between the two. It was inevitable that Adrian would be nervous about the change of regime.

'*I hope he sticks to the buildings and public affairs,*' thought Adrian. '*And I hope he gets another job to keep him out of our hair.*'

These were not generous thoughts, but they had some basis. The senior tutors of the colleges sit together on committees and Adrian was only too aware of some heads of house, as masters, principals, mistresses, and provosts, are collectively known, who thought that they were like head teachers and ran everything. It created all sorts of issues for the teaching staff and the welfare providers. For many of the heads of house, their only experience of a collegiate existence had been their public boarding school, where the head was the *de facto*, as well as titular, leading figure.

Adrian understood that being head of a Cambridge college was a subtle and extremely difficult role. First among equals. Unless a vote at the governing body was divided equally, the Master's vote counted only as much as the vote of the most junior member. It could prove difficult for outsiders to understand.

The morning after the election, Adrian sat in the parlour as usual, having a cup of coffee with the Bursar.

"We need to get him busy immediately," said Adrian.

"Yep," said Mark, looking up briefly from his newspaper.

"Let's get him to do a building appeal. We need a conference centre and theatre we can use for performances and larger assemblies. We could do it on the old car park site," added Mark.

"It would butter up his ego," said Adrian. "It would be his legacy. He would be remembered for ever."

"Need to start nudging the idea," said Mark. "Who should we get to start floating the proposal?"

They discussed who should put forward the suggestion of a new building. They were both subscribers to the Harry S. Truman philosophy that "you can get anything done in politics as long as you do not care who gets the credit." Just cut out the word politics and it applies to almost anything.

Adrian's forebodings about the new Master proved to be correct. He did want to have a finger in every pie. But Adrian and Mark managed him quite well. It took a few months, but they did manage to draw up boundaries, which the Master decided not to cross. They managed to get one of the lawyers to propose, and the governing body to agree, the campaign for the building of the conference centre, and that became the focus of much of the Master's energy.

In addition to the building project, the Master was determined to raise the profile of the college nationally. He invited a succession of senior politicians to come and address the college's political societies. The meetings were held in the entirely inadequate space of the current lecture theatre. It was the stature of the speaker, and the charisma of the Master, that made these occasions a success. External guests, carefully chosen, were invited to each of the sessions, feted and lauded by the Master, and put down for a generous donation to the New Building Fund.

The Master gradually recognised the competence of his back-up team and left Adrian and Mark to get on with what they were doing well. He nurtured the fellowship with several fascinating entertainments and visits that he was able to organise because of his status and networks.

After about a year, he had accumulated sufficient promises of funding for the building campaign to move to the next stage. The appeal would go public, but for that to happen a design brief would have to be agreed, architects would have to be appointed and a final design would need to be approved.

There was relatively little argument about the design brief. The only real concern of the fellowship was the loss of the parking spaces in the old car park. It was believed, quite rightly, that the City Council would withhold planning permission if those valuable car parking spaces disappeared. Traffic congestion in the centre of Cambridge is bad, and parking spaces are severely limited. The brief was to provide a conference centre without the loss of significant numbers of parking spaces.

There were three main approaches. One was the underground car park with a building on top. A second was a building that included two lower tiers of parking spaces reached by ramp or a car lift. The third solution was a building on stilts leaving the car parking spaces underneath.

Several firms of architects had expressed an interest in bidding for the commission and so the fellowship formed a committee to go and inspect the work of these different firms. It was another chance for the Master to use his influence to get the fellowship access to places from which the public is excluded and which, otherwise, the Fellows might never have seen. They managed to view the private rooms of one of Britain's greatest stately homes, they were invited into another college, in Oxford, to see the work of one of the candidate firms, and they were invited into a major London building to see refurbishment work that had been accomplished there.

Following a lot of argument about water tables, and flooding, and cost, a solution was envisaged which was to build the conference centre above an underground car park but keep sufficient of the old car park for delivery lorries to enter and unload on site. The architects who had made this proposal were commissioned to draw up detailed plans, and the campaign proper for raising funds could begin.

The Fellowship of the College was not the only group of people interested in the proposed new building. The discussions about the building, especially the cost, had led to some difficult debates at the governing body, and there were members of the college, who were somewhat opposed to the building itself, who wanted to stir up public opinion against the project. They leaked information to the press in advance of the planning hearings. The high public profile of the Master led to considerable coverage of the debate in the broadsheets, as well as the usual scandal mongering among some of the red tops. Despite that, the planning consent was given, and the scheduling of the construction process could begin. A model of the building was created as an essential part of the fundraising, which continued, and a photograph of that model appeared in the newspapers, and in one of the glossy society magazines.

Throughout London dissident groups had eyed the goings on at St Joseph's with interest. The regular stream of high-profile public figures coming through the doors to a relatively insecure public meeting whetted the appetite. Political groups, animal rights groups, ecowarriors, pro-life, almost any dissident faction was interested in these speakers. That no damage was inflicted on the participants was largely due to the excellent intelligence gathering of the various undercover surveillance teams and the subtle, inconspicuous, policing by Special Branch.

Detective Chief Inspector Jerry Gregory had been seconded to Special Branch following a long and distinguished career as a detective in both the Metropolitan police and one of the midland cities. He now found himself based in Cambridge in charge of security for the increasing number of retired high profile political, diplomatic, and military figures who were taking on roles as Heads of House in the University. His biggest Headache was Lord Fairfield of Chichester, the Master of St Joseph's, who almost every week brought a new and controversial figure to speak to the undergraduates. Jerry Gregory's job was to keep them safe.

There had been a few near misses. They had intercepted a would-be assassin on the train from Birmingham when the former Foreign Secretary, Lord Housedale, came to speak to the Cambridge Union, and was planning to stay the night with Lord Fairfield in the Master's Lodge at St Joseph's. The tip off had come from an undercover officer with the Met, working in the Finsbury Park area of London with a group of foreign nationals who objected to the British government giving aid to the government of their country, claiming that it was being used to purchase arms for suppression of the rebels, rather than for the humanitarian purposes for which it had been given. The interception had been handled with minimal publicity and the would-be assassin had ended up being charged with non-specific conspiracy to commit a terrorist act. A dangerous terrorist cell in that part of London had been apprehended because of the arrest.

A second, less serious incident, had involved the throwing of eggs by a committed group of student activists. In some ways, Adrian Armstrong felt himself responsible for this incident. The university has a freedom of speech policy which allows freedom of expression, within the restrictions of the law.

There are some circumstances in which invited external speakers are known to hold controversial views, such as the holocaust deniers, and these attract protests from within the college. The principle that anyone should be allowed to express a legitimate opinion is one that the colleges and the university hold dear. Unfortunately, many issues sharply divide opinion and there are almost always, in those circumstances, unpleasant face offs between the two opposing factions. The egg throwing incident was one such occasion. Lord Fairfield's guest speaker was the Prime Minister of a country which was held to have a poor record on human rights, and the human rights activists within the college packed the gallery of the old and inadequate lecture theatre, put their largest members in the aisle seats, put their most accurate egg throwers in the middle of each row, and threw upwards of a hundred eggs at the platform party before the proctors and the university constables could restore order. Mobile phones, the blessing, and the curse, of democracy, had a field day. Not a single national newspaper missed out on the opportunity for a front-page photo of the Prime Minister dripping egg yolk. It was either a headline criticising the regime in his country, or one decrying the inability of students to understand the realities of political life and thereby putting in danger contracts for arms and equipment that might mean the loss of hundreds of jobs for British workers. The new building was intended to replace this old theatre, which had been built in the 19th Century to house college lectures when the university itself had a distinct shortage of suitable lecture theatres.

Jerry looked at the design of the new building and had the same thought as many of the politically dissident groups. This is a terror magnet. Its location, its tiered design. All these made security doubly tricky. St Joseph's is situated very close to the rail and bus stations and London is only 45 minutes away by train. There were times when Jerry Gregory longed for the relative simplicity of policing a large midlands town.

It would be fair to say that Jerry Gregory harboured unkind thoughts towards Fairfield. He wished him gone. Every week many meetings, and a lot of Special Branch time, was taken up in dealing with the potential risk from Fairfield's generous invitations.

It would be fair to say that each of the terror groups hoped for a long continuation of Lord Fairfield's tenure as Master. Each was hoping for the opportunity for a statement terrorist action, based around the new conference centre. It lent itself to destruction.

The building operations began immediately at the end of one Easter term, as soon as the examinations had finished. The excavation of the car park site to a depth adequate to provide a high-ceilinged car parking area took the best part of three months, and then the rains came, which added delay. The demolition of the buildings around the car park area and the fact that the car park was out of use pushed several of the Fellows, and even more of the staff, into using their bicycles and an outcry about bicycle security, several bikes were stolen from the rather exposed college bike sheds, led to a modification of the plan for the new building so that a significant area of the garage space, in the centre of the building around the lift shaft, was designated for bicycle parking. A ramp down which cars and bicycles could be wheeled was a prominent feature of the southern wall of the car park. Access to the cycle store was by key fob RFID, Radio-Frequency Identification, improving the security considerably.

The stages of completion of the building were a little drawn out and were thoroughly exploited by Lord Fairfield to celebrate the brilliance of the architectural design and his own brilliance at bringing the project towards completion.

The foundation stone was laid in late spring a year after the excavations had begun and a large stone tablet, inscribed with the name of Lord Fairfield and the senior member of the royal family who laid the foundation stone, was suitably unveiled.

The building contained several public rooms, a student common room, some seminar rooms, a music practice room, and a large auditorium, with staged seating and a gallery. For Fairfield, ever the aesthete, its main attraction was that it tidied up a previously rather ugly area of the college and it mattered little to him that the construction costs, using some of the most expensive materials that modern architects could get their hands on, would make it one of the most expensive buildings per unit area built in the world in the 21st Century.

Adrian was excessively grumpy about the cost. He wanted the college money to be focussed on scholarship and welfare, and he wanted a student party room and other facilities for the students, but he had to admit that the increasingly high profile of the college was making fund raising, for all types of activity, considerably easier and encouraging many more students to apply for admission.

"Just so long as he doesn't stay long enough to spend all our money," said the Bursar.

The building, when it was finished, was magnificent. The whole underground car park allowed all the cycles belonging to the Fellows and staff to be safely stored, while still allowing many more cars than had parked before, to tuck themselves away from view. At ground floor level, the access to part of the old car parking area remained, tidied up of course, and delivery lorries and craftsmen working on the college site could access this area and park in comfort. All the ground floor rooms had very small windows and were heavily sound proofed. They were small supervision rooms, music practice rooms, seminar rooms. Many of these rooms could be used as breakout rooms for the conferences the college was planning to host there. The first floor contained a common room, at one end of the building, and more than two thirds of the floor area was occupied by the stage level of the theatre and the base of the raked auditorium, with an entrance foyer accessible from the main lift shaft. The second floor contained only a large reception room, to be used for events associated with the conferences and with any theatrical or musical events staged in the main auditorium. Access at this level to the auditorium led through to a gallery, with wall mounted seating. The vaulted roof of the auditorium towered above the audience and the stage, giving a great sense of spaciousness. It was lined with mature oak panelling and supported, cleverly, by stainless steel struts which gave it a truly modern feel.

Even Adrian, still sore at the cost of its production, recognised the sheer beauty of the design. It had the curious effect of calming people down. The colours, the warm sandstone, and the soft brown timber, had a calming effect that is often associated with the warm brown colours of autumn leaves in late Indian summer sunshine. Adrian sometimes felt guilty holding difficult meetings in the lecture theatre, a bit of a hypocrite for having condemned the waste of money that the building had represented to him.

Chapter 7

Martha McArthy had moved into the dorm at Stanford about a week before classes began in her freshman year. As was traditional at Stanford she was allocated a roommate, whom she had never met, and it was up to the pair of them to make it work. It was fortunate, or it was cleverly organised, that Martha's freshman roommate was also an athlete. Cecilia, Ceci to her friends, was a tennis player on the highly successful Stanford Women's Tennis team. She was intending to study medicine so was busy doing the appropriate pre-med classes with Martha. Like most athletes they had a big commitment to their sport. Training was compulsory and in addition to the training there were competitions at weekends and, sometimes, in the week.

Martha met Sarah, now Sarah McElroy, at the very first training session of the Varsity Athletics squad. Neither girl knew that the other had enrolled at Stanford. There had been no contact after Sarah moved to Chicago. There was a shock of recognition, there was a moment of painful recollection, and then there was delight. The two had always liked each other in high school, it was their friendship that had brought Martha to Robert Jackson's attention, and Martha had been very sad when Sarah and her family had moved away, although she had understood that it was necessary for them to do so. It turned out that they were living in the same dorm, that they both had opted for the same meal plan, and that they both had tennis players as roommates. Now they could make up for lost time and, the minute that the training session ended, they headed off together for supper in the Hall of Residence and started to talk.

Martha spoke first.

"Sarah," she said, "I've really missed you. I want to forget completely what happened that time in Mill Valley, and I want you to forget it too. I will never refer to it again, and I promise you that I'll never disclose anything about it to anyone with whom we come into contact. You are not your father, and you aren't responsible for his actions. I would really like to get back to friendship with you in the way that we did before. I want you to tell me all about where you moved to, and what you thought, and how it all worked out for you. Where do you live now?"

Sarah burst into tears, and the two girls hugged each other silently, for at least ten minutes. Sarah crying and heaving deep sighs, and Martha comforting her, and holding her tightly.

Finally, Sarah spoke, wiping her eyes and blowing her nose to clear away the tears.

"I missed you so much," she said. "We moved to Chicago and it was difficult. It was cold and I was lonely. Mum was very upset, and then there was the divorce. Training in Chicago through the winter was very hard, but I was determined not to let it slip. Remember how we used to spur each other on and train hard together? I missed that and I missed you and I felt so guilty about what had happened to you. I kept thinking that maybe, if we hadn't been friends, my dad would not have targeted you. And then I kept wondering who else he might have targeted. At first, I wished you had not done that clever thing with the coffee cups, but then I realised that you had probably saved someone else from being raped, and I knew that you'd done the right thing. I know we're going to be busy for a few weeks, with settling in, and enrolling in classes, and getting our books from the store, and, well, everything, but will you come home with me and meet Mum and my little brother Tim?"

"Sarah," said Martha, "You must be nuts. I'm not coming to Chicago right at this moment."

Sarah laughed.

"I forgot to tell you we've moved back to the Bay Area. We live over in Rockridge on the East Bay. We are all McElroys now, and Tim is going to Mater Dei Catholic High School over there. We thought it would be easier to be in the East Bay because too many people with long memories would still be around Mill Valley."

They talked, and talked, and, when, Martha returned to her room and chatted to her roommate, all she would say was that she had met an old friend, and it was as if they had never been apart.

Martha remembered that Sarah had only met Jonny once, before Robert Jackson had been arrested, and it was bothering her how she might deal with the situation. Jonny had met Mr Jackson on the afternoon of the track meeting, the one at which Martha had realised who the rapist was, and that was now some four years ago. It was rather obvious that Sarah and Jonny were going to meet again soon, Jonny had planned to cycle over to Palo Alto this coming weekend, as part of his training for the Bears' Triathlon. He was still cycling, running, and swimming, and Sarah was bound to be there at some point during the visit. Martha decided to wait and see if Jonny recognised Sarah before planning what to do next. It was important to Martha to protect Sarah, who was as innocent as Martha, of the goings on that had forced them apart.

For both Martha and Sarah, and over at Berkeley, Jonny, the next few days were spent completing much of the administrative detail that is associated with starting at university. There was enrolment in classes, making sure that they covered both their breadth and their specialist requirements. Sarah's specialist requirements were related to biological science so there was considerable overlap with Martha's. They also had fun picking one or two off-the-wall breadth requirements. It was partly tongue in cheek that they both chose to study Film Studies 442: Hollywood Musicals. They were saving the course on sleep for later in the year.

There was also the walk to the bookstore to collect the course texts. As athletes on a full ride they were able to get those free. There was also the possibility of extra tuition if they found themselves slipping behind because of training commitments or, as was the case with some athletes, they were not quite up to it, but with both Sarah and Martha having grade school GPAs around 4.0, and SAT scores close to full marks, the lack of intellectual ability was not going to figure in the equation.

They spent a lot of time together over that first few days and both became very sure that theirs was a friendship that, having been reforged, was going to last.

It was on the Friday evening of their first weekend as freshers, just after training, that Sarah asked Martha about boyfriends.

"I'm still with Jonny," she said.

"That could be awkward," said Sarah.

"You only met him the once," said Martha.

"True," said Sarah, "but I bet he remembers me. That was a very intense day we had."

"How do you think we should play it?" asked Martha. "I think if we talked to him, he would be very happy to let the past remain in the past. He is a really nice man, and we have talked a bit, while you were away, about how hard it must have been for you and your family."

"We don't really have a choice," said Sarah. "If he is someone nice, that you like, I'm sure he will be OK with it."

"Have you got a boyfriend?" asked Martha.

"Not really," said Sarah. "To be quite honest I was so upset, after what my father had done, that I went off the idea of relationships for quite a while, and so my social life took quite a beating. I have a friend who is a guy, but it isn't serious. He went off to Northwestern just as I came down here to Stanford. We chat a bit on the internet, and we watch each other on Facebook, but I don't think it's going anywhere."

"Well," said Martha, "there are a good few hundred freshmen here, and I bet at least half of them would love to date you! I reckon the world's your oyster."

"OK. Let's get over the hurdle of sorting out Jonny's reaction first, shall we?"

They stopped chatting for a minute and headed off to the Lakeside dining room for supper. They were supposed to watch a Fred Astaire and Ginger Rogers Musical as part of their Film Studies course, so they ate, changed into something a bit dressier, and headed off to the Art House Theatre where the film was showing.

When they came back that evening, there was the mother and father of all rows going on in the dorm corridor. The Stanford method of allocating roommates was a bit random; it was always given to two student room coordinators to pair people up. It was often well into the freshman year that roommates could work out why they had been paired. It might be that they shared a birthday; it might be that their names sounded good together, Grace and Kelly for example. It might also be that the coordinators got it very wrong, and this was the cause of the row going on when the two girls arrived back from the Cinema. For entirely undiscernible reasons, the coordinators had put Theresa, named after Saint Theresa, a devout Catholic, in a room with Sky, a devout cannabis smoker. For almost a week, Theresa had been arriving back in her room to find Sky, stoned out of her mind, sitting in a cloud of smoke, mellow to the world. It clearly could not go on, and the final straw had been when Theresa had, having said her prayers, and gone to sleep at around 9pm, been woken by Sky and her friends coming in for a party at midnight.

It had been the culmination of several serious disagreements, most of them based on Sky's slightly hedonistic lifestyle and Theresa's rigid adherence to Catholic dogma. Theresa had put up a pro-life poster in her room, Sky had ripped it off the wall, Theresa had put a poster for 'Save sex for marriage'. Sky had put up a legalise cannabis poster in her room, Theresa had ripped it down. Sky had put up a poster advertising birth control services, Theresa had ripped it down. Theresa went to Mass every morning, Sky slept in as late as she could. It was not exactly a meeting of minds.

For a normally peace-loving young lady, Theresa packed a heavy punch, and had almost broken Sky's nose with a left hook of which Christy Martin might have been proud. By the time order had been restored, and the blood had been cleared up, Sky was alone in the room and Theresa was sleeping on the floor on a mattress in Sarah's room.

Chapter 8

Sunday was a day free of formal practice for the athletes, although Theresa woke Sarah at 7 am to go to morning Mass. She was a little disturbed to find that Sarah, like Martha, was a 'lapsed' Catholic, but none of her cajoling would persuade Sarah to go to Mass, so Theresa went by herself, but not before she had explained that the final straw was that Sky, and one of the boys, had been about to have sex publicly in the shared dorm room, and, in the course of the row that followed, Sky had been less than charitable in her description of Theresa.

It was fortunate that a couple of students, withdrawing at the last minute from the freshman class had left a spare room, and the Resident Fellows were able to relocate Theresa into that spare room. This was all agreed before 9 am and, when Theresa got back from Mass, Sarah and Martha helped her move her stuff. Sky was still out cold in her room, recovering from a combination of over-indulgence, in alcohol and marijuana, and the bruised ego, and the sore nose that Theresa had landed her with. Sarah noticed that the birth control and legalise cannabis posters were back up on the wall, and there were used condoms in the waste bin.

Theresa was not really either Sarah's or Martha's type of person, but they were both kind human beings, and it was clear that Theresa needed support, so they took her with them to eat breakfast and chatted to her generally about how unfortunate the roommate pairing had been; in short, they said all the right things, even if they fundamentally disagreed with Theresa's hard core religious views.

Theresa went off to her room to study after breakfast and the other two girls went back to their rooms to change into their running gear. It was a warm, but not blisteringly hot, autumn day and the two ran at talking pace, which was still quite fast, for about 8 miles. They did the iconic Stanford Dish run, which, including the run from the dorm to the trailhead and back, gave them all the exercise they needed on a rest day.

When they got back from the run, Jonny was waiting on his bicycle outside Roble Hall where the girls lived.

"Hello Martha," said Jonny. He paused; stared very hard at the tall elegant young lady who had been running with Martha. She was a curly haired blonde, like Martha; she had violet eyes, she had freckles. They could have been sisters. He racked his brains for a moment and then said, "Hello Sarah." He smiled. "I know Martha missed you a lot when you moved away. What are you doing here? I mean, I don't mean that, I mean…" And he stuttered into silence.

"We'd better have a good long talk Jonny," said Martha. "This is Sarah McElroy. That's all you need to know for the minute."

"Sure," said Jonny. "Pleased to meet you Sarah McElroy," he stuck out his hand and they shook hands together, and then, somehow, they were hugging.

"You had better come and sit in my room," said Martha. "My tennis playing roommate is off at a tournament this weekend, so you won't be disturbing anyone, and Sarah and I can have a shower, and then we can all go and get a coffee and an ice cream somewhere. Does that sound good?"

They all headed off into the building and the two girls went and got showered and changed. Martha wore an orange sun dress that showed off her figure, her tan, her blonde hair, and green eyes, to perfection; Sarah wore a cream sundress that was equally stunning. Jonny felt somewhat underdressed in his Lycra cycling gear.

The three of them wandered off into the town, picked up their ice-creams from 'The Tin Pot Creamery', and took them, with take away coffees in their reusable mugs, over to Heritage Park to sit on the benches there, while the kids and families played in the playground, and several other people used the climbing rock. They all three had sugar cones.

Sarah told Jonny her story and, as she spoke, she realised that Jonny was deeply moved by what she was saying. When she finished, with the announcement that the family had moved back to the East Bay, she paused and let it all sink in.

They licked their ice creams in silence.

"Anyone want to try this pistachio flavour?" asked Martha. Jonny and Sarah both had a taste. Then they all had a taste of Jonny's pralines and cream, and, finally, they all tasted Sarah's very berry strawberry.

"Sarah," said Jonny. "I promise that you are Sarah McElroy to me, and always will be. I promise not to remember that I ever met you before today, and

I really hope that we can become friends. I know we can. Your family lives really near my dorm. Rockridge is just a walk, quite a long walk, from my dorm at Berkeley, but I go there a lot to Trader Joe's to buy stuff, so I'm bound to see you if you are around. Can I invite you and Martha to come to dinner with me one day next week? You choose the day, and it will be my treat."

Martha was smiling. She was looking at Jonny, she was looking at Sarah, she was just wondering whether the invite was for her, or for Sarah. She reflected on that a little. Did it matter? As a potential medical student, she was a long way from wanting permanent commitment. Had the decision to go to different universities been a signal that their relationship was strong, but more platonic than anything else? Too soon to start thinking about that, Martha was just going to enjoy the moments in the sun, the company of two good friends and the excitement of starting this new chapter in her life.

Theresa, meanwhile, was talking earnestly to Father Collins, the Pastor responsible for the Catholic Mission within the university. Stanford is a university which is unaffiliated to any specific religion and, to attend Mass every day, Theresa was using the Catholic churches in the vicinity, as well as the Catholic Mission within the university precincts. She had confessed to losing her temper and hitting Sky, and been given a suitable penance, but she had also explained that part of her anger had come from her commitment to the pro-life organisation and to the 'Save Sex for Marriage' campaign. Father Collins put her in touch with the local groups for each of these campaigns. Theresa resolved to keep a lower profile about her beliefs within the campus community, but she also began to become very involved with the local Catholic groups, and with other groups, working to bring sinners to repentance. She became part of a group of Stanford students who wrote regularly to Catholic prisoners in San Quentin, offering friendship and sharing the Christian experience. Her correspondence gradually focussed in on one prisoner who was serving a sentence for a crime of violence, he never told her that it was rape, a Robert Jackson, who shared her views on pro-life, although inevitably, he was long beyond the reach of the Save Sex for Marriage campaign. It was, indeed, Sarah's father.

****

Robert Jackson had already spent three years in prison. He had worked out very early on that his best bet to get out of jail as soon as possible was to be a model prisoner. He resurrected his Catholicism, as a foundation stone for the false persona he was creating, as soon as he met the Catholic Chaplain to the prison. He was kept in the Special Prisoner Unit, and had experienced a couple of near misses with being beaten up by fellow inmates, but there were other more notorious sex offenders in the jail and they were much more the target of the violent prisoners also housed on the special unit. He had befriended a particularly large, and rather simple, prisoner called Eddie and Eddie rather protected Robert. Robert was teaching Eddie, who was almost illiterate, to read and write, and the protection was a reciprocal part of the friendship. A surprisingly tough gang based on the Catholic subculture, formed around the nucleus of these two prisoners, and an unfrocked Catholic priest who had been jailed for child abuse offences.

Robert had no remorse about what he had done to Martha, his only regret was that he had been caught before he could repeat the events with further victims. Rather than feeling remorse, Robert felt nothing but anger towards Martha. It was not just anger that she had tricked him and caused his arrest, the deepest anger was for the fact that she had aborted his child. Robert became a strong pro-life advocate. He covered up all his feelings. His outward remorse was layered on, like thick plaster on a badly cracked wall.

Had Robert been honest in his dealings with the prison psychiatrist, there would have been no chance of early release. From the moment he had reached puberty, Robert had been sexually active, mainly with youngsters close to his own age. He had been a rather good-looking young man and had found it relatively easy to attract members of the opposite sex. His whole attitude to sex was totally irresponsible. In Senior High School, he had unprotected sex with classmates who were not taking any birth control precautions, and used them, and discarded them, like so many unwanted consumer products. Even at that early stage in his life, he had an unhealthy obsession with fathering children. It was a totally distorted interpretation on his part of the Catholic dogma about contraception.

More than one of his conquests became pregnant, and all but one had an abortion. This made him angry, and that was the point at which he first became interested in the pro-life movement. The one who did not have an abortion kept the baby, but refused to say who the father was, and denied Robert any access whatsoever to the child. It was a further factor in Robert's slide towards contempt for women, and a passion for breeding children in his own perfect image.

The irresponsible attitude had continued into university, but one of the very first conquests, who became pregnant, was Susan McElroy. Robert decided that she was pretty enough, and willing enough, for him to offer to marry her and, because she knew nothing of his past sexual history, and he was charming, and she was pregnant, she accepted his proposal. He had visions of breeding lots of children with Susan, but his whole attitude to sexual activity was so personally selfish that Susan soon tired of it and began to lose interest in sex with him. Robert responded by having a series of affairs with other students and, later, work colleagues, and it suited Susan to turn a blind eye to what he was doing. Robert remained irresponsible, he never used a condom, and he never bothered to check whether his sexual partners were using contraception. None of the partners became pregnant, all were much more mature than he was, and all used some form of contraception, or restricted their sexual activity with him to less fertile times.

Knowing that he would only ever have the two children with Susan was what finally tipped Robert over into deciding to rape younger girls. He reasoned that they were unlikely to be using contraception and so were very likely to end up pregnant. It was nasty, it was cynical, and it was entirely in keeping with his character.

Nothing of this came out in his interviews with the prison psychiatrist. He invented a persona which was loving and caring and devastated by the loss of his family. He wore a crucifix on a chain around his neck and prayed before every session with the psychiatrist.

Meanwhile, he was plotting and planning for the future, for when he eventually came out of prison. He had become completely obsessed with pro-life, partly because of his own obsession with procreation, his anger at Martha, and partly because he quite liked the idea of violent protest. He rejoiced when a pro-life group shot a doctor running a clinic in Tulsa, he rejoiced at every violent protest, at every threat to family or friends of obstetricians and gynaecologists practising abortion on a regular and legal basis.

As part of his plan, he kept himself very fit. He knew he would be in his forties when he eventually got out of jail, and he wanted to still be as young and attractive looking as he could, because he still had ideas of sexual conquest and breeding prolifically.

It was through the Catholic Chaplain, who was also in contact with Father Collins at Stanford, that he was put in touch with a young lady from Stanford University who wanted to save his soul.

It did not take Robert Jackson long to work out that this was a very naïve young woman, with a totally sheltered upbringing, that he could mould into a willing partner in his venture. She had just started university, that meant that she would finish in four years' time, and that would be when he would be very close to release. He decided that he was going to groom her for sex which, in the case of young Theresa, would mean he would have to marry her. But the strength of her commitment to the doctrines of the church led Robert to believe that she would be happy to breed children with him, there would be no question of contraception, and there would be no possibility of abortion. He thought he could settle for that, especially as he would always be able to work out a way to have relationships with other women, especially if Theresa was kept busy, either being pregnant, or looking after the huge number of children he was going to give her.

Chapter 9

It was Thursday evening before Sarah and Martha managed to find the time to drive over to Berkeley to see Jonny. Barclay's Restaurant and Bar in Rockridge was very close to where Sarah's family now lived, and they left the car outside the new home on Ocean View Drive and walked to the restaurant to meet Jonny who was coming up College Avenue from campus from the opposite direction. Barclays had a book in which you could write your name and record all the pints of beer you consumed. False ID was needed by all three of the students, because of the California drinking laws, but they were not intending to get drunk anyway, and, as Martha was driving, she was going to stick absolutely to non-alcoholic beverages.

The two girls got there first and when Jonny came in they both got up and gave him a hug. Martha noticed that the Sarah to Jonny hug was a little more prolonged, and she smiled inwardly to herself.

The food at Barclay's was always good, and they ate well. It was a very pleasant evening. At the end of the evening, when the time came to say their farewells, Martha managed to get Jonny to one side.

"It's OK," she said, "Go for it!"

Jonny looked at her.

"You don't mind?" he said.

Martha smiled, gave him a very nice hug, a huge smile, and a peck on the cheek and then she said: "I'm devastated," there was a pause, "if that helps your ego; or, if you prefer, of course not."

They gave Jonny a lift back down-town to his Hall of Residence and all agreed that they would meet up again in a few weeks' time for lunch at Jonny's home in Belvedere. Jonny would send an invite via email.

On the way back in the car, Martha told Sarah exactly what she had told Jonny, that she knew that there was something that might be starting up between those two, and that she, Martha, did not mind.

"Jonny and I have had a really great friendship, but, somehow, it was never more than platonic, and I don't know why, but there it is. I think we're even closer now than we've ever been, but friendship is useful for relationships, but you need more if you are going to live with just one person for the rest of your life. So you just go ahead and see what happens."

It was not late when they got back to the dorm; Theresa was still up in the common room area. She greeted them excitedly and began to tell them all about her latest venture, befriending a Catholic prisoner in San Quentin.

"He's clearly a good bit older than me, old enough to be my father in fact, but he's obviously a good man, a man who is deeply repentant about his past, and I think we are going to become quite good penfriends. He shares a lot of my views about pro-life and keeping sex for marriage. He won't tell me what his crime was, but he says it was a crime of violence and a foolish thing that he did. Let me read a bit of his letter to you."

Dear Theresa,

You cannot know how much it means to me here in this jail cell to know that there is a kind and thoughtful Catholic girl out there who is praying for my soul. I did a wrong thing for which I'm being punished. I shall be here for at least four more years. The crime itself brings too painful memories for me to tell you what I did, but you do need to know that I deeply regret my actions, and am now working hard, with the Chaplain here, to recover my faith, and rehabilitate myself within society. I share your views on the sanctity of marriage and the value of all life, even unborn life. I believe that we will enjoy our journey together as we campaign for the preservation of all lives, including those of the unborn child.

"I won't read you the next bit, it's a little embarrassingly kind. But he's asked for a photograph of me and wonders whether I could put it on a single piece of paper, with pictures of all the St Theresa's, there are lots of them. He says to make my picture the biggest one, and could it be of my doing something outdoor and active, as it will help him to feel free. He wondered about a photo by the swimming pool."

Martha and Sarah sat there, mouths open, aghast at the naivety of Theresa. They looked at each other. To say something or not to say something? Well, the guy was locked up in San Quentin for, according to his own words, at least four more years. Martha shook her head, Sarah agreed. Plenty of time for Theresa to become disillusioned with this obviously manipulative prisoner. Now was not the time to kick Theresa hard. She had barely recovered from the fight she had had with Sky.

Theresa went off to bed in her new room, and Martha and Sarah looked at each other.

"Bloody pervert wants a photograph of her in a swimming costume," said Martha.

"Let's deal with it. I'll offer to take a photo for her by the pool and I'll do it before she takes her robe off," said Sarah.

And that is what she did; and it was that photograph that Theresa sent to Robert Jackson, along with photographs of the paintings of other Theresa's, captured from the web.

Robert Jackson sat in his cell, on receipt of the return letter from Theresa. The photograph was very frustrating. He could see that Theresa was a very pretty girl, with a delicate face, very pale skin, and huge dark brown eyes. She had black hair. He guessed she might have Mediterranean ancestry.

He could not really see whether she had an attractive figure because she had covered herself up with a bathing robe. He was cross about that. The request for a photograph beside the pool had been as unsubtle a hint as he dared make that she might reveal herself in a swimming costume. Ah well, a request for a further photograph or photographs might be more revealing, in every way.

Chapter 10

The freshman year for Jonny, Martha and Sarah went rather well. Despite the high involvement with athletics, which gave two A grades every semester, and Jonny's commitment to the triathlon, all three of the students managed GPAs which kept them on the Dean's List. Martha was quietly picking off the necessary pre-med requirements and indulging her side interests in theatre and the performing arts. She and Sarah also took the neurobiology of sleep course that was available in freshman year. It was hard work, but interesting.

Sarah was following a lot of the same courses but was moving away from animal biology more towards plant physiology and genetics. She had become very interested in the problems of feeding the world in the 21st Century, and was fascinated by the difficulties of maintaining adequate crop production in the face of climate change, and seemingly more frequent periods of drought, in what might previously have been considered the perfect growing environments. She was already thinking about a career in research, looking at the possibility of inducing drought resistance in rice and certain grains. She knew that the Holy Grail of this research would be the introduction of C4 photosynthesis into currently C3 crops like rice and wheat. She knew that a lot of this research was being co-ordinated through the Plant Science Department in Cambridge, thanks to funding from the Gates Foundation. She was also interested in how the molecules involved in photosynthesis might be harnessed to provide alternative power sources for the generation of electricity. She was beginning to think about a Ph.D. at Cambridge University.

There was quite a cute, young, visiting post-doc from Cambridge, acting as a visiting lecturer on the plant physiology course, and Sarah persuaded Martha to come along. Sarah pointed out that many of the major drugs in use in modern medicine were derived from plants, so it would not be totally irrelevant. Besides which, focussing too narrowly on medicine is bad for the soul, at least, that is what Sarah told Martha and, even if she did not completely believe it, Martha decided to indulge her friend.

Jonny followed the standard elements of the engineering course, picking all those classes which would direct him towards a career in mechanical engineering. He was developing a taste for entrepreneurship and wanted to start his own business eventually. He believed the future of the internal combustion engine was limited, and that electric cars were the vehicles of the future, so, as well as gears and structures, Jonny was becoming very interested in electronics and batteries. He also dabbled a little in the computing skills necessary to at least understand, if not design, self-driving vehicle control systems. He became interested in artificial intelligence, simply because that related to the control of his beloved powered transport.

The 'cute guy' giving the plant physiology lectures, James Coghlan, was only about five years older than Martha. A fast-track genius, he had gone to university at 17, a year young, and had completed his B.A. at 20, his MPhil. at 21, and his Ph.D. at 24 years of age. The post-doc position at Stanford had been a logical next step for a high-flyer.

Martha sat in James's first lecture and decided that he was, indeed, cute. She decided that he was, in fact, cute enough for her to want to get to know him. At his second lecture, she sat in the front row and stared at him, intently, throughout the lecture. She could sense that he was beginning to feel a little uncomfortable at one point, so she let him off the hook for a while, and then, when she was confident that he had recovered enough, she turned the gaze on again.

At the end of the lecture, she took her time about gathering up her books, sat quite still, looking contemplative, and waited.

James Coghlan approached the bench where Martha was sitting.

"Miss…" he said.

"McArthy," said Martha. "Martha McArthy."

"Miss McArthy. You seemed rather intent on the lecture this morning," said James.

"Well, it was pretty good," said Martha.

James blushed.

"Glad you thought so," he said. "What are you planning to major in?" He was hoping it might be plant science.

"I'm a pre-med student," said Martha. And she watched as a slight frown of disappointment spread across his features.

"What are you doing in Plant Physiology 101 then?" asked James.

Martha gave him the spiel about how medicines are derived from plants and she did not want to become too narrow, and she rather hoped he was smart enough to recognise that for the bullshit that it was.

James was not arrogant, and it took him a second or two to realise that this very attractive young lady was teasing him, but, to his credit, it did not take him long after that realisation to do the sensible thing.

"I'm sure you have another class to go to now," he said. "Perhaps we could continue this conversation over dinner this evening?"

"I actually have athletics training to go to," said Martha, "But if you are asking me out to dinner, then I would really like that."

"Italian, French, Chinese, Mexican," said James, "What would you like? I can book a table. What time can you make? I guess you need to shower and change after training."

They settled on Mexican and 6.30pm.

Sarah was waiting for Martha outside the lecture theatre. She had a grin like a Cheshire cat. It was so wide a grin that there was hardly any space for any of her other features.

"Shut up," said Martha.

"I didn't say anything," said Sarah.

"That's why you're still alive," said Martha.

And that is how three became four, or that is the start of how three became four. It took more than one dinner date and Plant Physiology 101 to complete the synthesis.

Meanwhile Theresa was writing two or three times a week to the lovely man who she had befriended in San Quentin. She went every day to Mass, somewhere in the area, and lit a candle for her new friend. The letters which had started off 'Dear Mr Jackson' with a response to 'Dear Miss Moretti' quite quickly changed to 'Dear Robert' and 'Dear Theresa'.

Theresa chronicled her life in detail to 'Dear Robert'. She explained how lonely she felt being the only 'true' Catholic among her circle of acquaintances. He responded avidly to her letters which detailed the debauchery that she saw all around her. She reserved quite a lot of uncharitable vitriol for poor Sky, and Robert's vile imagination was fed by the picture of depravity that Theresa described. He began to lust after this Goth creature who, according to Theresa, seemed to have the morals of an alley cat.

Robert responded with bucket loads of false sympathy. He empathised deeply with her anguish, and, gradually, the tone of the letters changed so that, rather than Theresa writing to comfort Robert, Robert was writing to comfort Theresa. 'My Poor Dearest Theresa' gradually became 'My Darling' and the naïve young woman responded in kind.

She eventually sent him a photograph of herself in her bathing costume, and he realised that she was, indeed, a very beautiful young lady, fully grown physically, but with the mind of a particularly naive adolescent teenager. It whetted his appetite for what he had planned. Behind the ideal prisoner was a truly evil and depraved mind.

The relationship between James and Martha developed very quickly. The first dinner together, guacamole with tostada chips and fresh salsa, followed by chicken fajitas, was at Chilli's, a simple franchise eatery on El Camino Real. They cycled there from Martha's dorm and stayed a long time talking. James explained that his ambition was to become a university Professor in Plant Sciences, Martha explained that she intended to practise medicine.

James pointed out that the course at Stanford would cost her $300,000 and began to introduce the idea that Cambridge, and the graduate medicine programme there, might be a viable alternative. It would probably cost about $120,000 more, but she should keep it in mind. At that stage, it was more a wishful thought than a serious suggestion. James talked a lot to Martha about his college, St Joseph's, and told her that he would really like her to come with him next summer vacation to see the place. He was hoping to apply for a Research Fellowship back at St Joseph's when his current post-doc ran out in two more years.

They talked about family. James explained that his parents lived in a seaside town, called Ramsgate, on the Southeast Coast. His father was a Barrister. For a moment, Martha thought he had said barista. James had to explain to Martha what the equivalent of barrister was in American legal terms. He also explained that his mother was a General Practitioner, that too needed an explanation. He talked to her about how Ramsgate had been the point of departure for the hundreds of little boats that had evacuated the defeated British troops from France and Belgium, from the seaport of Dunkirk, in the darkest days of the Second World War.

His grandmother had been one of those who greeted and treated the wounded as they came off the little ships after their ordeal. He talked about the chalk cliffs and the sandy beach and the stone harbour, the Royal Harbour, given the title by George IV when he embarked from there to visit Hanover.

He talked about Pelosi's ice-cream parlour; he talked about the rock shop, where you could see the proprietor making rock, rolling it out on a marble slab in front of a huge plate glass window, as you walked down the long ramp from the cliff top to the sea front. James suddenly felt a little homesick; Martha began to hope that this very nascent relationship would fulfil its potential and she would get to see these wonders that James was describing.

Martha talked about her upbringing in Marin. She talked about the giant redwoods and the down-town tennis courts, where Martina Navratilova had once played a charity match to raise funds for breast cancer awareness. She talked about the legendary Mill Valley market, Mill Valley's answer to Trader Joe's, perhaps even more up market. She described her cycle commute from Blithedale Canyon down past the market and through the central square, with the imposing Bank of America building and the Depot Café, which served unbelievably delicious fresh sandwiches and soups and similar light meals.

She described the ride up Mount Tam, and the view from the top. She talked about the trips to Stinson Beach, the morning fog that she could see on the opposite hill side from the sunny side of the canyon on which her house was situated. She talked about the Strauss's swimming pool and lying on her back looking up at the giant redwoods, framed against the blue Californian sky.

James listened spell bound. Then he invited himself to Martha's for Sunday lunch.

When she got back to the dorm that night, Martha rang home and talked to her mother, Patti McArthy. She had obviously already talked to Patti about Sarah, and the whole of the McArthy family were in on the need to keep the past from destroying Sarah's life. She had also talked to the Strauss family, with the same purpose, to keep Sarah's past safe from exposure. All these thoroughly decent human beings were more than content to acquiesce to Martha's request.

The surprise for Patti was that Martha was calling to tell her that she had a new boyfriend and that, in boyfriend-girlfriend terms, Martha and Jonny were history.

"It was funny, Mum," said Martha. "The minute I saw them together, I knew that something had been bothering me about my relationship with Jonny. He never really tried even to get to first base when we were on a date. I thought that was because he was trying to respect me a bit too much, as he knew what had happened to me, but the thing is, I never tried to disabuse him of the need to treat me with kid gloves. I just liked his company, and we were, and still are, great friends. When I saw him look at Sarah for the first time, really look at her, I knew I was wrong and that we always were, and always will be, just friends. When I saw her look at him in the same way, I just decided to make it happen. I gave them both the word that it was OK by me. And they are now an item, very much an item."

"So why am I calling you now? I think it's because I'm falling in love with someone else. I get that empty stomach feeling when I look at him. I go all weak at the knees. I can hardly breathe. And this is only the second time I have seen him, and only our first date."

"Sarah's to blame. She told me there was this amazingly cute guy lecturing in Plant Physiology 101, and she persuaded me to take the course. I stared at him all the way through the lecture and, to cut a long story short, he asked me out to dinner tonight. He's an Englishman, a Plant Sciences post-doc, a few years older than me, and he just invited himself to Sunday lunch, so, if that's alright, I will be driving over for lunch with you next Sunday and you can meet James."

"Holy Moses," said Patti. "Where did this come from? Good for you, sweetheart. I hope you have a great time with him, and do you think he likes barbecued steak?"

"Mum, you're the greatest. Will you tell Dad for me? And do remind him not to give the poor kid the third degree on a first meeting. You know what he's like."

"I'm only going to bring James this time but, if it's OK by you, I would like to bring Jonny and Sarah in a couple of weeks. By the way, will you fill Vinnie in for me on how we're treating the Sarah issue please?"

"Sure Honey," said Patti. "Now you go and get some sleep. I bet you have Plant Physiology 101 tomorrow".

Martha snorted. "Just you behave yourself Mother!"

They laughed, blew each other a kiss down the line and went off to their respective beds. Matthew was away at a conference down near Moro Bay, so Patti was able to lie in bed and think quietly for a while before trying to fall asleep.

She too had always wondered whether the trauma of the rape, and the subsequent abortion, had left some permanent damage to Martha's ability to form relationships. She had noticed the lack of sexually charged intimacy between Jonny and Martha. She had read once that the Israelis had discovered that kibbutzniks, brought up together from an early age, sharing almost every aspect of their lives across family boundaries, rarely married, or formed sexual relationships with, each other.

It was a comfort to Patti to think that the physical coolness between Martha and Jonny was probably only a manifestation of the same phenomenon. She thought this James person must be quite special if he was having such a strong effect on Martha after only, what Patti worked out, was about thirty-six hours, presuming it was a nine o'clock lecture.

She lay there, remembering with pleasure, that breathless feeling that the first pangs of love bring, the intensity of being alive, with all your senses heightened; with a mixture of fear of the uncertain, and a craving for what might become. Each generation passes through those emotions on its journey through time, and, just like passing a baton in a relay, it moves the ownership of that intense pain and pleasure to the next generation. The baton is sometimes dropped, but it very rarely gets back into the hands of those through whom it has passed.

Martha, for the first time in many years, was unable to get to sleep. Her mind was racing, her heart was beating fast, and she was thinking about James. She suddenly realised that she had never been in love before, and she rather liked the way she felt about this stranger from England.

Chapter 11

The next morning Sarah pumped Martha for information, but Martha was giving nothing away. Finally, Sarah said that Jonny had sent the long-awaited email, asking Sarah and Martha to come to lunch on Sunday, and Martha had no choice but to say that she was otherwise engaged.

"You sly old thing," said Sarah. "That was fast work."

"You can talk," said Martha. "I saw you making calf-eyes at Jonny within two minutes of meeting him!"

"Breakfast and no cat fights," said Sarah.

"Breakfast, and you're just afraid you would lose the fight," said Martha. And they went off, arm in arm, to the dining hall.

When they got there, Theresa was already there. She had been to Mass, having fasted overnight of course, and was tucking into a plate of pancakes. She chatted a little and then excused herself to go off to a meeting with the Catholic mission.

"We're having a pro-life meeting this evening at the Memorial Church if you want to come," said Theresa.

"Thank you for asking," said Martha, "but I don't support the basic beliefs of the pro-life lobby, so forgive me if I refuse the invitation."

"Same for me I'm afraid," said Sarah.

Theresa gave them both a withering look and marched out of the dining room.

As it happened, she did not go straight to the Stanford mission but instead went back to her room and wrote another letter to Dear Robert, as he had now become.

Dear Robert,

I'm so grateful to have you to write to. You help me to reaffirm my beliefs in what we are striving for. Without your support I might well doubt myself and then I might just give up in the pursuit of the truth. I long for the day when everyone will recognise the sanctity of all human life and abortion will be a thing of the past. I know that the church believes that sexual intercourse is only for procreation, to make more human beings in God's image, but so many of my friends treat it as recreation and help it to lose its true purpose.

Why, only this morning, I invited my two friends, Sarah, and Martha, to join me this evening at the pro-life meeting in the Memorial Church. They stopped at laughing outright in my face, but they both clearly stated that they did not believe in the values of the pro-life organisation. I do wish you could be here to talk to them and convince them. I find your letters to me so persuasive and comforting. It must seem a very long time before you are eligible for early release, but I shall be patient and I hope that you can be patient too.

Sarah and Martha are a little bit silly; they are student athletes and they are very close friends. They both come from California as far as I can tell, and they compete against each other with no animosity. Martha is a pre-med student, so I suppose she has an informed view of abortion based on the information that medical students are fed by the murderers who perform abortions, but Sarah is interested in plants and plant science, and she wants to save the world. She says that there are already enough people in the world and that contraception is important for liberating women in developing economies. I think she has a new boyfriend called Jonny, and he used to be Martha's boyfriend. It strikes me as a bit odd that Martha has a boyfriend and then, a day or two later, he is Martha's best friend's boyfriend. I know it is not actually immoral, but it is not really decent either, is it?

Well, I have to go to my Mission meeting now, but I will write to you again soon. Is there anything special you would like me to write to you about? I will report on tonight's meeting.

With great affection,
Theresa.

It was a couple of days later when Robert got that letter. As he read it he had to remind himself that his only hope of early release was to remain calm and behave himself.

There were too many coincidences here. Martha and Sarah, Jonny, track athletes, Bay Area. Martha had to be that little bitch who had aborted his child, and Sarah had to be his little bitch of a daughter, who had cut him dead after his conviction. The communication with Theresa now had a new purpose. It was not just to keep Theresa on the hook until he could get his hands on her physically, it was also to keep tabs on the two girls that he most wanted to punish for ruining his life.

If that sexy little bitch of a daughter of his had not flaunted herself all the time in her track kit, he would never have gone to the track meets and formed his plan to rape Martha, and if Martha had been a more devout Catholic, she would not have murdered their child. Revenge is a dish best tasted cold. There would be permafrost on this dish before it could be tasted, but he promised himself that it would be tasted, no matter how long it took.

The reply that Theresa received from Robert Jackson certainly gave her pause for thought. He thanked her for writing to him and including him in her thoughts about her friends, and he began to ask her more questions about those friends. Theresa, naïve though she was, was not unaware that the course of Robert's enquiry was deviating from what she considered to be their main point of contact, the deep belief in Catholic doctrine.

She thought about it a bit and decided that the enquiries were probably only polite; after all, Robert had little else to do or think about in his cell at San Quentin. There was something else which came into Theresa's life which further diverted her interest away from Robert. It was to prove pivotal in the lives of Theresa and all her friends, and a further stimulus to the hatred and determination for revenge that was brewing in Robert Jackson's evil mind.

Track and field at American universities is a winter and spring sport, depending on whether you are at a semester, or a quarter, based university. It means there are indoor events in the first two or three months of the year and the outdoor season begins in earnest in late March or early April.

Unlike many other athletes, who often have individual competition during the fall semester and start their inter-university season after Christmas, the track and field athletes often simply train hard during the fall Semester or Quarter. It so happened that one week in early November Theresa found herself at a loose end, and decided to go and watch her two friends, Sarah, and Martha, training at the Stanford track. They teased her quite a bit and told her that she could only come if she was prepared to train with them. In the end, she accepted the challenge.

Theresa was quite tall, like both the athletes, and, as the knock-out blow to Sky had demonstrated, she was, behind that very shrinking violet image, tough and strong. The running turned out to be a revelation. She was quite fast, and, for an untrained competitor, she showed quite a lot of stamina. Much to Theresa's surprise, she absolutely loved running.

The three girls showered and changed out of their running gear and headed off to The Tin Pot Creamery for an ice-cream. They were sitting there, quietly chatting when Lucas, an African American member of the Track and Field Programme, came over to their table and asked, very politely, if he might join them. Lucas was a very popular member of the team. He was tall, well built, with a ready smile and a mass of tightly curled black hair. Martha jumped to her feet.

"It would be our pleasure, Lukey," she said. "What flavour ice-cream can I get you? Everyone, do you want a coffee now?"

Martha went over to the counter and ordered the single scoop pralines and cream for Lucas and three Americanos and one skinny cappuccino.

When she got back to the table, Lukey was just asking Theresa why he had not seen her before on the track.

"Well," said Theresa, "I don't do running."

"Whoa!" said Lucas. "You don't do running and, I had the clock on you for that four hundred metres, you come out and run a time like that. Where have you been Theresa? Didn't you run at high school?"

"I didn't go to high school," said Theresa. "In fact, I've never been to school since 6th grade. I was home schooled."

Suddenly, lots of things were clear to Sarah and Martha. The unworldliness, the lack of easy social interaction, the lack of boyfriends and, even, girlfriends; all this now began to make sense. It also made sense that Theresa would not have known how to handle Sky, other than by socking her one. If you don't have the cut and thrust of negotiation with your peers, you never learn how to deal with 'issues'.

Martha, a bit like a Jane Austen heroine, was highly tuned in to emotional vibes. Lukey was not here to talk to Sarah and Martha; Lukey was here to talk to Theresa.

"Well," said Lukey. "You're a good runner and, if you like, I can help train you up so that you give these two a run for their money. You might not catch them quickly but if you want to I bet you can be up there with them by the time we graduate."

There was a bit of breath holding by Martha and Sarah. Would she, wouldn't she?

"It surprised me how great it felt running, and feeling the wind in my face, and just getting in touch with my body," said Theresa. "I think I want to do that more and more. I feel very alive. Do you always feel like that after training?"

"Except when I feel completely knackered," said Sarah.

"I take it that is a yes then?" asked Lukey.

Theresa gave the biggest smile any of them had ever seen her give.

"It's a yes. And thank you for offering," she said.

That evening, Theresa sat down to write again to Robert. This time, the letter, after giving a brief account of the previous week's pro-life meeting, went on to talk about what had happened that day and how she had met a very nice young man called Lucas, because she had gone training with Martha, and Sarah. She explained that Lukey was a male sprinter, and he had a mass of tight curly black hair and the most gorgeous smile. Theresa had no idea how much this would stoke the flames of Robert's hatred and resentment.

A week later, Robert sent his reply. By this time, Theresa had had three more training sessions, and was beginning to look forward to them as much as any of her Catholicism-based activities, indeed, if she were honest, more than the sacraments of the church.

She was not expecting the vitriol in the response, about opportunistic young black men. Robert assumed a sprinter with a mass of tight black curls was black. Robert said Lukey would only be trying to seduce her from the path of virginity, and of saving sex for marriage.

Theresa couldn't understand why there was such venom, and where the sexual implication had come from. All Lucas had done was offer to train her. He hadn't even asked her out on a date. As she thought about that, she was surprised to find that she rather wished he had.

The morning after the letter came, Theresa was sitting at breakfast with Lucas and Martha. They had gone for an early training session, and Theresa had decided that running, provided you thanked God for your ability to do it, was as much worshipping Him as going to Mass, and a lot more fun. She decided to show Martha the letter from Robert and ask her what she thought was going on here.

"I can't understand why this lovely devout man is so racially bigoted and so opposed to my enjoying the running. I also can't understand why he doesn't see that I'm beginning to worry about the behaviour of our pro-life leaders, that violence is not God's way, and yet some of them are doing all sorts of violent things to the innocent families of some of the doctors who perform abortions."

Martha had the letter in her hand and was about to start to read it when Sarah joined them.

"What are you doing with a letter from my father?" she said.

There was a stunned silence.

"What?" asked Martha and Theresa simultaneously.

"That is my father's writing," said Sarah, "How did you get it?"

Lucas and Theresa were immediately sworn to secrecy and then the truth came out. Theresa was close to tears, but they were tears of frustration, of disappointment at her own naivety.

Sarah did not say that it was Martha that her father had raped, that was not necessary for the resolution of this situation, but she did make it clear that her father had raped a young girl and was serving a ten-year sentence in San Quentin for that crime.

"I'm so sorry," said Theresa. "I'm so naïve. I just wish I had gone to school like the rest of you. It's taking me ages to catch up on all this emotional development, and I make such stupid mistakes. I've told him all about you and he now knows where you are. I guess you would have preferred him not to. Look, even if he behaves perfectly, you will have graduated before he comes out, won't you? I'm going to write immediately and tell him that I know who he is, and that there will be no more contact from me. I wonder why he's so violently into pro-life. He clearly is."

They all went off to their different classes and agreed to meet at the track that afternoon to do some more training.

It was difficult to say who was more shaken up by the events. For Sarah, it was a reminder that her father was still out there, no matter how hard she tried to exclude him from her life; for Theresa, it was a reminder of the dangers of her trusting innocence; for Martha, it was a reminder that ten years seems hardly long enough to keep this evil guy out of circulation.

Theresa brought all the letters she had exchanged with Robert to the track with her and, after the training session, they sat and looked at them together. It was obvious to the more experienced girls, and to Lukey, that Robert had been grooming Theresa.

They could see the progression, and the 'My poor little Darling' letter, that was the last one before the wheels began to come off, was the final proof to all of them that Robert had rather unpleasant intentions towards his pen pal.

They could see how far Theresa had come on her journey to a more worldly view when her response was simply:

"The effing bastard. I'll castrate the bastard if I ever get my hands on him. Do you think we can use this to delay his release? Should I write him one final letter?"

Deep inside, Martha rejoiced at this. Theresa was going to be alright.

Lukey said, "Don't waste the paper and the ink on him. Write to the prison warden telling him that Robert Jackson has been deceitful and has tried to lure you into an inappropriate relationship. He's also been pumping you for information about his daughter and her friends, and don't forget to tell them that he got you to send him a photograph of you in a swimming costume. That should fuck up his chances of release; oops, sorry, didn't mean to swear but it makes me very angry for you."

"Please don't let him know that I'm no longer Sarah Jackson," said Sarah. "He doesn't know my new surname and I would like to keep it that way. It will make it just a bit harder for him to trace Mum, and me, and Tim, when they do let the pervert out."

There was a bit of silence and they all took drinks from their training water bottles.

Lukey finally broke the gloominess of the mood.

"Now you no longer have a geriatric boyfriend. Would you let me take you out to dinner tonight?"

Theresa's eyes lit up and her face beamed.

"About time you asked me," she said.

And that is how four became six, because Jonny came over that evening from Berkeley and Martha and James, Sarah and Jonny, and Theresa and Lucas all went together to the Tai Pan restaurant on Waverley Street. Robert Jackson had fried catfish and potato wedges, it was not 'haut cuisine' in San Quentin, it was Friday!

Chapter 12

That Sunday was the first time that the McArthys met James. Martha drove James out to Mill Valley and gave him a running commentary all the way. They passed Mill Valley High School, with the red outdoor running track where Martha and Sarah had begun their athletics journeys. Martha couldn't resist taking James to the Depot Café and Book Store in the centre of town, for a coffee and one of their exquisite croissants. James spent the whole time staring at the giant redwoods.

"We have a metasequoia by the pond in St Joseph's," he said. "I think they call it the Dawn Redwood. It was thought to be extinct, but someone brought a live specimen back to the college from China. It had been found in a small clump of trees by someone during the Second World War. It's lovely, but these things are just magnificent."

"If you behave, I'll ask Mark and Sarah if we can have a swim in their pool, but not today. It's a bit too chilly. Maybe, next spring when things start to warm up. I love lying on my back looking up at the blue sky through the branches. I'll show you the pool, we go past it on the way up to our house."

They finished their late breakfast and drove up the canyon to the house on the hillside just off West Blithedale.

When they arrived, Matthew and Vincent were tending to the barbecue. Funny how, even in late October, it was still warm enough to barbecue out of doors. The decking at the house was a sun trap, the coastal fog was more a summer phenomenon, and the deck was well sheltered from any breeze.

Martha introduced James to each member of the family in turn and they all duly shook hands, except Patti, who gave James a quick hug of welcome.

It was not exactly the third degree but there was a lot of asking about family, and career, and interests, and the sort of thing that you ask about when you are being sociable, and you think that your daughter might be a little bit serious with this new boyfriend. There was also a lot of polite interest from James in Vincent.

James asked about Vinnie's career plans. He discovered that Vinnie had an eye on a basketball scholarship at Cal and was hoping, like Jonny, to do engineering there. Vinnie's engineering interest was more around electronics and control systems than mechanical, but he liked that he could pick a bit of everything until he specialised in the upper class-man years. Martha, with her Jane Austen antennae out, realised that James and Vinnie were getting on well.

Matthew was, as he always was, much more reserved. It was curious how reticent Matthew could be in meeting new people because, once he got to know folk, he was often the life and soul of the party. It was a little bit strange watching him being so careful around James. It might have stayed a little bit distant if James had not suddenly asked Matthew if he could show him round the garden.

"I noticed you had a really well laid-out garden and some very interesting plants. Many of them are new to me. I'm a botanist, but my interests are in food producing plants and photosynthesis and bioelectricity. I'm not that great on taxonomy."

The pair of them filled up their glasses with another beer and headed off into the garden. By the time they came back, all the reserve had gone, and they were virtually bosom buddies.

From that point, the time flew by and, as it started to get dark, James and Martha said their goodbyes and headed back off to the dorms.

"I have a small flat in one of the campus buildings," said James, just as they were leaving, "I wonder if all of you might like to come over sometime and have lunch with us. I'm not cordon bleu, but I can manage a few quite passable offerings and I know you haven't really been over to see the campus much. You could watch Martha and Sarah train. I would probably invite a few of our friends, I'm sure they would love to meet Martha's family. She's quite the focus of our little circle."

"Do you mean an apartment?" asked Matthew. That triggered a conversation about language differences and a quick rendition, in his terrible singing voice, of 'Let's call the whole thing off.'

It was agreed for the weekend after Martha's birthday. James also offered a bed for the night of the birthday to Vinnie. That too was agreed.

Martha's roommate, Cecilia Tan, had trained at Nick Bollittieri's academy from the age of about 11. She had risen quite high as a junior, both in the States and internationally. She had played in all the Junior Grand Slam events, Wimbledon, Roland Garros, US Open and Oz. They got on very well together, but it took them almost the whole quarter before they managed to work out why they had been put in the same room together. They were both pre-med, but the second thing they had in common was that they shared a birthday, 31st October.

Martha and Ceci organised a joint birthday party, and this was the beginning of a further developing friendship for Martha and her five close friends. Ceci was lively, intelligent, chatty, and friendly, and she soon became an additional member of the group. The friends would go to the Stanford Tennis Centre to watch Ceci's matches and Ceci would often come along on the many occasions when they all went out to dinner together.

On the weekend of the party Vinnie, only fifteen months younger than Martha, was driven over to Palo Alto by his father, Matthew. Vinnie was going to stay at James's apartment. It didn't occur to Martha that a romantic attachment might develop for Vinnie with any of her friends, after all, he was her little brother. Martha's usually reliable Jane Austen's heroine mode must have been turned off by her current total absorption in her relationship with James because she missed the chemistry developing between Vinnie and Cecilia.

Vinnie was tall and handsome, quite mature for his age. When he danced with Ceci, he towered over her, but he danced almost every minute of the party with her, and they talked and talked, to the exclusion of almost everyone else, until the early hours of the morning.

Vinnie stayed overnight with James, and, by the morning, he began to wonder whether Stanford might be a better bet for him than Cal. Jonny, who had also been present at the party, mostly wrapped around Sarah, tried to persuade him otherwise.

It was strange for Vinnie to meet Sarah again. Sarah had been a great support to Martha during the period between the rape and the termination, and right up until the meeting at which Martha had identified Robert Jackson as the rapist. Vinnie had not seen her since then and only knew that she was back because Patti had told him and warned him not to reveal the back story. Vinnie had enjoyed Tim's company before the tragic events and he asked Sarah, very discretely, if she thought Tim might like to meet up again.

Sarah promised to find out. Vinnie was too shy to ask Cecilia out on a date, and he really didn't have the wherewithal to do so anyway. He did not have a car and he did not have the experience to be confident about dating a girl who had travelled all over the world playing tennis and was so much more worldly wise then he.

Theresa began to question all her previous beliefs. The first thing she decided to do was to go and study some biology. Her mother had been a creationist and had refused to let Theresa read or listen to anything about Darwin and evolution. Theresa decided that majoring in religion was not going to happen. She stopped going to Mass in the week, she went running early mornings instead. She still went on Sunday to Mass, but without the same fervour that had infused her during the first couple of months of her time at college.

She talked a lot with Lukey about pro-life, and she began to see that there was an alternative view, that the potential to become an independent being was but one of the definitions that might be used to define a life. She listened to the arguments about sentience being the dividing line between an individual and a mere collection of cells.

The one thing Theresa was unwavering about, at least at this stage, was saving sex for marriage. Lukey found no problem with that. It was not an issue between them. They both behaved as if their relationship was one for the long term.

Before the quarter ended, Theresa sought out Sky and apologised to her for having hit her and having been so antagonistic towards her. Sky was much less outrageously dressed than in the early days, still a Goth, but a clean and tidy Goth. She was no longer smoking, not even cigarettes. To Theresa's amazement Sky asked Theresa to join her for a coffee and started to explain herself. It turned out that Sky had adopted her cannabis habit, and her Goth dress sense, and her promiscuity, as a coping mechanism following systematic abuse as a young teen.

It also turned out that, like Theresa, she had been home schooled. In her case, it was a deliberate attempt to hide the abuse that was happening to her. There is more than one form of child abuse and the two girls soon realised, as Theresa also began to tell her story to Sky, that they had both been victims of abuse, in quite different ways. It was something that Sky said towards the end of their little chat that gave Theresa the push towards the next step on her own journey.

"You're so easy to talk to," said Sky, "I hear you are now going training with some of the other freshers. Can I come training with you next time you go? I think I need to sort myself out physically. I used to be quite a good gymnast, and that's when the abuse started. I miss being fit and healthy. Can I join you, please?"

Of course, Theresa said that Sky could join her. She knew that Lukey wouldn't mind and, anyway, lots of people were always there at the training sessions. The thing that made the difference to Theresa was that she had never before thought of herself as a good listener, and yet here was Sky saying that she had found her easy to talk to. It was a bit of a damascene conversion, but suddenly `Theresa knew she was going to be a psychology major and train as a clinical psychologist.

When Theresa told Lukey about her plans later that day, he said, "Where did that come from? I like it but I didn't see that coming. You will be great at it."

Theresa could not really explain how she had decided on this vocation, but she told Lukey about the meeting with Sky, and Lukey was not surprised when, a couple of days later, Sky and Theresa moved back in together.

There were a few sheepish grins, but there were also some big hugs, lots of tears, and several late night sessions in which both of the girls unburdened themselves. Theresa bought Sky a legalise cannabis poster and the two of them fell about laughing. And Sky became part of the ever-expanding circle of friendship that was spreading out from Martha and Sarah.

In San Quentin, Robert Jackson was called into the warden's Office to explain the letters he had been writing. Silver tongued Robert managed to convince the warden that he was merely acting as a sort of surrogate father towards the girl. He explained that Theresa was obsessed with pro-life and Catholicism, and he was trying to create a relationship with her which would enable him to wean her off the more dangerous aspects of these things. He apologised and he even started to cry.

"I had no idea she was so naïve," he said. "I felt sure she would understand what I was trying to do. I just wanted her to understand that she was not alone in her Catholic beliefs, that there was someone like me who was as deeply moved by the church as she was."

The rest of the conversation was equally nauseating, although the warden, himself a practising Catholic, was wanting to be convinced and allowed himself to be deceived into believing Jackson. The upshot of it was that Robert Jackson remained on track to be released after seven years for good behaviour. The warden told him so.

Chapter 13

At the end of the quarter, the freshmen went out of residence for a couple of weeks over Christmas. Martha asked her parents if James could come and stay for a few days since he was not going back to England for the Holidays. They had met a couple of times since the first Sunday when Martha took him home to Mill Valley.

The first occasion had been when all of them came over to James's place for a cold buffet lunch one Sunday. James served Coronation Chicken, cold salmon, lots of salads, wonderful sourdough, and a dessert called Boodles Fool, which is full of cream and orange and is delicious and was invented as a dish at Boodle's Private members Club in London. Lots of the gang attended, including Sky, who was now a very close friend of Theresa's.

On the second occasion James, Sarah, Jonny, and Martha had gone over to lunch one Sunday, after the party. It was the first time since Sarah and her family had left for Chicago that Martha's parents had met Sarah. Jonny, James, and Martha, left Sarah alone with Patti and Matthew for a while, and Sarah updated them on all that had happened to her, and to Susan and Tim, since the conviction.

"Does James know what happened to Martha?" asked Patti.

"I don't think she has told him," said Sarah.

"I think she's going to have to," said Patti. "If she is serious about him, he will need to know. It did happen. It was not her fault. If he really likes her, it will not change things."

"I guess everyone has been so kind protecting me," said Sarah, "That they haven't thought through the situation for Martha. I'll talk to her later this week if you think I should."

"I think you should at least discuss it with her," said Patti. "And now let's go back and join the others."

In San Quentin, Robert Jackson was mixing with a lot of very dangerous sexual predators. He was learning from them all the time, taking note of every trick that they had to try to avoid forensic detection. He was beginning to form some new ideas about how he might avoid detection when, and not if, he committed his next rape. His plan to use Theresa as a surrogate rape victim had been blown out of the water by that daughter of his, and her friend, the baby killer. He was beginning to think that a rape, followed by an attack on his daughter and that Martha girl, and then an escape to South America, would be a really good way to celebrate release.

Only just over three years away now if he behaved himself. He asked some of the more knowledgeable criminals about how to get false documentation and was building up a dossier of the things he would need. There was a need for money, but he had always had bank accounts in another name that Susan and his family knew nothing about. He had never been sure why he had set them up, and in a false name, but he was glad that he had done it, as it would facilitate all his intended crimes, and his eventual escape.

The one big issue he had was that his fingerprints and his DNA were now on the data base, but he thought he had an idea how to deal with both those problems. As far as he knew, his ideas were original, and he was not about to let anyone else use the ideas first. Being patient was remarkably hard. The food was shit; the company was shit. The time went by 'real slow'.

All the friends stayed up a little after the end of instruction for the quarter. Theresa and Sky talked about going home. Sky felt that she could not face going back to where she had been abused for so long. Theresa felt that she was now old enough for the constant indoctrination at home not to matter. She had never been physically mistreated, there had always been food on the table, and the freedom to go anywhere, if it was related to the church and the church community.

She reasoned that taking Sky home with her would free her of that burden, and demonstrate some independence, and might help her to rebuild her relationship with her mother on a more adult plane. It would be easy to resent the lost opportunities caused by home schooling, but it would be completely futile. Moving on was now the name of the game for Theresa, so she rang her mother and Sky was booked in as a house guest for the entire vacation.

Lukey was from the East Coast, upstate New York to be exact. His Father was a Professor of African and African-American studies at Cornell University and his Mother was a Museum Curator at the Corning Glass Museum. Lukey was flying home for the vacation.

Jonny and Sarah lived on opposite sides of the Bay. They decided that it might be a little too early to spend Christmas away from their families. Jonny's parents, and his little sister, Iris, were desperate to see him, and Sarah's family were also very keen to have her home. They decided to settle for regular meetings, either in downtown San Francisco, or near to one or other of their home bases.

All these youngsters were still training hard, especially the runners, because the indoor season began very shortly after the start of the Winter Quarter.

It wasn't until they were all packed up and about to leave for their holiday destinations that Martha suddenly realised that Ceci was not going home and was going to be by herself for the whole two weeks that everyone else was away.

"I can't afford the flight to Florida," Ceci explained. "My family moved there when I joined the Bollitieri Academy, and all the family money is tied up in that home or was used for paying for my coaching. If I didn't have my full-ride scholarship for tennis, I couldn't possibly be at Stanford. But please don't worry about me. I've been alone a lot on tour before coming here. I'll just get on with some work and beat the heck out of the lot of you academically."

Martha said nothing immediately but made a couple of phone calls. She called her mother on her cell, and then she called James. There was no hesitation from either of them. Martha went back to the room she shared with Ceci. Petite, tough, resourceful, Ceci, was sitting there, staring into space, and looking very down.

"Pack your bags, Ceci," said Martha. "You've got twenty minutes and then I'm going without you!"

The smile was worth a million dollars.

"You mean it? But what about James? What about your family?"

James happened to come into the room just as Ceci said his name.

"We're going to get plenty of time together," said James. "After all, Martha tells me that you are going to be studying hard in order to kick everyone else's arses."

It took Ceci five minutes to pack her clothes and then another five to get her books and her sport stuff together.

"Will you be able to take me past the campus shop before we leave?" asked Ceci. "I really can't go to your house for Christmas without picking up a present or two for your parents and for Vinnie."

Jane Austen was back on duty. '*For your parents and for Vinnie, not for your family*,' thought Martha. '*I'm going to watch this space.*'

The more she thought about it, the more she realised that every telephone conversation she had had with Vinnie, since the party, included Vinnie asking after Cecilia, and every time she had told the group she had called home, Ceci had asked how Vinnie was doing. Nothing obvious but this might just be an interesting vacation.

'*Well, well, little brother*,' thought Martha.

On the way back up to Marin, Martha explained to Ceci that there were excellent tennis courts down in the centre of Mill Valley. She also said that she knew a couple of guys who played Division One tennis at university and would also be home on vacation.

"They're nice guys. They usually play a couple of hours a day in the vacations, and I'm sure they can give you a good game," said Martha.

Ceci had never seen the giant redwoods, and James had never been to Muir Woods and Muir Beach, so, on the way home, Martha made a big detour and took the pair of them to have fish and chips at the Pelican Inn, and a small jug of English beer. The Reception Centre at Muir Woods was open, and they went for a walk around the giant trees. It was mind blowing for both James and Ceci.

The welcome given the group when they reached the house in Blithedale Canyon was everything Martha could have hoped for. As always, her parents were welcoming to James and they made a special fuss of Ceci. Vinnie was unusually shy, but Patti told Martha, when they were alone, that Vinnie had been very excited to learn the Ceci was coming to spend Christmas with them.

"I think he rather took a shine to her when you had him over to Stanford for your party," she said.

Christmas served only to reinforce the friendships that were forming among the group. There was very little academic work done by any of them, except James, who was busy writing up some experiments for the research group he was working with in his role as a post-doc. With James working, it was very pleasant for Martha to have the company of Ceci. Given that Ceci had spent most of her formative years playing tennis, and had been home schooled, it might have been thought that her social skills and her general development would be limited, but that was far from the case. Home schooling for Ceci had been organised by her father and involved all kinds of extracurricular, as well as standard curricular, activities. It had not been entirely restrained by syllabus and so it contained some fascinating high spots, such as regular visits to theatres and museums. Ceci had taken ballet lessons before she had been 'discovered' playing tennis in the local park, and she had maintained her interest in ballet and dance right through her school days.

She had so much to tell Martha about her upbringing. The San Francisco Ballet was putting on a production of 'The Nutcracker' at the Opera House on Van Ness Avenue, and Ceci persuaded Martha, James, and Vinnie, to go with her. For Vinnie, it was one of the highlights of that Christmas.

By the end of the holidays, there was simply no question, Vinnie was applying to Stanford for his engineering.

Sarah and Jonny came over a few times, Jonny had a car and he brought Tim with him, and Iris, Jonny's younger sister.

Ceci reflected on how much nicer the Christmas had been for her than it would have been had she stayed at Stanford, working, but by herself. She managed to play tennis regularly with the local guys that Martha knew, and they asked her out, but she politely refused. Martha thought it might just have something to do with not wanting to upset Vinnie.

The 'gang' all returned to Stanford, and, in Jonny's case, Berkeley, very early in January. The Winter Quarter, the first part of the Spring Semester at Berkeley, seemed to fly by. All the students were now beginning to think about their majors and the course requirements, so the academic work took on a new significance. Perhaps, it was the presence of James, with his received pronunciation English, that turned thoughts in that direction, but several of the gang, except perhaps Lukey, Theresa and Sky, started to think about going to the UK to study after graduation. The two would-be medics were talking about whether they would be able to take a year out to study at Cambridge for a masters, between completing their pre-med and going on to med school. James was going to try to get back to Cambridge when his post-doc work at Stanford finished, either on a Royal Society Research Fellowship or, perhaps, a college Junior Research Fellowship. Sarah had plans for a Ph.D. in the Plant Sciences Department and Jonny was looking at the Engineering Department. They were all looking at various scholarship opportunities, including the Gates Foundation awards. Lukey was just thinking about where Theresa might be going, and he was planning to stay somewhere near her.

The rest of the year passed in a welter of athletics competition. Ceci's tennis team won the NCAA Division 1 National Championships, for the second year in succession. Large barrels of Gatorade were thrown everywhere and the traditional dogpile on top of the coach took place, after the final ball was hit. Sarah, Martha, and Lukey had successful track seasons, but the overall track and field performance was good rather than outstanding. It had been a long time since the Stanford Track and Field had won the intercollegiate title. Individuals did well, and both Sarah and Martha improved their personal best times, and both got to the National Individual Championships, but there were no gold medals. Ceci and Ronnie (Sarah's room-mate Veronica, a vet pre-med) won the NCAA Doubles Championship. There were All Pac-12 awards and some All-American awards. It was a good year for all of them.

Alongside the group's activities the campus was aflame with the issue of sexual harassment. It was all triggered by evidence of sexual harassment at other universities, where football players and other athletes were not investigated adequately, after claims of sexual assault were made against them. Theresa, moving ever away from the zealous pursuit of the pro-life mission, turned her attention to the whole question of sexual abuse and harassment. Sky joined her in taking a very active role in the movement to create more social awareness and better education programmes for both men and women. Martha could not help being affected by all that was going on and started to question the whole issue of sexual discrimination and bias in academia and the professions as well as in everyday life. Martha and Sarah started to become active in the Rape Crisis and Anti-Harassment movements; it was, eventually, to blow the cover off their own histories.

It was about the middle of May when Martha, at a Rape Crisis meeting, became slightly irritated by a girl who was suggesting that the morning after pill should not be routinely administered to all victims of rape. Perhaps Martha was physically and mentally tired, perhaps she was emotionally tired of hiding her experience and pretending it had not happened. Whatever the reason, she decided, there and then, that the time had come to talk to James, and her other close friends, about the rape incident, about her abortion, and about what it had meant for her. She rang James and told him that she had something very important to talk to him about. Would he be able to meet her after her 5 o'clock class?

It might have been one of the hardest things Martha had ever done. To some extent she had survived by ignoring the whole incident, wiping it out of her mind. Now it was surfacing, and she was having to confront some of the emotions that she had buried for almost four years. It would not only be Martha that would have to revisit and recalibrate her responses, but it would also be Sarah, Sarah's and Martha's families, and many others, the Strauss family, Jonny, the home schoolers, among them.

James arrived looking very apprehensive. His worry was not helped by the fact that Martha looked, for the first time he had seen it, seriously depressed and anxious.

"What's the matter Martha?" asked James. "Can it be so bad, that you look so sad?"

"I've got to tell you something James, and I don't know how you are going to handle it."

James went pale and started to tremble.

"You aren't planning to chuck me, are you?" he said, stumbling badly over the words.

"No," said Martha. Then she paused.

"It's about something horrible that happened to me when I was a very young teenager. I thought I had buried it but all this debate about sexual harassment has brought it back to me, and you and I cannot continue our relationship until I know how you feel about it, and you know how you feel about it."

James looked almost relieved. He was confident he could handle almost anything, as long as it did not involve Martha and he breaking up.

"I'm just going to tell you bluntly," said Martha. "I can't do this sugar-coated."

There was a pause.

"I was raped on my way walking home from babysitting one evening when I had just finished 9th grade. I got pregnant and had to have an abortion at seven weeks. That's how I met Jonny because his dad was my gynaecologist. Perhaps, I should have told you sooner, but it's complicated, and if I tell you the full details, some more people are potentially going to be damaged by the revelations."

James's reaction was immediate. He jumped up from his chair, rushed round the table, grabbed Martha from her seat, wrapped her in a bear hug and started to kiss her passionately, almost insatiably. It took her about a milli-second to respond, and then she was kissing him back, more passionately than she had ever kissed him before.

They might both have burst into tears, but that was not the nature of the beast. Instead, they eventually tore themselves apart, much to the relief of all the onlookers who were totally unsure what was going on.

James just would not let go of Martha's hand. They somehow managed to get the table between them again and sit down, still with her hand firmly clasped in his.

James broke the silence.

"I'm so sorry," he said. "Please, tell me only what you're comfortable with telling me. If you want to know how I now feel, all I can say is that my respect and admiration for you has gone off the scale. You've always amazed me, but you now amaze me even more. Where does that steel core of yours come from? And yet…"

There was a silence, filled with the two of them just staring into each other's eyes and now holding both hands across the table.

"Pure gold," muttered James.

"What was that?" asked Martha.

"I said 'pure gold'," said James. "I caught the sun shining on those gold flecks in your eyes and it just sort of slipped out."

"Trust me, James. I can't tell you any more now. I need to clear it with a couple of other people before I do. But I will try to clear things with them, as soon as I can, and then I will tell you the rest."

James thought about what he had just heard. He also thought about the passion in the kiss they had shared. It was as if a dam had burst, and Martha, for the first time, had let her emotions run riot. He could feel the magic in that kiss.

Martha was thinking about Jonny and her. Had that rape been why she and Jonny had been platonic friends? Might things have been different without the shadow of Jackson's deed hanging over them? Would things now be different with James? That kiss had been something different. Those bodice-ripper stories where the earth moves; they don't often end up in bed, except by implication, but Martha had a feeling that this kiss might just end up in bed, and not in theory either.

Two very happy young people went about the rest of the day's business. That evening Martha went round to James's apartment, and her guess about where the kiss might end proved to be accurate.

Next morning, James and Martha were sitting in the dining room having breakfast when Ceci and Sarah came down to join them. Ceci, somewhat naively, said something about Martha not coming back to the room that night, and Martha said she had been talking to someone rather late, in their room, and had decided it was unfair to come home so late, and wake Ceci up, so she had slept on the couch there. There were many things about that statement which were untrue, sleeping was one of them, on the couch was another. Sarah was just about to take a sip of coffee when Martha said this, and found herself spluttering, having snorted a large noseful of coffee, accidentally, as she tried not to laugh. Martha kicked her under the table.

Sarah could hardly wait to get Martha by herself so that she could pump her for information. The opportunity did not come until just before afternoon training. Then the whole story was revealed.

At first, the two girls agreed that James did not need to know that it was Sarah's father who was the rapist. Martha would just explain that it was a school friend's father. Then they recalled that Theresa, who was part of the group, did know about Robert Jackson, and that Sarah's mother had changed the family name to protect herself and her children, so they agreed that Sarah and Martha would talk to James together that evening.

The conversation between Martha, Sarah and James took place outside one of the local bars where James, who was clearly over-21, bought the drinks. There was nothing but sympathy for Sarah's predicament, and James was able to praise her too, for the courage and perseverance that had let her emerge, relatively unscathed, from such a different, but, in many ways, no less traumatic, past. He made it clear how happy he was for both Martha and Sarah that they had managed to remain Best Friends Forever.

Over the next few weeks, the whole story, including the change of name for Sarah, became generally known on campus. Martha talked about her rape at the Rape Crisis and Sexual Harassment meetings, and Sarah explained how the event had impacted on her, and her mother and brother, as purely innocent parties. This had quite an impact on some of those present, particularly the male members of the group. It was not always thought about, by perpetrators of these crimes, what a devastating impact their actions might have on their family and friends.

Theresa had a very long conversation with Martha and realised, finally, that her sympathies for the pro-life organisation were now totally undermined, and that abortion was a much more complex issue than she had previously thought. She could not condemn Martha for what she had done, and she wondered what other circumstances might make abortion a morally justifiable option. She started to look at the biology of pregnancy and reproduction, and to listen to arguments on both sides. Theresa remained quite conflicted, but the pro-life movement itself was jettisoned completely.

"Today's news is tomorrow's fish and chip wrapper" is a well-known British saying, and the story of Martha and Sarah soon faded from the limelight. There were more important crusades around women's rights and harassment to occupy the time of the activists.

To all intents and purposes, the end of the freshman year marked the end, for Sarah and Martha, of the episode that had dogged them for four years. For Robert Jackson, it meant only a further three years to wait before he could start to act out his revenge.

Freshman year at university is often a time of huge change, and a time when friendships, that will last forever, are forged. Sophomore and junior years are times of consolidation. In some ways, they can be magical, especially if you are living in the climate and ethos of the Bay Area.

The revelations of the rape and the name change soon faded into the background, and the group of friends simply carried on with their lives, building the foundations for future career choices. Susan McElroy and Tim were soon a part of a support network for all the undergraduates, especially Jonny, who was very definitely deeply in love with Sarah. Sarah had developed a real love of cycling and would often head off into the countryside with Jonny on relatively long bike rides. Mount Tam was almost a none challenge to the pair of them by the time they reached their final year. In that final year, Sarah began to focus more on the cycling and to think about adding the swimming, that she would need for triathlon, to her athletic repertoire. She remained competitive as an 800m runner at intercollegiate level, but her 400 metre times started to slip as the training she was undertaking became more endurance and less sprint focussed.

Martha remained focussed on track. Secretly she did not mind giving up the cycle trips she had undertaken previously with Jonny. Martha's times went from strength to strength and she began to add the 400m hurdles to her repertoire at a competitive level. Depending on the meeting, the availability of other athletes, and the strength of the opposition, she would be asked to run in any event of 800-metres or shorter distance.

The one significant change to the group dynamic was that Vinnie arrived as a fresher at Stanford a year after his sister. The dynamic changed because, as Martha had thought it might, the relationship between Vinnie and Ceci had somehow taken off. Vinnie was playing basketball on the Varsity Squad and Ceci was playing tennis. Their social lives, as well as revolving round the already formed friendships with Martha and the gang, began to expand to include the other tennis players on Ceci's team, and the basketball players, especially the other freshers, in Vinnie's squad.

Chapter 14

By the end of the junior year, the undergraduates were beginning to think more seriously about destinations for after graduation. James had submitted his application for Junior Research fellowships in Cambridge, most notably at St Joseph's, which had been his undergraduate college and where his Ph.D. supervisor held a professorial fellowship. The work he had been doing in Stanford had proved to be very productive. He had managed to harness the photo-activation of one of the steps in the photosynthesis chain, to movement of ions, to create an electrical gradient across an artificial membrane. This created a sort of battery, which could then be used to create a current flow, and so the whole system worked as a sort of light to electrical energy transducer. The thing about James's biological engineering was that the efficiency of the process was much better than the efficiency of the best solar panel. There was a reasonable chance, as James had already applied for a patent under the auspices of Stanford, that James and Stanford were going to make a lot of money. The supply of the photo-transducer components was potentially huge, since all you needed was some maize from which to extract the molecules, for the photo-transducer, and the ion exchanger, and the artificial membranes were as cheap to manufacture as a supermarket plastic bag. They could be made of biological and degradable materials. James's JRF application was linked to his application for the Royal Society Fellowship. The college element would be without pay but would enable him to have a link to a college, and to supervise students if he wished.

The medics were choosing the medical school to which they would apply.

Jonny had already decided that he wanted to go to do a masters in the United Kingdom, possibly even a Ph.D. Deep down he wanted to get into Formula 1 as an engineer, but he thought he might just have to get some UK experience before being taken on by the mainly European based teams. He was applying for a Gates Scholarship.

Theresa and Sky were both planning to take masters courses, Theresa in Psychology and Sky in Social Work. They did not plan on moving far either, Berkeley was their top degree choice.

Sarah was following up on her plan to do a Ph.D. at Cambridge in the Plant Sciences division. James would have been prepared to take her on as his own Ph.D. student, had he held a faculty position, but for the moment he simply put her in touch with Professor Arnold Raum, the plant scientist who had supervised James's own thesis. A Gates Scholarship was how Sarah planned to get herself funded, but she was also applying for the scholarships offered by St Joseph's, knowing that, in the first instance, these were not full funding. She was determined to go, and she would be taking out loans, if she failed to get funding from the host institution.

Ceci and Martha were both applying to medical schools but wanted, if accepted, to take a year out before taking up their places. They wanted to go to Cambridge. The top applications from the two pre-meds were University of California San Francisco, Stanford, Northwestern, and Columbia. There were also five scholarships, funded by a legacy from a Stanford graduate, which were designed to allow graduating students, who had contributed in either athletics or music, and had very high GPAs, to take a year out from their studies and go to Cambridge to study a masters course of their choice. Ceci and Martha were each applying for these awards. Ceci wanted to take a Masters in Translational Research in the Department of Physiology, Development and Neuroscience, and Martha wanted to study for a masters in Obstetrics and Gynaecology. Ceci teased Martha that, coming from an American background, she would have to get used to spelling Gynaecology properly.

The first part of the Senior year involved all of them putting in their applications. It was a rigorous process in each case. They were all applying to top schools for the courses they wanted to pursue, and, even having outstanding GPA's, which each of them did, was no guarantee of acceptance.

James heard from St Joseph's early in the year that he had been given a Research Fellowship, and they offered him a salary as well, so he at least knew he was heading for Cambridge that summer. He flew over to the UK for interviews in April for the Royal Society Post-Doctoral Fellowships, and he heard from them at the end of May that he had been successful. The Department of Plant Sciences was very keen to welcome him back. Stanford offered James a permanent post, but he had no interest in remaining in the Bay Area. He was anxious to get back to his old department and pick up with Prof Raum where he had left off.

Gradually, over the course of the Winter Quarter, and, in the case of Berkeley, the Spring Semester, each of the hopeful undergraduates received their acceptances from their top choices, and Ceci and Martha chose UCSF, Sky and Theresa chose Berkeley, and Jonny and Sarah, were accepted at Cambridge, subject to finance and completing their degrees with high GPAs. Ceci and Martha had applied to Cambridge for their masters courses before the outcome of their medical school applications were known. They also were successful, subject to finance and good enough GPAs.

Sarah and Jonny were awarded their Gates Scholarships in early February. They had 72 hours to accept the offer once it had been made. It took them about 72 minutes, each.

There was a bit of a wait while the finance was sorted out for Martha and Ceci. The process of awarding the Stanford Scholarships was rather unusual. Former holders of these awards, which had been running for about thirty years, formed a committee which interviewed the candidates. The criteria for the award included not only academic ability, that was almost a given, but a sense of how the award holder would represent Stanford in an almost ambassadorial way in the Cambridge context.

These interviews took place at the end of the Winter Quarter, and Martha and Ceci were both given scholarships. That meant they had fulfilled the trickiest of the acceptance requirements, and it also meant they now had to negotiate a year's deferral for the UCSF medical school places. Fortunately, holding scholarships and places in medically related courses was deemed a strong enough reason for deferral, and so Ceci and Martha were lined up to go to Cambridge, and, with James as an influence, they both chose St. Joseph's as their graduate college.

On graduation, Theresa and Sky would be moving across the Bay to Berkeley, and everyone else, except Lukey, would be going to Cambridge, and, more specifically, to St Joseph's.

Lukey, by now, was completely committed to Theresa and she to him. Lukey had majored in Computer and Information Science and he had done very well. He had no difficulty in obtaining a job in the Computing Service at the University of Berkeley, even though he had left it until Theresa knew where she was going before he had applied.

Berkeley graduation day took place in early May. Jonny's family, Sarah's family, Martha's family, and the friends from Stanford all attended the event and afterwards joined Jonny and his parents at one of the Chinese restaurants on Durant. Jonny had achieved the GPA he needed for his Cambridge admission and, with his Gates Scholarship assured, the celebration was truly joyous. It did go on rather late into the night, including a trip to Barclay's up on College Avenue in Rockridge, for the younger members of the team. The parents departed leaving the youngsters to it. Tim and Vinnie were old enough to get away with staying, even though they were strictly underage. There was a bit of a debate about whether Iris, Jonny's little sister, could stay with them. Part of the problem was that she was very small for her age, and, at only eighteen, she was easily the youngest of the group. Tim and Vinnie were now juniors, about to go into their final years. In the end, Iris stayed, much to Tim's delight, and they got away with it. False id is a very useful thing.

Jonny, after the ceremony, had an extra month of kicking his heels while he waited for the Stanford commencement. He spent a lot of time getting really fit, and working on his cycling, which was rapidly becoming more of a focus for him than triathlon. He still liked triathlon and had an ambition to do an iron-man one day, but his swimming was not as strong as his other two events, and he was concentrating on distance running, and road cycling, more and more as he grew older. Following graduation, he moved over to Stanford on virtually a full-time basis and Sarah and he began to sleep together almost every night. Sarah had opted for a single room in the senior year, as had Martha and Ceci; Theresa and Sky, against all the early odds, were still sharing.

Graduation at Stanford was a big event. This graduation year was the one in which the university got the chief executive of a major tech company, based locally, to come and give the commencement address at graduation. Jonny was invited over from Berkeley by Sarah. Theresa's mother arrived, Sky's parents did not come, there was too much bad blood between her and her parents over the abuse, and the traumatic upbringing, but Sky, somehow, did not mind. She was made a part of every one of the families that did attend, and, in the evening, the whole group of them went, with their families, for a private celebration at the seafood restaurant in Sausalito, overlooking the Marina and the Bay. Jonny and Martha were able to offer beds to everyone, including their families, either directly at home or by calling in favours from friends. Theresa, Sky, and Theresa's mother, stayed with Martha and James at the McArthy home; Sarah and her family, and Ceci and Lukey, stayed with the Strauss family down on Blithedale. Vinnie was a little grumpy about this, but the walk down to the Strauss house was not that far.

The following day was a bit like a wake. It seemed entirely appropriate to think of it in terms of Rudyard Kipling's poem, Recessional. The poem he never copyrighted and which he donated to the Nation.

"The tumult and the shouting dies;

The Captains and the Kings depart."

The slightly downbeat mood lasted a short while. The departing athletes, for which Martha was almost a poster girl, gave their interviews to 'The Bootleg' and the Stanford Daily campus paper. The articles highlighted, for all of them the essence of the student athlete, the combination of sporting and academic excellence that each of them had achieved.

And then it was time to plan and move on. Theresa and Sky were looking at accommodation in Berkeley and decided to move into an apartment with Lukey, who would now be working there. Apartment hunting took a little while, but they were helped by the Catholic Chaplain, with whom Theresa was still in touch. He had contacts in the East Bay, and long before the end of August, the three were settled somewhere down in Rockridge, quite close to where Sarah's family lived.

Sarah, Ceci, Martha, and Jonny were allocated accommodation by St Joseph's. Ceci and Martha were given two of the rooms in the very oldest residential building on the main site. These rooms were reserved for the two Stanford Scholars who were accommodated there each year. Sarah opted to share with Ceci in the second bedroom on her set. Martha had a spare bedroom, a perk of being the top Stanford Scholar in her year. The rooms were beautiful, in an early 18th century sort of way. Beams and leaded windows, but they had recently been up graded to 21st century standards by having bathroom pods fitted discretely into one corner of the main sitting room and overlapping onto the staircase. Jonny had graduate accommodation in a house overlooking a large common area, on the boundary of St Joseph's, but accessible from the main college site, as well as from the road bounding the common.

Chapter 15

Robert Jackson too was making plans for the coming year. He had served seven years of his ten-year sentence and was considered a model prisoner. That reputation had come at a cost. After Eddie had been paroled, six months earlier, some of Robert Jackson's protection had disappeared, and he had been the victim of a couple of assaults, one of them of a distressingly sexual nature. He became much more careful after that, worked out a lot in the gym, and generally beefed up, and learnt to defend himself. He got quite a reputation, in the end, for being too tough to tangle with, and he wondered why he had not bothered to do that earlier in his sentence. He became even more bitter towards his daughter and Martha. He focussed on learning as much as he could from the criminal fraternity, about how to obtain false documentation, and how to plan a hit. He also decided to learn something about bomb making. It would have been easier to do something like that using the internet, but prisoner use of the internet was closely monitored and, with what Robert had in mind, attracting the attention of the law enforcement agencies would have been counter-productive; it would almost certainly have meant that he would not be released early.

Robert expected the conditions of parole to include a prohibition on his free movement, a stipulation about his place of work, regular meetings with an appointed officer, a ban on association with young girls, and his name would be on the sex offender's register. He knew all that and was thinking hard about ways to get round some of the difficulties that it might create for him. He knew that it was probable that the police would be monitoring his bank account, so was pleased that he had several accounts, in different names, which they knew nothing about. He knew he would need more money than he currently had, if he were to carry out his planned revenge, so he tried to make contact with some of the gangs running organised crime in the East Bay. Seven years in prison had turned him from an opportunistic, if calculating, rapist, into a determined criminal who had an agenda of his own. That agenda was fuelled by hatred and resentment.

By the time he walked out of San Quentin that September day, he had acquired a lot of highly dangerous skills. The first thing he had to do was to put himself in the position to use them.

Eddie had kept in touch with Robert and came with a friend, Joe, to collect Robert on his release. Eddie and his friend were muscle for a mob working in Richmond on the East Side of the Bay. Robert had agreed with his parole officer that he would go and live with this friend in Richmond. The friend had no criminal record and was 'deemed suitable' to take in a lodger on parole. The friend, who owned a garage and cycle repair shop, used as a front for recycling stolen vehicles, had also promised Robert a job. Robert would be working in the shop repairing motorcycles, mowers, rotavators, bicycles, chain saws, and other similar items; anything relatively small and mechanical, whether driven by electricity or by gasoline. This job was going to provide money for Robert's basic living, while he built up his reserves from the illegal activity with which he was going to be associated.

Robert found it very hard to stick to his plan. Very soon after his release, he started to notice attractive young teenage girls, roughly the age that Martha had been when he raped her, and he had to keep telling himself that patience would be worth it in the end. He confided in Joe that he was having trouble with his lack of ability to satisfy his sexual appetite, and Joe arranged, through the mob, to fix him up with some young-looking hookers, who were being managed out of San Rafael, just across the bridge from Richmond. It helped Robert to keep his focus on the plans for revenge, although it irked him that he was having to pay for the sex, when rape would have been free.

One of the terms of his probation was that he was not allowed to access internet porn of any sort and he was not allowed to use computer wiping programs on his machine. His parole officer regularly checked Robert's phone and laptop for evidence of sexually sensitive content. There was no privacy. This, of course, was a farce. Using false identity, provided by his new 'friend', Robert was perfectly able to access anything he wanted on computer, including material on the 'dark web'. He refined his knowledge of explosives and bomb making, eluding forensic detection, and laundering money that he acquired through the illegal activities.

The first 'job' that Robert went out on was a robbery at a supermarket in the East Bay, one that was not paying protection money. Robert, Eddie and Joe, Eddie's friend, got to keep and share the several thousand dollars they came away with. As far as the gang was concerned the protection money, 10% of the profits going forward, was what they were interested in. There were quite a few more jobs like that, easy money if you did your homework and made sure that there was no chance of anyone getting hurt. The three stooges were paid a retainer as well, and were sent on collection rounds, for the protection money, all over the East Bay.

The evening side-line was stealing very expensive cars and rapidly giving them a makeover at Joe's garage in Richmond. Robert was a 'very moral' person and refused to have anything to do with drugs, Joe and Eddie were less scrupulous and made a bit more pocket money helping distribute for the mob.

Throughout his time in the East Bay area Robert played the part of a thoroughly contrite and now totally honest citizen. He was careful not to live beyond his means. He was careful to never miss an appointment with his parole officer. He was particularly careful to attend Mass every Sunday, and to cultivate a relationship with the Catholic priests who celebrated Mass with him.

It took Robert six months to save about $150,000 to add to the $100,000 he had already stashed in his secret bank accounts; with $250,000 in the bank he was ready to move to the next stage of his plan.

The next thing Robert did was to start to talk to the priest at St Xavier's, the church he attended each week, about his early years in San Quentin, and how he had come to rely on the communications of a delightful young Catholic student, called Theresa, to keep him focussed on redemption and salvation. He explained that, for some reason, she had stopped writing and so he, Robert, had had no way to let her know how wonderful her letters had been, and how grateful he was to her for what she had done for him. He now wanted an opportunity to thank her for all her support. Would there be any way that the priest could find out for him where this young lady might have gone after, as he now believed she must have done, she had left Stanford? He recalled that her full name was Theresa Moretti. He so desperately wanted to repay her for her support. The words were sweet, the thoughts behind the repayment option were very dark indeed.

Father Francis agreed that he would make enquiries of the Catholic Mission at Stanford. He had no idea what he was setting in train.

The next part of Robert's plan was to find out all about sperm banks at cryo-storage facilities in the Bay area. He knew that his criminal background would exclude him from donation at most properly run clinics, but he wanted to know the location, and he had something other than sperm donation in mind.

Chapter 16

Back at St Joseph's the four graduate students and the newly elected research fellow were settling in well. The initial culture shock of the weather, the language, the narrow streets, the driving on the wrong side of the road, and the somewhat old-fashioned accommodation arrangements, had given way to the positive phase of exploring new delights. They had found Savino's coffee bar, with its near perfect coffee, so one of the most frequent complaints of American visitors to the United Kingdom had been removed at an early stage. The outdoor track facilities at Wilberforce Road, and the University Sports Centre out on the Madingley Road, kept Sarah and Martha happy as far as fitness was concerned. There was even the college gym, a bit limited in its provision, but more than adequate for a quick work out.

Ceci was far better than any of the other women playing University tennis. It was not a big issue for her, she had long ago decided that medicine and not tennis was the way forward. Ceci was good enough that she was invited by the men's Blues Squad to train with them, as well as the women, if she wished, and she did choose to do so. The amount of indoor tennis time available in Cambridge to the university teams was still very limited; the indoor University Tennis Centre was still a long way from being built, and the teams hired the two indoor centres in Cambridge City itself to get reasonable court time during the winter and spring. Ceci brought to the team a new sense of importance for fitness and general flexibility. She was also able to provide an example of good match play, both singles and doubles. Ceci's National Doubles title was a springboard for the women to develop their doubles skills as a team; during the coming competitive season it was to prove crucial in bringing the team success.

Jonny and Sarah, now focussing on their triathlon skills, found that the lack of hills in the Cambridge area was a big culture shock. They were worried about resistance training at first, but one weekend they decided to go for a bike ride, which involved their taking the train to Ipswich, and cycling back along National

Cycle Route 51. The distance, about 112 kilometres, was something they would have done comfortably in a day around the Bay Area, even with the hills. They rather expected it to be a lot easier here on the flat. Unfortunately, they chose a day when there was a stiffish breeze from the Southwest, the standard wind direction in this part of the country. That was the last time they complained about the possible lack of resistance training. Halfway back when they reached Bury St Edmunds, they rang James's flat and got hold of Martha and begged her to cook an evening meal for all of them. They just knew they would be too exhausted to do anything when they lifted their Lycra clad corpses off the saddle. Martha collapsed in gales of laughter. She had heard the conversations about lack of hills.

Rather than transport their bicycles over from California, short of flying them at great expense, the delay in delivery was going to be a big unknown, Sarah and Jonny had purchased new road bikes, and town bikes, from the cycle shop in Mill Road. It had been recommended to them by the porters at St Joseph's.

"Everyone gets their bikes repaired there, and so do the University Cycle team," said Susie, the porter on duty at the time they asked.

James, Martha and Ceci also bought town bikes there.

"Get yourself a very good cycle lock, and always lock the front wheel, and the frame, to something immovable, when you leave your bike unattended!"

That was Susie's parting shot to the group, and they duly did purchase the best locks they could find. They were allocated bike parking spaces in the cycle shed under the new conference centre building. Looking around, when they first parked their bicycles, there must have been about 200 or more bikes there, all locked to bike stands. Most were in good repair, but some were falling to pieces and one or two had even had a wheel or some other part stolen. The numbered cycle racks were for the more serious cyclists and for those who wanted to look after their machines. It did cost a small fee to buy a special electronic key to access the numbered racks, which were in an inner cage of about twenty dedicated slots, right at the centre of the underground store. This area was monitored by CCTV which switched on and recorded briefly whenever the gate to the cage was opened.

The conference centre was right next to the Master's Lodge and DI Gregory had insisted that the place be fitted with lots of CCTV cameras as part of his brief to protect the new Master. The Fellows, staff and students using the building were probably the most monitored people in England, if not in the whole world.

DI Gregory was getting very tired of his role with the Special Branch. There had been nothing in the way of genuine threats in recent months and he was missing the cut and thrust of investigating serious crime. Monitoring terrorist activity, or potential terrorist activity, is hardly the most exciting thing. Over 99% of all the intelligence information that comes through from the surveillance teams, and from GCHQ, is not of significance, the great problem is to identify the 1% that leads somewhere serious. There are times when the serious piece of information is put on record and noted, but temporarily leads no further. Recent intelligence, from a far right and racist section of the potential terrorist spectrum, reported the influx into The Home Counties of a large quantity of Semtex. It was not known who the storekeeper was for the Semtex, nor was the intended destination of the highly malleable and very effective explosive known.

There was a rumour that an attack was likely to be made on one of the larger football stadia in the area. The Arsenal Stadium in Finsbury Park was the first one that was cited as a possible target, but regular searches and constant surveillance showed no threat, at least to the present date.

Jerry Gregory was well known for thinking outside the box. There were the obvious terror threats, the Al-Qaeda, the far-right groups, the politically motivated terror groups, but for Jerry Gregory the net needed to be cast much wider than that. Almost every political, religious, or ethical conflict in the world was represented in Cambridge. The Cambridge Union housed major debates and attracted high profile politicians and racial and religious leaders. Security at the Union was relatively easy. Surveillance cameras were situated in sensible places, and the location between Bridge Street and Park Street made the perimeter relatively easy to patrol.

It was in December of that year that Jerry was sitting down with his wife, Marianne, in their house in North London. During the week Jerry regularly stayed in a college owned flat in Warkworth Street, just behind the police station, but at weekends he tended to head home to London. Jerry's eldest son James, Jim to his friends, had just obtained a place to read Physics at St Joseph's, their daughter, Audrey, was in the final year at the local comprehensive school, and was applying to read English at Cambridge, although Jerry was convinced that Audrey really wanted to go to Cambridge for the theatre scene. Jerry was thinking it might be time for Marianne and himself to move out of London. He was looking at a position in a city, within easy commute of Cambridge and

London. There were positions in Cambridge, but Jerry had almost had enough of that.

"I really am sick and tired of student antics, low key protests, and providing security and wet nursing to a group of retired important people. There've been eggs and tomatoes thrown, and things like that, placards, and protests, but nothing genuine since we arrested that would be assassin on the King's Cross train."

"Well, it suits me to know that you're relatively safe," said Marianne. "But if you want a bit more excitement we need to think about where we might move to. Any jobs coming up soon that you know of?"

They talked about some of the older DCIs and Chief Constables. Jerry had a good track record. Being based in the Met, for all those years, he had been involved in solving crimes in homicide, narcotics, prostitution, child abuse, and organised crime, and now he had a developing profile in anti-terrorist work. There ought to be something suitable. They decided to take a watching brief. With Jim and his sister both about to go away, a move in a years' time would make sense, and it did, usually, take a year to find a position with a serious promotion opportunity.

Jerry did not know how soon his wish for excitement was going to be fulfilled. He might have found his hair standing on end if he had realised the significance of the article he read, in the student newspapers, on the Monday morning when he headed back to Cambridge.

"The heir to the third richest man in the world is coming to St Alfred's College in January to read for a Ph.D. in Translational Research."

Jerry knew what was said about this man's particular business empire. It was said that it had been built on the blood, sweat, tears, and dead bodies, of persecuted and exploited ethnic minorities in parts of the old Soviet Union, large parts of Africa, and South America. The truth was very different. Anton Stanislowsky had built his empire in troubled times, but he had been more ethical than most, and he was currently a major advocate for human rights in his own country. Much of the bad publicity was propaganda spread by the reactionary forces wishing to suppress the campaign for human rights that Stanislowsky was heading up.

Jerry was convinced that this arrival was going to mean trouble, and that, before long, significant attempts at kidnap or murder would be appearing in the intelligence literature. He would watch very carefully for anything in the intelligence briefings that mentioned Cambridge.

Ceci read the same article.

"Oh damn," she said. "This guy is coming to do translational research. I reckon the security is going to go over the top. Thank God, I'll only overlap two terms with him."

Chapter 17

Robert, meanwhile, was continuing to accumulate cash, and continuing his quest to find Theresa. His breakthrough came when Father Francis met Father Collins at a convocation of local Catholic priests in the Bay Area. Father Collins remembered Theresa Moretti and agreed to find out what had happened to her on graduation. He had not been party to the discussion between the warden and Robert Jackson, and knew only that, at some stage, Theresa had become less observant of the sacraments and had stopped writing to Jackson.

Robert got the information that Theresa and two fellow students had moved into an apartment in Rockridge, the address of which was known to Father Collin's friend, the priest in charge of a local Catholic church in Rockridge itself. Father Collins gave Jackson a letter of introduction to the priest and, armed with this, Jackson obtained Theresa's address.

By this time, Jackson was developing many white supremacist tendencies, as well as his loathing of abortion, and his lust for young teens. He watched one afternoon and early evening in January, and saw Theresa come home, arm in arm with Lukey, accompanied by another very attractive young woman, dressed in the style that the Japanese call Gothic Lolita, with make-up to match. This had two effects on Jackson, one is that he was angry that Theresa was obviously dating an African American. In his mind, he used the 'n' word. The second was that he was incredibly turned on sexually by the Goth woman, and fantasised about assaulting her, before he fled the scene to finish his revenge on Martha and Sarah.

Robert racked his brains about how to approach the further information gathering he needed. He was sure, from the way Theresa had written warmly about Martha and Sarah, that she would know where they had gone after graduation. He also recognised, from what Theresa had said, that they were high profile, so there might be information about them on the Stanford website, or in the Stanford Daily.

Without privileged access to the website, the amount of public information available to Robert Jackson was very limited. He could find out about Martha's sporting activity, and he came across the name and picture of Sarah McElroy. Searching the Track and Field Archives he discovered that Sarah was described as having come from Chicago. That was the first time he had realised that his family had changed names, as well as location. It gave him something to go on, but it was all very limited. He had no idea where his family were living, Chicago was a long way from the Bay Area, and the parole meetings limited his ability to travel and hunt them down. Sarah was not his main priority anyway. It was Martha, and revenge on her for aborting his child, that Robert Jackson wanted. He had no reason to believe that Martha's family would have moved, so that was another approach to finding what he needed to know. A visit to Mill Valley and Blithedale Canyon was certainly something he might consider.

He began to realise that there was probably going to be no way of obtaining the information he wanted, other than through direct contact with someone who knew Sarah or Martha. It was clear to him that Theresa, or Sky, or the young man who was clearly sharing their apartment, would have the information he needed, but any direct approach to them would be a problem. A direct approach to Theresa would almost certainly cause her to clam up, and complain to the prison authorities, and that might impact upon his parole.

The timing was not good. Had it been outdoor track season he might have gone along to a meet and casually engaged some of the athletes in conversation before pumping them, discretely, for information about the two very good middle-distance runners who he had 'seen running here last year'. That could have been a way to start to extract much more information. But indoor track season was not a good time to be hanging around the meetings. There were very few spectators at the indoor meets, other than athletes and athletes' friends, and he could not risk drawing attention to himself.

Several years earlier he might have managed to gain information by monitoring the post boxes of Martha's family, and of the kids in the apartment in Rockridge, but, these days, most communication was done by email, and unless there were birthday cards, or goods being transferred, the major content of mailboxes was flyers and junk snail mail.

Robert was trying very hard to think of a way to get the information he wanted, without raising an alarm with Theresa and Sky. He began by following them as they went off to class and, gradually, came to realise that they almost always met mid-morning for a coffee at a coffee shop on Telegraph Avenue. They almost always sat at the same window table, and their arrival time was almost always a quarter of eleven, or quarter to eleven as the English would say. For a couple of days, Robert arrived fifteen minutes earlier than the two girls, and sat at the table near them, in comfortable eaves dropping distance. There was little in the conversation to interest him in the first two days he sat there, it was all about the courses they were taking, and domestic matters, like who was cooking dinner, and what they were going to have. It was the third day of patiently sitting there that finally gave Robert a clue, two clues, in fact. Lukey arrived to join the girls and sat down at the table with his coffee.

"I had a message from Martha," he said. "She says it's pouring with rain and cold and damp and she misses the California climate."

"Well, what did she expect in Cambridge?" asked Theresa. "It always rains in England, doesn't it?"

"Yeah, guess so," said Lukey. "Her main complaint is that her college is so old, it started in the 16th Century, and she says they still haven't put decent central heating in. She wants us to send her a very good Stanford waterproof to wear around the town. Have you got her mailing address? I didn't put it in my phone, I relied on you guys."

Sky dug her phone out of her pocket and looked up contacts.

"Yeah. Do you want to put this into your phone now?"

Lukey got his phone out and started to type as Sky read out to him the address. It was all Robert needed to get a fix on Martha's location. St Joseph's College, Cambridge, England, and then the postcode. They had a long debate about post codes and zips, so Robert just could not have missed noting it accurately. The postcode for St Joseph's was unique to St Joseph's, and, even if he had forgotten everything else, he would have been able to locate her from that.

Then came the second piece of luck.

"Is that the same address for Sarah?" asked Lukey.

"Yeah," said Theresa.

Robert got up and left quietly making sure not to draw attention to himself.

So, the two main targets, apart from that little cow Theresa, were in England at Cambridge University. Robert needed to work out how to get over there, and, when he got there, would need to work out how to take his revenge.

This was all going to have to be carefully choreographed. He needed to go to the United Kingdom to complete his revenge, but, as he was not intending to return to the US after dealing with the two girls, if he wanted revenge on Theresa, he would have to get it before he left the country. He would have to deal with Theresa without compromising his main mission.

So, he had to disappear, very soon, deal with Theresa, get to England, and take it from there. He reckoned he needed another quarter of a million dollars in funds before he could confidently leave. He knew where and how he could get that. Eddie, and Eddie's friend Joe, especially Joe, had much more than that, hidden away in a safe at the apartment. He would have to remove the cash and take it with him, on the day that he left for the airport.

Robert, as soon as he got back to the apartment, went online, and ordered a spy-cam. It took about a week to arrive. He then waited until he was alone in the apartment and set it up to record the actions of anyone opening the safe. Either Eddie or Joe opened the safe just about every day, they used cash for most of their transactions, or they had cash from their criminal activities that they wanted to stash. Within 24 hours of installing the camera, Robert had the combination to the safe. He removed the spy-cam and hid all traces of his having used it.

It cost ten thousand dollars for Robert to get false papers, passport, social security, and driver's licence, in one of the names he had used for his hidden bank accounts. He had more than one set of false papers made, each with a different passport photograph, it cost him a little in hair dye. He began to withdraw money from his other accounts and exchange much of it for pounds sterling. His intention was to have relatively small denomination notes, no more than £20, and live a cash-based existence in the United Kingdom while he got himself established. It cost him an additional five thousand dollars to have fake fingerprints made for all ten of his digits.

By the end of January, he was ready to move. He explained to Father Francis that he was planning to join a different church and asked for a letter of introduction to the new community. Father Francis innocently provided such a letter. It was neutral enough to be usable on Robert's arrival in England. It contained no mention of his surname, only the Christian name. Robert persuaded the priest not to use his surname; he argued that it might be hard if someone in the congregation were able to find out about his past before he had had time to show them what a good citizen he had now become.

On the Monday before his intended flight to the UK, Robert visited one of the brothels run by the mob for which he had been working. He carefully collected all the used condoms he could find and put them into a plastic bag he had brought with him. Then he found the youngest looking of all the girls working there and, rather roughly, had sex with her. It was not as good as rape for him, but it was the nearest he could manage on this occasion.

He put the plastic bag of used condoms in his fridge for safekeeping.

Over the next few days, he arranged an Airbnb near Cambridge, England, and arranged several courier deliveries to that address, to await his arrival. They contained most of his money in pounds sterling. The money was carefully hidden in 'presents' for his non-existent nephews and nieces.

The day before his flight he had a final meeting with his parole officer, not that the parole officer knew that this was the final meeting, not until Robert disappeared off the radar. He removed all his body hair, including shaving his head, then he packed his cases, had a shower, and got himself a good night's sleep.

Friday morning, Robert had discovered, was a day when Theresa slept in, and the other two left the apartment early, not to return until late afternoon. If he could not get the Goth woman, he could try and get Theresa. That morning he left his apartment with all his worldly possessions and went to the bus station. He caught a bus down to Rockridge. He left most of his belongings in the lockers at the station. He was wearing a track suit and trainers. He had a change of clothes in a small sports bag, along with duct tape, his knife, a syringe full of other people's sperm, his mask, and a hood.

At about 9 am that Friday morning, Theresa woke up to find a man, in a hood and stocking face mask standing over her. He had a knife in his hand and some duct tape. He duct-taped her mouth, taped her hands behind her back, turned her on her front and taped her legs to the foot of the bed. He used the knife to cut away all her clothes and then he raped her. He did not use a condom. He sat for some time staring at her, she could feel his eyes boring into her back. He raped her once more about an hour after the first rape. He did not speak once during her ordeal. Before he left, she felt him insert something hard into her vagina and squirt into her something cold.

Robert left the apartment as quietly as he had come, completely unseen and avoiding the CCTV that he knew covered part of the front of the building. He had changed his clothes. He was wearing a face concealing large Stetson hat, cowboy boots, jeans, and a fringed shirt, like a latter-day Roy Rogers or Lone Ranger. He put the discarded clothing into the Rockridge Clothing Bank and disposed of the syringe and other items, except the knife, in a garbage can near the mall. The knife he took with him. He did not dispose of it until he was at San Francisco International Airport security check. He put it into the container for dangerous goods not allowed on the flight.

The Bart journey to the airport took about an hour. He arrived at San Francisco International Airport, some three hours before his flight, checked in his luggage, and went to the first-class lounge, he was flying Virgin Upper Class. His hand luggage contained lots of 'papers', which he needed for his visit to the UK. The 'purpose' of his visit was to attend a conference in Cambridge University.

Robert was in the air before the rape in Rockridge first appeared on the news bulletins.

Lukey and Sky arrived home late afternoon to find a deeply distressed Theresa still lying taped to the bed. She was, by then, very dehydrated. They called 9-1-1 and were strictly instructed not to touch anything. That was so hard. To see someone you loved lying there in distress, and not to touch her or help her, was heart-breaking, but they did as they were told. The police were there within ten minutes of the call, and Shapiro, it was the same detective who had dealt with Martha's case, took over. The police moved swiftly to gather all the forensic information they needed. They took the tape, the semen samples, took swabs from Theresa's body, vacuumed the sheets to try to find any hairs that might have been left, and completed the rest of their forensic work, photographing the scene, and searching the room for clues. It was horrendous seeing the poor girl lying there, face down, spreadeagled and strapped to the bed. As quickly as was compatible with their investigation they freed her. They gave her lots of fluids to drink. She had been in that hot stuffy room for nine hours before the other two had come home, and the paramedics put up a drip to rehydrate her before taking her to the hospital.

Theresa turned to Lukey to be cuddled and comforted. Lukey wrapped her in her warm white cotton bathrobe, and Lukey, Sky, and Theresa clung together for a long time, Theresa and Sky sobbing. Sky was experiencing her own trauma. Lukey and Theresa both remembered that Sky had suffered sexual abuse as a child, and it was a measure of Theresa's humanity and compassion that she was aware of this, even during the immediate aftermath of her own terrible experience.

Lieutenant Shapiro was patient and thoughtful. He waited until a degree of composure had returned before he continued his questions to Theresa, and then to the other two. Theresa described how this powerful man had surprised her in her sleep, had stuck the duct tape over her mouth even as he had woken her. He had quickly taped her hands behind her back, turned her on her face and cut her clothing away. He had used the sheets on her bed to keep her constrained while he dealt with her hands. She could tell that he was white, because she saw his hands; she said that the knife had an orange and black handle. He had not spoken a word to her throughout the ordeal.

"I think we need to take you to the hospital for an Ob-Gyn doctor just to check you out," said Lieutenant Shapiro. "I will come down and ask you a few more questions later, but I have all we need for the moment."

Lukey and Sky were allowed to travel with Theresa in the ambulance which took Theresa to the hospital for a further medical check by the police surgeon.

The similarity of this rape to the one committed by Jackson on Martha seven years ago was obvious to Lionel Shapiro. The duct tape, the rape from behind, the knife, with the orange and black handle. It was too much of a coincidence, and when Shapiro discovered that Jackson had been released on parole only six months earlier, that there had been correspondence between Theresa and Jackson during Jackson's time in San Quentin, he was almost certain that this was Jackson's second rape. The slightly puzzling thing was the description from Theresa of the rapist inserting something into her vagina and squirting in something cold. Shapiro's first thought was that it might be something to try to destroy the DNA evidence, but Theresa had not felt any pain or discomfort after the injection of material, and Shapiro's second thought was that it had to be something to confuse the DNA evidence. Theresa had said that she felt the man's body was smooth, he had no body hair, and he had no pubic hair that she could feel as he raped her. Shapiro was not then surprised that they found not a single hair that was not from one of the inmates of the house.

Shapiro, while he had been waiting for Theresa to recover enough to talk to him, had soon established the whereabouts of Jackson for the past six months and had had a conversation with the parole officer. It did not take long to work out how Jackson had located Theresa using the naivety and kindness of the Catholic priests.

While he was travelling down to the hospital, after leaving the scene of the crime, Shapiro was thinking about what the hard object and the cold material inserted into Theresa's vagina might have been.

He was as certain as he could be that the rapist's sperm, and hence DNA, was in there. The injected material had caused no damage or pain and, as far as the surgeon could tell, there was only semen in the vaginal swabs they had taken. Shapiro had a suspicion that what had been injected after the rape might be other people's sperm, collected from a different source. He had read in the Police Gazette that it was possible to amplify the DNA from a single sperm and get a DNA profile. He arranged for the sperm sample to be sent to the lab as quickly as possible, and he called the forensic guys to tell them that he thought the rapist had tried to confuse the analysis, by mixing of multiple sperm samples. It was less than eight hours after the rape that the samples were obtained, and the lab were able to identify some sperm still alive and wriggling in the specimen they received. They selected the healthiest looking sperm they could find and ran them through the new protocols for amplification of the DNA. Within a week, Shapiro had his DNA match to Robert Jackson, proof that his initial assumption was correct.

When he got to the hospital, Shapiro sat down beside Theresa's bed and began to update her on his thinking.

"You were targeted," said Shapiro to Theresa.

"I think it may have been someone called Robert Jackson."

Theresa shuddered. She knew who Robert Jackson was, and his relationship to Martha and Sarah.

The old Theresa, the naïve young lady who came from the home-schooled background, would have been broken by what had happened, but the new Theresa was made of sterner stuff. Like Martha she was determined not to let this event define her life, but, like Martha, she was angry.

"Lieutenant Shapiro," said Theresa. "If he targeted me, he's also probably going to target Martha and Sarah. I think they're safe now because they're both in England, at Cambridge University, but when they come back, I reckon he will be after them and, if you haven't got him by then, I think he might even want to kill them. Can I email them and warn them? Will that be alright?"

"I met Martha," said Shapiro. "I would be happy to talk to her if you prefer, but I think you are right to warn them, and they will probably want to warn their families too."

Lieutenant Shapiro thought for a moment.

"This was a carefully planned and researched attack. Do you think that Jackson might know where his daughter and Martha are? He knew so much about your movements he must have been watching you for a while. We'll look at the CCTV pictures around here. Is there anywhere else you might have been that he would have been able to get information from? Have you seen anyone suspicious around at any of your normal hangouts?"

Lukey and Sarah were present during the questioning and Lukey responded to Shapiro's question.

"There was a guy who started coming to the same coffee bar about a couple of weeks ago," said Lukey. "He came for a couple of weeks and then I haven't seen him for at least a week now. I didn't think anything of it really. We usually left before he did, but now I come to think about it, the very last time we saw him he left before us. That was…" Lukey paused, and then continued.

"That was just after you told me Martha's address so that I could send her the Stanford top."

"Look, it's probably nothing," said Shapiro. "But just to be on the safe side I would like you to have a look at a couple of pictures and see if you can identify the man." He paused, called through to the police control station, and asked for a picture of Jackson to be sent to him immediately.

"That's him," said Lukey when Shapiro showed him the mug shot of Jackson. The other two agreed with Lukey.

Shapiro paused for a moment and then he said, "We need to consider that Robert Jackson may have headed over to England to complete his revenge, highly unlikely when he can just hide and wait. Nevertheless, I'll contact the Cambridge police and alert them to the situation, and I'll make sure all airports have a picture of Jackson and we monitor all flights to the UK. Meanwhile I'll get on with filling in the details of Jackson's last few months here, since he got out of San Quentin, and get a nation-wide hunt going for him. We must assume he has left the Bay Area and gone underground. We can put an alert on his bank accounts and credit cards, but he's going to be too smart to let us find him that way, and my guess is that he will have bought a burner phone and be using that, rather than continuing to let us get him through his cell phone."

Despite her Catholic upbringing, Theresa had agreed to the use of the morning after pill. The debate around it prompted her to say a bit more to Lieutenant Shapiro.

"My initial contact with Jackson developed to the point where I thought he was a bit over the top about abortion and pro-life. I confess I was a pro-lifer at that stage, but nothing like Jackson. He seemed to think they could do no wrong. He hated contraception and thought all intercourse, even rape, should be allowed to proceed to pregnancy. Pregnancy was what sex was for. I wouldn't mind betting that he attended pro-life meetings during his six months out of jail. I still accept a lot of the Catholic faith, but not the obsessive misinterpretation that Jackson was putting on things."

Shapiro thought about that comment. Useful, and something he ought to put into his communication with Cambridge just in case Jackson found himself over there.

After leaving Theresa and her friends, Shapiro went to visit Eddie and Joe at their apartment. They described Robert as someone who had fitted in well, leaving out that he had been useful in their criminal activity. Joe had no rap-sheet, so Shapiro had no reason to suspect anything when Joe told him that Jackson had scarpered taking all their money with him.

"The motherf***er must have found our combination and emptied the safe before he left," said Joe.

"How much do you think he got?" asked Shapiro.

"At least fifty thousand dollars," said Joe. "We keep the money there to pay our taxes at the end of the year and they were due very soon."

Joe did tell Shapiro that he thought Jackson had been visiting a local brothel and seemed to like the younger looking girls. That was not exactly a surprise to the detective. Joe also said that Jackson had gone out regularly to the local church and had attended pro-life meetings. Joe and Eddie knew this because Jackson always returned preaching pro-life and denouncing the use of contraceptives.

"I think he was a bit obsessed with it," said Joe. Eddie added that Jackson had been obsessed with pro-life when he was in San Quentin and had told him, Eddie, that he intended to kill the girl who had aborted his baby and the bitch of a daughter who had helped her. If he could get the doctor who had carried out the abortion, that would make his day complete.

Both Eddie and Joe knew that fifty thousand dollars was a huge underestimate. They were going to be in a lot of trouble with the mob, because they had only just finished a collection round, and there were several tens of thousands of dollars in the safe, which they were due to take to the mob bosses later that week. They were very scared about what might happen to them. They made sure they got a crime number from Shapiro and, as soon as Shapiro had gone, they called their mob contacts to explain what Jackson had done. Several years of good service, plus the inconvenience of setting up a new collection round, were the things that kept Joe and Eddie alive. A contract was immediately taken out on Jackson, a top hitman from Chicago was sent over to find him and kill him.

None of the conversation with Joe and Eddie made comfortable hearing for Shapiro. The need to find Jackson was ever more urgent. He went back to the station and looked up the records in the Martha McArthy case, found out that Dr Robert Simms had conducted the procedure, and immediately contacted Simms to warn him about Jackson and his intentions.

"I guess I have to start looking under the car even more carefully and trying to avoid too much routine," said Dr Simms. "Thank you for letting me know. I've been living with this for years now."

There was an air of resignation about the way that Dr Simms responded.

Lieutenant Shapiro contacted the Dean's Office at Stanford and asked for contact details for Martha and Sarah. He also contacted Martha's parents and asked them to warn Martha that Jackson had committed another rape, this time on Theresa. He also informed Sarah's mother, and Tim, that Jackson had committed another rape and was on the loose, possibly in the Bay Area. Shapiro warned them to be careful as he believed that Jackson was still very angry with his family for disowning him and distancing themselves from him. He then called Martha and Sarah, separately, to warn them what had happened. Over the next few weeks Shapiro kept the Cambridge police informed about the progress, or, rather, lack of progress, of the investigation. The Cambridge police contacted Adrian Armstrong, the senior tutor at St Joseph's, and asked him to let the porters know to be on the lookout for strangers with an American accent hanging around the college, especially if they were watching the American students.

There were a lot of tears, and a lot of anger was expressed, when Martha, Sarah, Theresa, Sky, and Lukey had a video conference later that week. For the next couple of weeks, Martha and Theresa spoke together almost every day; it was a useful part of the healing process for Theresa, and the fact of the rape had aroused feelings in Martha that she had thought to be long buried. It was therapeutic for them both to express their anger and determination. It was important for them all to plan ahead, to think about the future rather than to dwell on the past, so during the now regular video calls it was arranged that Sky,

Theresa, and Lukey would come over to Cambridge in late July and they would spend some time in England before going off on a trip around Europe together. James, Jonny, and Cecilia would go with them. Martha and James were still an item, even more so than before, and Jonny and Sarah also.

Chapter 18

Robert Jackson, now known as Robert Jones, sailed through Heathrow, with his false fingerprints and his brand-new fake passport, and got his taxi to the Airbnb near Cambridge. Robert Jones arrived at the Airbnb to await the parcels he had sent himself, and to recover from the flight.

He had a plan. The first things it involved were finding somewhere to live, getting a job, ingratiating himself into the local community, and then working out how to get at his two targets, and anyone else he fancied raping or killing along the way. The rational and reasonable human being that had been born Robert Jackson, was giving way to a very disturbed, hedonistic, human being, currently going under the name of Robert Jones.

Jerry Gregory had unearthed a snippet of information that a substantial quantity of Semtex had found its way to the Cambridge area and was likely to be used in a terrorist attack. It could either be an attack on one of the research establishments around the university, or it might be an attack on individuals and groups. Animal Liberation groups were threatening, as always, some of the high-tech companies on the Bio-Medical site. There was no shortage of high profile political and scientific individuals attending Cambridge to give public lectures. The proximity to London, and the appetite for Cambridge colleges to seek the Great and the Good, from all walks of political and public life, to lead them in the 21st Century, meant that Jerry's work was cut out deciding from what direction, and against whom, any attack might come.

Alexis Stanislowsky had arrived in Cambridge at the beginning of January, right on time, and Jerry and his security team had spent time with both St Alfred's College and Alexis himself, advising on security measures to keep him safe. The college had allocated Alexis a room on Second Court, close to the Master's Lodge, where security was already very strong. There was no immediate access from outside the college and the area was well covered by CCTV. All the accessible windows on the ground floor of the building were alarmed. The staircase was secured by key card. An additional key card operated a fireproof and bullet proof door which was installed at the entrance to Alexis's suite of rooms. He had a sitting room, a bedroom, and a bathroom; there was a small kitchen. This was not the regular accommodation for a student, the suite was more usually occupied by a resident fellow, but the rooms had been vacant, and the security issue was acute; hence it provided a good solution to a problem that had been thrust upon the college at the very last moment. A bed was set up in the outer room of the suite to allow a permanent bodyguard, provided at his father's expense, to protect Alexis, at all times. This reduced some of the pressure on Jerry's team but there was still the possibility that an attack might be mounted in a public arena, and without any regard for the safety of others. The politically motivated hatred of Alexis's father was that extreme. Jerry's hidden Semtex could be heading in that direction, among all the other possibilities.

Robert Jones found himself a flat in Gwydir Street, very close to one of the major cycle repair shops in Mill Road. He observed the cycle repair shop for a few weeks, buying himself a bicycle there. One evening he followed home the middle-aged man who worked in the shop. The man lived in a one-bedroom flat, down by the river in Chesterton.

The arrival of Alexis Stanislowsky triggered an idea in Jerry Gregory's mind. It is one very useful thing about Cambridge, if you are a policeman, that graduate students come and go at different times of the year, not just once a year in October. There were so many politically active student and town groups in Cambridge that it was impossible to predict which one was most likely to get its hands on the Semtex. Jerry knew, from the intelligence services, that the Semtex had come up the train line from London; there were undercover officers in London who had provided the basic information, but even they had not yet been able to discover the intended recipient, or recipients, of the explosive material.

Jerry was talking to Sergeant Jeff Glover of the local Cambridge police, a well-informed detective who had been seconded to work with Special Branch, and Jerry Gregory in particular, when Jerry arrived from London. Jerry had been told he could have the pick of the local Detective Sergeants to act as his personal assistant, and the local chief constable had recommended Jeff, fresh off the solution of a rather difficult, racially motivated, murder in the Abbey district of Cambridge.

"Jeff," said Jerry. "We need to beef up our intelligence. So far, the threats we've dealt with have come from outside the city, mostly on the bloody Fen Flyer!"

Jerry was referring to the train that went from King's Lynn to London King's Cross and took about 45 minutes to get between Cambridge and London.

"We know that there is Semtex coming our way. If the intelligence is to be believed, it's quite a big package, more than enough to set off at least a dozen significant explosions. What we have no idea about is to whom the explosives have been distributed. Has it gone on to Peterborough? Has it gone to Huntingdon? Is it still here in Cambridge? I think we need to set up our own local intelligence gathering. We need to get some young coppers, preferably smart ones, to start joining, under cover, some of the bigger dissident groups. We are only a couple of weeks into the Lent term so we could easily bring them in, claim they were doing a Ph.D., or coming as post-docs, and start the intelligence gathering. What do you think?"

"Well, we would probably only need half a dozen. The groups are so interlinked, with the nasty boy fanatics just looking to join in anything that might give them a chance for a punch-up and a bit of civil disorder. I think it's a great idea Jerry. Might be a bit of a stretch to get the powers-that-be to agree, but you could point out how much cheaper it would be than rebuilding the centre of Cambridge."

Jeff was nodding his head in agreement the whole time he was saying this. He had a habit of either nodding or shaking his head as he talked, you were never in any doubt about whether he did or did not agree with something.

"I'm on it," said Jerry. He picked up the telephone and called Special Branch Headquarters in Scotland Yard.

Robert Jackson, now Robert Jones, was growing back his hair. Having shaved it off for the Theresa rape he now decided to grow hair everywhere he could. Never having had a beard before, he was struggling to recognise himself in the mirror, as a luxuriant facial growth happened far more quickly than he could have imagined. He had decided that his naturally light brown hair colour needed to be disguised so he made it much darker, with easily applied hair colourant. He knew this was going to be needed every week or so, but he could cover for any lightness of the roots by pretending that he was going grey. He ordered online a pair of photochromic sunglasses with plain lenses and started to grow his hair long. He had never had a very nasal American accent, so it was relatively easy for him to work at softening his pronunciation still further, and by the time he had finished growing and colouring his hair and beard, wearing glasses, and speaking English, his own daughter would not have recognised him. That, of course, was exactly what he was hoping.

Robert Jones reasoned that his daughter, if she still went to Mass, would probably go to one of the churches in town, so, to make sure he avoided meeting her, Robert took his letter of introduction to the Catholic church in Cherry Hinton, on the outskirts of the town. It was a useful way to start to build a new persona. His American contacts had sold him false documentation for use in England, under the name of Robert Jones. He had a birth certificate, a driver's licence, and a National Insurance Number. He had his eyes set on a job at that cycle shop on Mill Road. Not long after he arrived in Cambridge Robert had staked out St Joseph's College and had spotted Martha and Sarah coming out of the front entrance of the college, pushing bicycles. The bicycles had a Yellow patch sticker on the frame. Robert had seen those stickers on other bikes around the town. They had the address of the Mill Road cycle shop printed all over them. He also noted that some bicycles had registration numbers painted on the frame, and, when Sarah and Martha were safely out of the way, he wandered into St Joseph's and saw that almost all the bicycles there had some indication that they had been in the Mill Road shop at some point in their lifetime. He narrowly missed being seen by one, or both, of the girls when, about half an hour later they returned to the college and went down to the bicycle racks in the conference centre. Robert saw enough to realise how things were arranged in the basement there, and Sarah and Martha, accompanied by a boy that Robert realised might have been Jonny, came out of the bicycle store, Jonny and Sarah pushing their road bikes, and Martha just chatting, and clearly going somewhere other than on a training run. Even more than before, Robert wanted that job at the cycle shop. He did not know how it was going to help him, but he had a feeling that the revenge he was seeking would come out of that shop.

A couple of weeks later, Jerry Gregory and Jeff Glover sat down with their six new intelligence recruits. One, Arthur, Jerry already knew. He had met him while investigating a murder, or rather a series of murders, a year or so earlier. Arthur was an undercover narcotics squad copper who had been brilliant during the previous investigation. Arthur was going to keep his eyes and ears open for anything that might be related to big crime and might involve Semtex. Arthur was the longest shot in all this intelligence gathering, but some drug addicts, between fixes, are very into anti-establishment activities, so Arthur might be useful.

The next person on their list was a young woman who was 'studying' ecology and conservation. She was going to keep an eye on the Eco-warriors, Greenpeace, and Extinction Rebellion, quite a portfolio, but all seemingly linked.

The third recruit was a 'veterinary graduate student' who was going to keep an eye out for animal liberation movements and other protest movements looking to reduce the exploitation of animals. That group had been known to be violent before, with car bombs and other very dangerous actions against individuals.

There were some ethnic minority students who were monitoring the activity of various political pressure groups, the far right, and one or two ethnic groups.

Finally, there was one girl who was asked to keep an eye out for pro-life and anti-medicine groups.

It was quite a formidable and extensive team by the time it was set up, and the communication methods were agreed (the usual use of one-off burner phones, and a continuously monitored number, to which only Jerry and Jeff had access). There were also occasional in person meetings, where they could be arranged without arousing suspicion.

As far as was possible the two policemen sat down together at least once a week and tried to estimate the potential danger from planned controversial meetings due to happen over the following six months. They hoped they could narrow the options down to a smaller number of societies and dissident groups they could focus on, but every one of the likely suspects was holding a meeting, a conference, a rally, or a workshop, in the six months leading up to the summer break. When they included the colleges, there were two or three danger spots each week.

"I hope the team get us something soon," said Jerry. "I just know something is going to happen."

Chapter 19

The American students at St Joe's were enjoying the freedom of a research-based degree. No need to get up every morning very early to get their training in and then attend class. There were some lectures that they attended, simply because the depth of content at Stanford and Berkeley had not been as great as in Cambridge, what they lacked in depth they had made up for in breadth. The biggest difference for all of them was the ability to train at sensible hours. For Ceci, the tennis player, there were still early mornings, simply because the lack of university indoor tennis courts meant that the teams had to train at hours when the public did not want to use the commercially available facilities. A combination of the County Tennis Centre at a local sixth form, and a commercially available centre out near Cherry Hinton, offered some help, but Ceci was amazed by the difference in provision at Stanford and that at Cambridge.

The university track and the fitness centre out on the Madingley Road were always available for the other athletes to keep up their fitness. Martha was still running very competitively. She trained almost every day, either alone or with the university athletics club. The senior tutor of St Joe's heard that Martha was sometimes running alone on the Coton footpath, or out to Baits Bite Lock, and he advised her against it, especially as it was still quite dark in the evenings and early mornings. She began to find running partners from within college and from among the athletics club members. Sarah sometimes ran with her. Most of Sarah's training was now for longer distances, and for swimming and cycling. Sarah and Jonny were both members of the University Triathlon Society and the Cycling Club.

For Sarah and Jonny, the University Cycling Club offered regular competition in the British Universities and Colleges Sport competitions, but, as with many Cambridge clubs, the focus was on the Varsity match against Oxford, which was to be held at Cambridge in early June. The match took place during the BUCS 25mile Time Trial. Several universities competed, but Oxford and Cambridge took the finishing positions of their own competitors and used them to decide, separately from the overall race results, the outcome of their own separate Varsity match. The time trial would be carefully and professionally monitored. As is often the case with university sport, it was almost professional in its approach to events, including things like weighing bikes and riders before competition, and after, and providing the best level of marshalling and first aid support that could ever be imagined. Most of the competitors in the time trials had excellent road bikes but did not have the much less manoeuvrable time trial bikes, that bit heavier than the road bikes. Jonny and Sarah both had road bikes that weighed in at 7.2kg every time they competed. This was just above the 6.8 kg minimum weight for a competition bicycle.

The University Cycling Club had an arrangement with Sean's Cycle Emporium, the Mill Road cycle shop, to service and maintain their machines at a discount, and Jonny, Sarah, and most of the other members of the club, would put the machines into the shop for service, before any major time trial, road race or, on vary rare occasions, track event.

Robert Jones, meanwhile, was extending his circle of acquaintances. The first thing he did was to get himself involved with the local pro-life group. He found there several different nationalities and ethnic origins, all united by a strong belief that the foetus had a right to life from the moment of conception. Robert believed only that he had the right, and perhaps duty, to father as many children as he could, and that anyone, such as Martha, and his ex-wife Susan, who prevented his fathering a child, had somehow violated his human rights. He made a mental note that when he had finished here in Cambridge he would have to go back and deal with the unfinished business of revenge on Susan, who he had now added to his hit list. That presented him with another task. To find Susan's address. He thought he knew how he could do that.

The original simplistic plan to revenge himself on Martha was simply to rape and murder her when she was on one of her runs, hide the body in the Cam, and disappear back to the States, or, perhaps, Canada. He began to plan how he might do that, but, as he was planning, a new thought came to him. A way in which he might deal with Martha and Sarah at the same time.

For Inspector Gregory and Sergeant Glover, the first breakthrough in the surveillance came in early April. Intelligence work can be slow and heavy going, but when it starts to bear fruit, swift action is always needed. One of the undercover team attending the pro-life meetings heard an unguarded remark from Sean O'Connor, the secretary and chair of the pro-life group, in which he commented that the next stem cell conference in Cambridge might be more exciting than the participants could ever imagine. The agent, Kesandu, had asked Sean what he meant, and he had immediately retracted, and said that he meant nothing by it, but that some disruption of the conference was a must.

"They use stem cells from aborted foetuses," said Sean. "We have to stop that. We must make them think twice about it. How would you like to be torn apart and have bits of you used to grow things or test drugs, or even be implanted into animals to try and cure diseases?"

Kesandu had agreed that she would not like that and asked how Sean intended to disrupt the conference.

"Something big," was all Sean would say.

Jerry and Jeff looked at the schedule of public events and noted that the stem cell conference was due to be held in the first week of July, with delegates staying at St Joseph's College, and most of the main presentations taking place in the nearby lecture theatres on the New Museums site. There was plenty of time to prepare for the security sweeps that would be needed, and to vet and monitor everyone who might be involved in preparing the venues. It did not make much sense to think that anything would happen on the college site, the delegates would be too widely dispersed, but the Main Lecture Theatre there on the New Museums site, would be an obvious place to try something. It was almost certain that any demonstrations or marches would have a focus on Downing Street and the New Museums site.

"We have to guess that this might relate to explosives," said Jerry. "We certainly have to assume it does and act accordingly. We need to up the surveillance on all the pro-life members that we know about, and we have to monitor the New Museums site very carefully for the next four or five months."

Jeff agreed with him.

"We have to put a tail on Sean O'Connor in particular. We also ought to run a check on the other attendees at the pro-life meetings. One of them might just have a track record with us."

"Yep," said Jerry. "But we don't let up on the other groups just yet either. There are plenty of other possible targets over the next year or so. I still think that Alexis Stanislowsky is at risk. Probably not from a bomb, although a personal bomb can't be ruled out. More likely a kidnap attempt or a shooting.

HQ reported that several known political opponents of his father have arrived in the country. I hope they're all being closely monitored, and we will be told if any of them are heading in our direction."

"I'll check on that if you like," said Jeff.

"Stanislowsky is at St Alfred's, isn't he?" asked Jerry.

"He is," said Jeff, "I'll go and see the senior tutor there if you like. Nice woman, name of Professor Marjorie Grey."

Jerry responded: "I think it would be very good if you just gave her a courtesy call, and while you are there you could check out his living arrangements, you know, the security, any enhancements you think might be needed. No harm in checking, even if 'daddy' has provided a personal bodyguard."

Jeff Glover went to see Marjorie Grey the very next day. He walked through the ancient archway into the first court at St Alfred's, turned right through the gate, and walked towards the ivy surrounded doorway with the letter 'A' above it. He found the senior tutor's office at the foot of a staircase, knocked on the outer door and was called to come in.

Marjorie Grey's personal assistant was sitting there, behind an old wooden desk, working away on a very modern desk top computer.

"Detective Sergeant Glover to see Professor Grey," said Jeff.

"Thank you for coming," said the P.A., "Marjorie has just popped out for a second and she is expecting you. Please take a seat. Would you like a cup of tea or coffee while you wait? I'm sure she will not be long."

Jeff opted for a coffee, he had not yet had lunch and it was very close to one o'clock. The P.A. busied himself making Jeff a coffee and had just completed the task when the formidable form of Marjorie Grey, only a tad over five feet tall, entered the room.

'*How is it that some people immediately command your attention,*' thought Jeff. '*My ten-year-old niece is probably taller than Professor Grey and yet, the minute she walked into the room...*' He left the thought there.

"Sergeant," said Professor Grey. "Thank you for coming. The policeman who arranged this appointment for us suggested that you might want to talk about Alexis. Shall we go through to my office?"

Jeff followed Marjorie Grey through to the inner sanctum. It was obvious that this was a working study as well as an office. There were scholarly tomes lining the walls and some volumes were open on a second desk near the window, a desk without a computer and just notepaper and writing instruments. Jeff could not help noticing that some very neat and flowing writing had taken place on the top sheet of paper on the pad. Marjorie Grey could not help noticing him noticing!

"Sergeant," she said, "I'm an academic first and senior tutor second. If I had wanted to be an administrator, I would probably have gone into the Civil Service." Marjorie smiled, and Jeff looked a little bit sheepish.

"All a bit new to me," said Jeff. "Looks as if you're interested in Chinese history."

"I am, but I'm particularly interested in the history of medicine, including Chinese medicine, and the development of Chinese scientific thought. You must come to one of my lectures sometime. I do some more popular lectures for the extramural studies, and I should love the chance to tell you all about the history of medicine. But you haven't come here to talk to me about this. How can I help you?"

Jeff took a sip of his coffee, put the cup down and said.

"I think you already realise that I am here to talk about young Alexis. I can't go into details, but we have reason to believe that several political enemies of his father have entered the country and may be planning some sort of action against him. I just wondered if you could tell me how he has settled in and whether he has been making any friends while here."

"Well, strangely enough, I was just thinking about Alexis. He's not had a very high profile within the college, but he's made some friends because of the course he's studying. He seems very fond of a young American girl who's studying translational research, like Alexis. From the track suit I saw her wearing, she's a university standard tennis player, and, from the scarf she was wearing, I think she's at St Joseph's. I've seen the two of them with some other St Joseph's students wandering round the College and using the Middle Common Room. I suppose the advantage of having this room in first court is that relatively little goes past these windows without catching my eye. I sometimes feel I ought to get some net curtains and stand there staring out like any nosy old lady in a village."

"Sergeant, while you're here, would you like to have a look at Alexis's rooms and remind yourself of the security arrangements?"

Jeff politely agreed that an inspection of the security arrangements was exactly what he had in mind.

Marjorie Grey led Jeff Glover over to the staircase in Second Court where Alexis had his suite of rooms. Jeff had to agree that short of surrounding the place with armed guards the security was as tight as it could be. He looked at the positioning of the CCTV cameras and thought they covered all the important areas of the courtyard and buildings. He tested the alarms on the various windows and doors, just making sure that they were in good working order, and then he and Professor Grey walked back together to Front Court where Jeff went into the porters' lodge and reviewed the bank of screens monitoring all the areas of the college.

Professor Grey escorted Jeff Glover back to the main gate and thanked him for his concern about her student.

"Just doing my job Professor," said Jeff, "and you've been very helpful. I think I might just go and talk to the tennis player. You said she was American?"

"Yes, she looks East Asian, but when I heard her speaking, she had an American accent. I saw her in a Stanford University Tennis tracksuit top on one occasion. I expect it will be easy for you to identify her. There are not that many blues squad players."

"Thank you, Professor. As always it was a pleasure to talk to you, and I *will* come to one of your history of medicine lectures one day, I promise. Please let us know immediately if anything unusual happens around Alexis."

"I won't hold you to your promise about the lecture," said Marjorie Grey, "but I will let you know if anything happens."

And with that, and a friendly handshake, they said their goodbyes and Jeff Glover headed back off into the city to meet Jerry Gregory. The two of them were sitting together in Savino's coffee bar when Jerry suddenly said: "Did you say the girl had a Stanford connection?"

"Yes," said Jeff.

"That young woman who was raped in Berkeley, the one that Lieutenant Shapiro called us about. She was Stanford, wasn't she? I might give him a call and see whether he's making any progress. He did call to warn us that the Jackson guy might end up over here trying to do something to those two St Joseph's students. I know it's a long shot, but the guy sounded dangerous."

The telephone call with Lieutenant Lionel Shapiro almost caused Jerry Gregory's hair to stand on end. He put the call on speaker phone and Jeff Glover listened in.

Shapiro, to try to get a lead on where Jackson might have gone, had visited San Quentin where Jackson's new cell mate, after Eddie had left, was still serving his life sentence for rape and murder of two women. Shapiro told them about the interview:

"I asked the inmate about Jackson and he was scared. He said that Jackson had become one hardnosed motherf***er and nobody crossed him. To the warden and the prison guards he was sweetness and light, but to the inmates he was Mr Nasty, you didn't cross him. He had worked out every day, he was as strong as an f***ing ox, and he knew how to hurt people. He also had three or four improvised knives. He seemed to like knives. The prisoner was far too scared to tell me anything more, and I was about to leave when he suddenly said, 'He was really into explosives.' I asked him what he meant, and he said that Jackson had quizzed everyone in the prison who had made or used explosive devices, and had written himself a coded notebook, full of all the information he could get on how to make a bomb, and how to trigger a bomb by timing device or remotely. I'm sitting here hoping like hell that Jackson doesn't get his hands on any explosives, although I gather his notebook includes information on how to make your own from fertiliser and things. I just hope he's not planning some big bang in this state, or, at least, in my territory."

"So, you reckon he might be, in theory at least, a bomb maker?" asked Jerry.

"Some of those guys in San Quentin are pretty damned good at explosives," said Shapiro.

"Oh shit!" said Jerry, under his breath. "Did you tell me he was a pro-lifer?"

"Big time," said Shapiro. "Big time."

"Do you reckon he could handle Semtex?" asked Jeff Glover.

"No problem," said Shapiro. "I reckon he could handle almost any explosive and, as I said, he could probably make his own with what he learnt inside that jail."

"Houston," said Jerry, "Or perhaps, I should say Berkeley, we have a problem. If Jackson is over here, and you seemed to think he might be, we have some missing Semtex, we have a Translational Medicine conference, we have a very active pro-life movement, and we have some California girls who might be considered a Jackson magnet. I think I need some Valium. Is there any way you can find out if Jackson did come to England? I don't know how you use facial recognition over there but is there a way, even if he had a false passport in a false name, you could check if the photo on his real passport and that on a false passport matched?"

"Robert Jackson never had a passport. On the way out, we don't keep the photograph of US Citizens for more than 12 hours. I'm real sorry, but we cannot help you with that. We didn't send a photograph of Jackson to the airports and other travel terminuses until more than ten hours after the rape so he could have got away in that time frame without any chance of our catching him. It didn't go world-wide until even longer after that.

"My hunch is that he got out of the country. He took money with him. We interviewed a couple of people he shared an apartment with, and he robbed their safe before he left. We circulated his picture to all the banks in the area and one of the people recognised his mug shot. He was using a false name, Robert O'Reilly, and he had a few thousand pounds in an account which he had held for more than ten years.

"A couple of weeks before the rape, he had used the account to buy pounds sterling and then closed the account, telling them he was moving to Idaho. We followed this up by asking each bank if someone called Robert had closed a bank account with them in the weeks leading up to the rape. There are dozens of little banks in the Bay Area and I was betting that he'd put money in small amounts into lots of them. It's a big area for tourism so foreign exchange is real easy. We think that about fifty bank accounts, each with somewhere between one thousand and ten thousand dollars in them, had been closed by Robert something or other in the three weeks leading up to the rape.

"If I were a betting man, I would say he is with you somewhere over there with more than a quarter of a million dollars in cash, plus whatever he stole from his housemates. They said it was fifty thousand dollars that he stole, but they were very nervous when we talked to them, I think it was much more than that. How much would that translate to in sterling?"

"Probably about a quarter of a million," said Jerry, "more than enough to get by for a year or two."

"He's one smart son of a bitch," said Shapiro, "I hope you or we catch him real darn soon, before he does too much damage. I reckon he pulled the wool over the eyes of the warden, the parole board, and the prison psychiatrist."

When the telephone call ended, Jerry Gregory and Jeff Glover took stock.

They were just about to begin talking when the phone rang for Jeff and, as he listened, his face showed real concern.

"OK," he said, "so you're telling me they have disappeared without trace, and you now have no idea where they have gone, is that right?"

There was a pause.

"Can you send us pictures anyway of the men you think are a risk to Stanislowsky please?"

Jeff put the phone down.

"I guess you got that. The people who are anti-Stanislowsky seem to have completely disappeared. They followed them from Heathrow into the centre of London and then lost them completely in the maze of platforms and tunnels that make up the King's Cross and St Pancras underground network. They have no idea where any of them are now."

"Well, we really needed that," said Jerry, "Now we have a posse of political hardliners, who might be a threat to Stanislowsky, we have a shed load of Semtex, and we don't know where either of them are. And we have Robert Jackson, probably, heading in our direction. Maybe pro-life is going to be the least of our troubles."

"We need Kesandu to keep a really good eye on the pro-life lot and we need to keep digging for the whereabouts of that Semtex. My money is still on something to happen, with the explosives, and that Translational Research and stem cell conference, but we're forewarned, and I think we can deal with the threat." There was a pause, "I hope!"

Chapter 20

By a curious coincidence, one of the days that Robert Jones chose to visit St Joseph's College coincided with a visit by Jeff Glover. Robert Jones was intent on finding out where his ex-wife Susan and the family now had their home in America. He was hoping that the American habit of putting the return address on the back of an envelope would help him. He had discovered that the pigeon-hole room in St Joseph's, the place where student mail was left, although it had CCTV, had no other security measures, and anyone could look through the partition containing anyone else's letters. He had been going into the college regularly for a couple of weeks, looking into Sarah's pigeon-hole on the pretext of dropping off flyers for the Catholic church and for pro-life. The porters had become used to his visits, they did not associate him with the warning about strange Americans.

Jeff Glover did not give a second glance to the dark haired, bearded, middle-aged man walking around the Front Court of the college. Jeff was off to keep an appointment with Adrian Armstrong, the senior tutor of St Joseph's, to find out the name and arrange a meeting with the young lady tennis player that Professor Grey had mentioned during their conversation the day before. He had had previous dealings with Adrian, who was the secretary of the university's Senior Tutors' Committee, as well as senior tutor of St Joseph's. Previous conversations, and presentations to the Senior Tutors' Committee, had concerned freedom of speech and the university's duty to uphold the rights of free speech, within the framework of the law. Jeff Glover had been sent to one of the committee meetings to provide a police perspective on the issue. He remembered Adrian as an intelligent and cooperative man who had listened intently, as had all the senior tutors, and asked excellent questions at the end of the presentation.

As he walked into the outer room where Adrian's P.A. was sitting Jeff began to think that all senior tutors must have had the same interior designer, sometime in the fifteenth or sixteenth century. The outer office with the P.A.'s desk, the inner sanctum, where the senior tutor conducted her or his own research, and held the private conversations, all had the same feel about them. The confidential interviews must have been a big part of the senior tutor's job, just as the interrogations conducted in the interview rooms at a police station were, for Jerry and Jeff.

Adrian Armstrong was a coffee addict, well, anyway, very keen on his fresh ground coffee. He could not always get away to Savino's, so he had his own bean-to-cup machine, in the gyp room attached to his outer office. Jeff was offered a cup of coffee, and duly accepted. When they were seated in the inner sanctum and the coffee had arrived, they stopped their idle chatter and Jeff got down to business.

"I'm sure you know that Alexis Stanislowsky is studying at Cambridge, at St Alfred's. That's what's bringing me here. We have reason to believe that Alexis is likely to be a target for some of his father's enemies and we know that at least half a dozen of Stanislowsky Senior's enemies, from his home country, have entered the UK within the past two months, during the time that Alexis has been here. Unfortunately, we don't know their whereabouts, they gave our agents the slip shortly after they passed through Heathrow. What I'm going to tell you next must be kept in strict confidence. If I could get you to do it, I would get you to sign the Official Secrets Act, but I think I know you well enough from our past dealings, so here goes anyway.

"We have intelligence that a few kilograms of Semtex have made their way to East Anglia and we are concerned that they might be coming our way here in Cambridge. Alexis is studying Translational Research, particularly stem cell Translational Research. We know that there is a huge stem cell conference here in July and that you will be housing the delegates while they attend meetings on the New Museums site. We have some intelligence that the pro-life groups here in Cambridge are intending to disrupt the conference, but we also think they might try and do a bit more than just disrupt. The thing is that Alexis will almost certainly be at the conference, and that's going to be an additional risk factor.

"So, we're trying to get as much information as we can about Alexis, his friends, his movements, and his involvement with the conference.

"I saw Professor Grey yesterday and she told me that one of his closest friends is a girl tennis player, on the same course, who she thinks may have a Stanford connection and a St Joseph's connection. Have you anyone who fits that description?"

Adrian had listened intently to what was being said, and his normal poker face was beginning to show some signs of concern. All the delegates were staying in St Joseph's. St Joseph's had a big perimeter, very close to major parts of the town, like the central park area, the main shopping centre, and the bus station. Alexis would be moving into temporary accommodation in St Joseph's for the duration of the conference. It was not going to be a peaceful first week of the Long Vacation!

"We have a young lady who fits that description," said Adrian. "Her name is Cecilia Tan. She's a student studying here for a year doing a master's degree in Translational Research. I think she is going back to the States to the Medical School in San Francisco. We have a regular arrangement with Stanford, and we have four students from there this year. They're very active in the college and the university, and they work very hard, from what I can see. Two of them are university cyclists and triathletes, there's the tennis player and then the other one runs, very fast, middle distance for the university. I'm sure they're no threat to Alexis but, of course, you will probably want to see Cecilia and maybe the others. How would you like me to fix it?"

"I guess I can ask to see them and warn them that the American police think Jackson may be in this country? I would be happy to see them all together. Could I ask you to fix it and could I come here please? I think that would be less alarming than having them come to the police station."

The two men agreed on some possible times and Jeff said his farewell and returned to base.

Meanwhile, Robert Jackson had finally got his address. The dark haired, bearded, middle-aged man walking around the Front Court of the college, to whom Jeff Glover had paid no attention, had lucked out in the pigeon-hole room. Sarah's birthday was in March, and Jackson had been visiting the pigeon-hole room on a regular basis, with his flyers, waiting to see if a birthday card arrived. It did indeed arrive, in good time for Sarah's birthday. He found it in the pigeon-hole that morning. He obviously recognised his ex-wife's writing, and copied down the address; Ocean View Drive, in Rockridge. His immediate thought was that he had missed an opportunity. When he had been in Rockridge raping Theresa, he could easily have gone round to Susan's home and taken care of business there. But by way of consoling himself he decided to look forward to returning to finish the job, after he had finished in Cambridge. Rape and, this time, murder was what he had in mind.

That evening Kesandu called Jerry on the burner phone and asked for a meeting. Jerry was in London, having gone home, as usual, for the weekend. He arranged to meet Kesandu, with Jeff Glover, at a safe house in the village of Bar Hill. There is a very big superstore there, and several students have been known to go there on shopping expeditions. The bus service is not great, but at least there is a bus service.

The house used by the police had two ways in, one at the front, through the front garden, from the ring road running round the village, and one through the garage at the back of the plot. It was easy for people to meet, without being seen gathering.

The meeting took place on the Sunday. Jerry came back early from London. Kesandu began her report:

"I was at the pro-life meeting, and Sean O'Connor was talking to this new guy who had started coming to the group about five or six weeks ago," she said. "The new guy has an American accent, and he was sounding off about the pro-life movement in America and how it's losing its focus. I distinctly heard him say that they had not shot or blown up anyone for quite a few months now, and he thought that was a shame. His exact words were 'If you don't keep reminding the motherf***ers that all life is precious, they f***ing soon forget and start murdering babies again.' Then he said he knew how to make bombs and he was probably going to go back to America to start helping people to blow up these bastards.

"I thought O'Connor was very interested when this new guy, I think he's called Robert, said he knew how to make bombs. I listened very hard, without being obvious, and I heard them talking about fertiliser bombs, and pipe bombs; and then they said something about using Semtex as a primer. It sounded like the guy, Robert, knew what he was talking about. He said it was easy to get all the equipment you needed to set off the bomb, from a local electronics store. O'Connor and this guy then went off into an inner room and I couldn't get anything more."

"Do you know where the new guy lives or works?" asked Jerry.

"I know nothing about him," said Kesandu. "Nobody does. He just turns up and then disappears immediately after the meetings. We meet at the Friends Meeting House, and he seems to head off towards the town after we break up. Our next meeting is Friday next week. Sean called a meeting to discuss how we are going to organise the protest in the summer, but I get the distinct feeling that we are going to be used as a distraction, with placards and a demonstration, while the real protest action could be much more serious."

"Can you give us a description of this bloke?" asked Jeff.

"I can try," said Kesandu. "But there isn't too much to go on. He's about 6ft tall, perhaps a bit more, he's powerfully built, I reckon he's about mid to late forties, he has very dark hair and he's growing a beard and sideburns all over his face. He may have recently been clean shaven because the beard is not that long. I don't think he trims it. He has slightly lighter hair roots, so he may be dyeing it. He has very good teeth, a real American mouthful."

"It could be Jackson," said Jerry. "The hair colour is wrong, but the build is right, and he is calling himself Robert, a lot of people stick to their first name when they choose an alias. It's easier for them."

"Who's Jackson?" asked Kesandu.

"An American rapist who we think might have come over here looking for a particular group of victims," replied Jeff.

"This guy goes to church regularly," said Kesandu. "That doesn't totally fit with a rapist, does it?"

"Going to church is apparently what got him out of prison early," said Jerry. "He uses it as a smokescreen to hide what he's really like. The minute you see him I want you to call us and tell us where you are. We need to see this guy as soon as possible."

The two detectives and Kesandu went their separate ways back to Cambridge. The bus service is so bad that Jerry told Kesandu to go and do a big grocery shop and get a taxi to come and pick her up, all at police expense.

It was a lot for Jerry and Jeff to take on board. On the way back in the car, they were very concerned that this American might be Robert Jackson. It was clear that they were going to have to locate him and talk to him. A lot of things fitted. Right height, right age, right build, could have dyed his hair, interested in bombs, pro-life and calling himself Robert something.

Jerry contacted Shapiro immediately and asked for further pictures and descriptors, such as likely height and weight, just to see how closely it fitted Kesandu's description. Jerry also asked if there was any CCTV footage of Jackson, or any other video material involving him. Shapiro said there was nothing immediate, but he promised to see if any of the television footage of the trial, seven years ago now, had survived at the news station. Jerry and Jeff wanted to show it to Kesandu, just in case she could give a more positive id.

The conversation In the inner room, which Kesandu had not been able to overhear, was very direct. Sean was clearly not yet ready to trust Robert Jones, but he was intrigued, and he asked Robert if he could arrange a demonstration of a remotely triggered device.

Robert was all theoretical knowledge to this point. He had never actually made a bomb. He was going on the conversations he had had with the various bombers in the special wing at San Quentin. He decided it would be a great chance to practice making devices, a useful skill for his future criminal intentions, and he had a suspicion that Sean might want him to do something with a bomb here in Cambridge, or elsewhere in England, in the not-too-distant future.

"I need about £200 to buy some components," he said. "I'll make a couple of devices and we can go out into the fens, along the river path if you like, and I can show you how to work them. We don't want too big a bang, we don't want to draw attention, so I'll get the device to set off a very small explosion for you. Do you have any explosives?"

"I don't," said Sean. "I guess I could ask around among my contacts to see if anyone has some small quantity of a not too powerful explosive, or maybe you could make some from fertiliser and stuff."

"OK," said Robert. "Give me a week or so and I'll get back to you with a suggestion for a demo out along the riverbank."

When he left the meeting, Robert was more animated than he had been for a very long time. He was relishing the thought of trying to put his theoretical knowledge into practice. He would build a device that could be triggered by a clockwork mechanism, and he would try various mixtures of chemicals, to see which gave the best bang. Even if Sean did not want his skills, he had a feeling that they would be useful for revenge or might give him an opportunity to contact other groups and carry out terrorist activities for them. True to his promise he spent the next week gathering the materials and making a couple of relatively simple explosive devices, with a little bit of fertiliser-based explosive to be used to show that it worked. He was not going for sophisticated, just a simple timer device. He knew exactly what he would do for a remote, but he wanted to take this slowly. No risk but lots of reward.

The meeting with the students and James took place the next day. Adrian Armstrong had booked the large room, which was used for several committee meetings, the anteroom to the Long Gallery; the Long Gallery in which the governing body of the college met. The anteroom contained numerous works of modern art. Jeff was looking at one of them, a sort of scrubby version of a green tree. He was not impressed, until someone told him who had painted it, and what it was worth. There must have been nearly a million pounds' worth of modern paintings in the anteroom, and a few million pounds' worth more of paintings in the long gallery, plus a couple of sculptures.

The college had provided some coffee, water, and those packets of expensive biscuits, that have two or three in, rather than the cheap packets that tend to have four. Being students, the Americans made a beeline for the biscuits. Having a sweet tooth, Jeff Glover did likewise. James simply had a coffee and shared one of Martha's shortbread biscuits.

"There isn't an easy way to tell you this," said Jeff, "and I don't mean to alarm you, but we have some reason to think that Robert Jackson might be here in Britain and might even be in Cambridge looking for you. We think you would be wise to be watchful and we do *not* want any of you, particularly the women, to go running out in the countryside early morning or late evening and never alone, please. Walking around the streets at night alone is also a bit risky, especially for the ladies. We have some leads as to where he might be, and we are going to try to find him, but in the meantime until we do find him just be very careful please."

There was not much else to say about that. Ever since they had been told about Theresa's rape the six of them had been extra careful and Martha had stopped doing the Baits Bite and Coton runs alone.

What Jeff said next did suddenly change their demeanour.

"Lieutenant Shapiro, I believe you know him Martha, went to interview one of Robert Jackson's cell mates from San Quentin, and it turns out that your father, Sarah, had been taking a crash course in bomb making. We have no reason to believe that he's making bombs to attack you, but there are some things you can do to take precautions just in case we're wrong, and Jackson is targeting one or more of you."

"I spent years with my dad looking under cars and not opening suspicious packages," said Jonny. "I guess I can go back to that for a bit, until you catch him. I seem to remember it was also a case of not following routine, but that's difficult here given that the city is so small, and we are all working in a particular laboratory or workshop, and we all live in the same college. There's also a bit of a timetable effect, we have to be in certain places at certain times."

"I get that," said Jeff Glover. "I'm not convinced that he's going to go for you individually with a bomb, but we do have a suspicion that he's working on a bomb for a bigger purpose. I think that some of you are going to be around in July when the big Translational Stem Cell medicine conference is taking place. We think there's a good chance that the pro-life group are going to target it, and there's a possibility that Robert Jackson is going to make their bomb for them."

"I need to tell you that our intelligence sources say that a large quantity of a very powerful explosive has found its way to East Anglia, possibly to Cambridge. That's why I want to talk to you Cecilia. That and the fact that you know Alexis. We think that Alexis may also be a target, for dissidents who are enemies of his father. I think you're a friend of his?"

Ceci nodded.

"Are either of you presenting any work at the conference?"

"Yes," said Ceci. "We are both giving poster presentations of our research work, in the foyer to the conference building here in St Joseph's, or in the large Laboratory in Physiology, Development and Neuroscience. We are not yet sure which one. They are running a satellite session for M.Phil., M.Sc., and Ph.D. students, and we will be part of it."

"What about the main conference. Are you attending sessions there?"

"Yes. All the department's graduate students have been invited to attend any session they want, including the opening address by the Nobel Prize winner, Lord Guerney."

"OK. Thanks for that. I didn't know for sure what was going on, I expect the exact programme is still being worked out. Ceci, how do you find Alexis, is he alright here? It must be hard for him with a constant bodyguard and all the security issues of being Stanislowsky's son."

"He's a very nice guy," said Ceci. "He doesn't flaunt his wealth and he's absolutely dedicated to trying to improve the health of the people in his homeland, and around the world, by developing medicines and treatments that rely on stem cell therapy. I don't know if I'm supposed to tell anyone this, but Alexis, we all call him Lexi, has persuaded his dad to make a gift of twenty million dollars to the Stem Cell Research Institute, and another ten million to plant sciences, for research into improving crop yields in staple food plants. I think they intend to announce it at the conference in the summer."

"That's great," said Jeff. "Look, Ceci, without being desperately obvious about things, would you mind watching out for Alexis a little for us. We know he has a bodyguard, so that's fine, but would you keep your eyes and ears open for anything that happens around the two of you, anything that makes you suspicious that someone might be watching him, or tailing him, or otherwise doing something that could mean potential harm to him. Just anything unusual really. The same goes for the rest of you as you go about your daily business. Anything at all that you notice."

Martha, sitting there next to James, spoke for all of them when she said, "I guess we're all a little nervous now. Are there any special things we need to do to try to keep safe? How big a threat do you think this is? We have some friends planning to come over around the time of the conference, should we stop them coming?"

"I don't think it has reached that point yet. We aren't certain that he is here, and we don't know for sure what the pro-lifers are planning. It could all be just talk, a bit of bravado by the organisation. It could end up with throwing a few eggs and rotten tomatoes. But we promise you that if we think it is getting more definite, we will get back in touch with you. Meanwhile, as Jonny said, try to vary your routines a little, try not to open any suspicious packages, bring them to us at Parkside Police Station and we can X-Ray them before you open them. Look, enjoy the rest of your time here, I'm sure you'll be alright, but be a little careful too."

They had another cup of coffee and first Sarah and James, then the other three in turn, explained to Jeff the basis of the research they were doing, and what they hoped to achieve by it. Jeff was fascinated, fascinated enough to have another two packets of biscuits without really noticing he was eating them.

The meeting did put a little bit of a damper on things for a while, but after a few days the sensible precautions became routine, and life settled back into a pattern, a less predictable pattern, but a pattern, nevertheless.

Chapter 21

Robert Jackson, also known as Robert Jones, was the only American at the pro-life meetings. His years in jail had made him very aware of when he was being watched. It was a protective instinct, if someone was watching you, they were thinking of targeting you. It could be a potential knife in the back when you were going to the library, or it could be an attempt to rape you when you were in the showers. Nobody watched anyone in jail without intent. The instinct had served him well. Mostly.

He was beginning to find the pro-life meetings a bit uncomfortable. Someone was watching him. He was not sure who, but he could feel that prickle at the back of his neck, the hairs standing on end. He wondered who it was, and why. He realised that he did not need to know, but he also realised that it might be time to disappear from the scene. He asked Sean if he could speak to him privately in the office.

"I have a couple of devices ready for testing," said Robert. "Is there a day that would suit you?"

"How about tomorrow afternoon?" asked Sean. "Have you got a decent bicycle?"

Robert admitted that he did have a decent cross-country bike with wide tyres and good gears.

"Got it from the shop in Mill Road," he said.

Sean said nothing, he just smiled at that.

"I'll meet you at Baits Bite Loch at about 1pm," said Sean. "We can go on beyond the Loch towards Ely. Not much interference up there. There's a coppice or two and there are crow scarers going bang all the time up on that route. Should be easy to avoid any attention."

They went back into the main meeting room and Robert, again, felt sure that someone in the room was watching for him to come back. It was time to leave; he would *not* be coming back.

"Just off for a pee," he said, rather too loudly. And then he was gone. He went back to Gwydir Street. As far as he knew, nobody who might mean him harm knew where he lived. He felt comfortable staying there, for the time being.

While Robert and Sean had been in the inner room, Kesandu had called Jeff Glover and told him the American was at the meeting. Shortly after Robert had left the meeting, a police car drew up outside the Friends Meeting House. They waited patiently while the meeting concluded and then watched for the American among those leaving the scene. But they were too late.

The next day Sean and Robert met, as agreed at Baits Bite Lock at 1pm.

"We had a police car draw up outside our little meeting room last night," said Sean.

"Well, I'm very glad I wasn't there," said Robert. "I might not be here now if I had been there. I'm not exactly a legal alien."

Sean noted that comment, but decided not to press for further information, for the time being anyway.

They cycled on towards Ely. They stopped in the little coppice that the path goes through just before Dimmock's Cote Road and Bridge.

Robert set up his little bag of tricks and invited Sean to set the timer. Sean chose one minute. They retreated. One minute after the retreat there was a perfectly satisfactory bang. More smoke than substance. It was enough to convince Sean that Robert could do the job he was asking him to do.

"Do you think you could make a trigger with a remote control?" asked Sean.

"I could," said Robert. "It would just use the radio or phone signal to close the circuit instead of the mechanical alarm that you just set off. It would be better if we could buy one of these new electronic detonators. Then it would be very easy. Trouble is I don't know where to get hold of them. It might take a bit of work to find out. I may have a contact in America who could get them for me. What sort of explosive are you thinking of?"

Sean paused for a moment and then decided he was going to go through with it and use Robert as his bomb maker.

"I think I have contacts to get the detonator and the explosive for you."

"What's the explosive going to be?" asked Robert.

"Semtex primarily, but I also want you to make some fertiliser explosive. You can set off the Semtex as your primary explosion, just as you told me last week, and then a big bag of ammonium nitrate can go off as a result. Dead easy

133

to get ammonium nitrate around the fens, with the agriculture industry, and growing all that produce."

"How much Semtex?" asked Robert.

"A few kilos," said Sean.

"And where are we going to put this stuff?" asked Robert.

"I'll tell you exactly where we're going to put it once I have the timetable for the conference. In the meantime, just think about how you could get enough ammonium nitrate into the basement of a building, over a period of three or four weeks, and how you could get the Semtex there with a suitable detonator and in a sealed container so that it would not be detected by sniffer dogs or one of those chromatograph devices. Just plan the logistics. Assume I'm going to get you those fancy electronic detonators."

"OK," said Robert. "Now it's my turn to trust you. I was in jail before I came over here from America, and I developed this sixth sense. I think you have someone in the pro-life group who's a security risk. I think there's someone there reporting to the police. I haven't been able to pin-point who, but I just know there is someone. I'm not coming to any more meetings. I'm going to disappear. I stick out like a sore thumb. If the police do come calling, and from what you said it looks as if they are already suspicious, they'll pick me up for certain. I bought two burner phones before I came here today, and one of them is for you. From this moment forward, I suggest we communicate only by the phones, and not by text messages either, because they get stored. And I suggest you try and find out who the mole is. If you can't find him, or her, then I suggest you work only with the people you really trust, and I wouldn't let anyone, other than just you and me, know about the bomb."

"Thanks mate," said Sean. "I think you could be right, and I understand why you want to go very low profile. I'll get everyone else working on the demonstrations and the rally. Now let's get back to Cambridge."

They got back on their bikes and headed back down the footpath and cycle track towards the city. On the way back, just as they had gone under the A14 road bridge, they passed a couple of girls running towards them. It was Martha and Sarah. Robert was rather pleased that neither of them batted an eyelid, just acknowledging the two gentlemen on bikes going in the opposite direction. It suggested to Robert that his disguise was effective; if those two didn't recognise him nobody would. He had tried not to stare but, looking at Martha, he was reminded of that night in Mill Valley, and he found himself unable to look away.

In fact, he stopped his bike, and turned to stare at her as she went off towards the Lock. Martha looked back and noticed him watching. She was used to it, not nice, but inevitable with some men. Why did it feel uncomfortable? She put it down to a heightened awareness following Jeff Glover's briefing, but something was bothering her. Sarah looked back too and felt the same unease.

"I think we should just tell Sergeant Glover," said Sarah. "It's a bit unusual for men to actually stop their bikes and stare. There's something didn't feel right about the way they went past us and then stopped. It made me feel very uncomfortable."

It was not difficult for Robert to keep a low profile, living, as he did, in Gwydir Street and working an entirely cash economy. The nearby shopping centre had a couple of large supermarkets; the variety of shops in the Beehive Shopping Centre, meant that he had little reason to expose himself to surveillance.

In terms of picking him up as the American stranger at pro-life meetings, the two detectives had missed the boat. After the next pro-life meeting, Kesandu called Jerry to report that the American had missed the meeting, and that the pro-life group was focussing on organising the demonstration to protest the use of stem cells. It would take place on the first day of the conference, during the opening speeches and the first plenary session. The protesters would picket the lecture theatre and harass the delegates as they went into the session. They would make a lot of noise. They had banners and drums and trumpets and other very noisy instruments and devices. They were planning recruitment in local schools, and across the university, as well as at all the local churches. They were even talking about a leaflet campaign to get a turnout from the villages around, and they were asking the more tech-savvy younger members of the group to plan a social media campaign against the conference. The demonstration would start on Parker's Piece and march through the bus station and past numerous colleges on a circuit through the Market Square. There would be an address by a guest speaker in the Market Square, outside the Guildhall, and then a walk along Corn Exchange Street, to Downing Street, and onto the New Museums site, where the final protest would take place outside the Babbage lecture theatre, where the plenary session was taking place, and the main conference papers were being presented. Kesandu reported that there had been no more talk about further elements of disruption, and Sean was playing up the protest as a very big event, as if it were certainly the main event happening that day.

The information from Kesandu suggested strongly that the intensity of protest about the conference was much closer to the normal pattern of demonstration, placards, a few eggs, and tomatoes, that sort of thing.

"What do you think?" asked Jeff. "Was this a false alarm?"

"I'm not sure," said Jerry. "That previous conversation seemed a little bit earnest to me, and a simple protest against activity in the Babbage is far too easy for us to police. There aren't that many entrances to the New Museums site, and we can easily stop the protest going through the archway from Downing Street, and the passageway into Free School Lane. I still think these characters need watching. I would still like to trace the American. Until we find him, I'll not rest easy."

Jeff asked, "What does this Sean guy do for a living. Have we got anything more on him?"

They set the intelligence network and the local police the task of unearthing all the information that they could on Sean O'Connor. There was a lot of it. Nothing definite but a lot of smoke, and, as the saying goes, there is no smoke without fire.

****

Sean had been brought up in the Finsbury Park district of London. Born in 1978 he had attended local schools. He had been in and out of trouble at school. Never enough to get himself permanently excluded, but enough for him to be a real nuisance to his teachers, and a very disruptive element in class. He was, however, very clever and had managed, despite his appalling behaviour, to get seven GCSE's, with good grades, and move on to a cycle maintenance apprenticeship. The one saving grace when he was at school was that he had been a keen cyclist and had joined a local cycling club. It had kept him off drugs, something that many of his contemporaries had become involved with during their out of school hours. He had tried to be a professional racer and had won a couple of minor road races on the British Tour, but he had not made the grade to the really high-powered professional teams. It was before British Cycling really took off, and long before Sky moved in on the big tours. His apprenticeship paid him enough to keep going, and the firm he was working with bought him decent road bikes, it was a good advertisement for them to have a 'tour' rider working in the shop. Eventually he had got enough money together to set up in business for himself and, after a few successful years in North London, he had bought the shop in Mill Road. It was doing well.

That was the simple side of the story. What intelligence picked up on was that Sean's father and mother had moved to Finsbury Park in the early 1970s, from the Bogside in Derry. They were quite old at the time, both in their forties. Sean was a late birth, an only child. One of Sean's uncles, Patrick, had been convicted of terrorist offences in the 1980s and had been imprisoned in the Maze Prison. Patrick's son, Donald, was now a porter at St Joseph's, and had shown no evidence of involvement in Irish politics.

GCHQ was asked by Special Branch to see what they could find about Sean's social media and internet activity. It was not difficult for them to find out that Sean was continually accessing information about Sinn Fein, the IRA, and the provisional IRA. There was nothing to directly link him with any of these organisations but there was a lot to suggest that he had maintained a very active interest in them.

There was also a single report that Sean O'Connor, then aged about 19, had been seen on a protest march against the Orange Parades in Derry in 1997. There was a hospital record that he had been treated for an injury caused by a rubber bullet. There was no further record of active involvement in the Nationalist movement.

Jeff and Jerry reviewed the information that had been sent to them. Given the history of the troubles in Ireland and the previous report from Kesandu they decided that keeping a watch on Sean O'Connor would be a prudent thing to do. They set up a regular patrol past the cycle shop on Mill Road and sent officers in, from time to time, to ask for repairs and spare parts. It was all the budgets would run to at this stage.

Sean, while keeping his head below the parapet, had maintained his links with his uncle, and his sympathies were still very much with the aspirations for a United Ireland. That was not his motivation for most of his protest activities. Deep down, Sean O'Connor was someone who liked a fight, who enjoyed the adrenaline rush of running battles with authority. The surveillance records did not show him taking part in the London Riots of 2011, but he had been there, and he had thoroughly enjoyed himself. He had been in a few other minor skirmishes, but that was the highlight so far of his rioting career. He now wanted to take things further, he wanted to plan and execute a large-scale violent act. The cause did not really matter. It was the destruction that motivated him. Sean contacted his uncle and asked to meet him. He was hoping that Patrick O'Connor could direct him towards someone who could provide what was needed to make a bomb. He had the bomb maker, most of the ingredients were sorted, he now needed a few components to make the task easier.

A telephone call to Uncle Patrick allowed Sean to do what Jerry and Jeff had been unable to do, it allowed him to contact the quartermaster of the group holding the Semtex. The man lived in Ely, a handful of miles north of Cambridge. Sean decided to cycle to Ely again, along the footpath by the river. It was easy to avoid surveillance, and avoiding any possibility of surveillance, especially if Robert was correct and there was a mole in the group, was high on Sean's priority list. He thought it would be good to take Robert with him, so he called Robert, and they agreed to meet, again, just beyond Baits Bite Lock.

Chapter 22

There was a bit more conversation this time as they headed up the path to Ely. Robert asked Sean what he did for a living and was absolutely delighted to discover that Sean owned the cycle shop in Mill Road.

"I nearly told you last time," said Sean, "but I wasn't sure then I could trust you and I didn't want to give you too much information in case you took it into your head to come after me."

A few nights earlier Robert had lain awake for an hour or two thinking about possible ways to fix the last part of his plan for revenge. He wanted to get a job at the cycle shop in Mill Road, that was essential for what he wanted to do. He came up with all sorts of ideas to get rid of or disable the present assistant there, but everything he could think of would lead to a police investigation, and that would probably compromise his ability to remain below the radar.

"Can I come and work for you?" asked Robert. "I followed that old chap who works for you, and who sold me the bike, to his home on riverside. To be honest I was thinking of ways to make him disappear, but I was afraid anything I might do would bring the cops down on me. I'm getting a bit bored with nothing to do. I did a lot of cycle maintenance when I was in San Quentin, and I worked in a small garage in Richmond when I came out. If you need a spare pair of hands, I'm sure I could be helpful. In fact, I would do it for nothing if you want."

Sean was beginning to realise what a nasty piece of work this Robert Jones was, making poor old Ravinder disappear sounded a bit drastic, but Sean thought he would be able to handle the American, if he had to, and he wanted to use the expertise and determination that Robert had on offer.

They agreed that Robert would start work at the shop and, to avoid paperwork, Sean would pay him a small amount, off the books. No National Insurance and no PAYE. Sean thought it might be a good thing if Robert used the garage at the back of the premises to build the bomb. Out of sight of everyone, including the regular shop assistant, but where he could repair cycles as a cover for his other activities.

By this time, they were nearly at their destination. They had watched Ely Cathedral, 'The Ship of the Fens', growing larger and larger as they finished the cycle ride along the riverside path. The last part of the path to Ely runs past the King's School playing field, and then the railway station, before it reaches Station Road. A left turn on Station Road, and right turn on Annesdale, took them to the pub where they were to meet the quartermaster.

They sat for about twenty minutes at a table with a view of the river, and, just as they were beginning to get a little concerned, the quartermaster arrived. They had booked a table in a false name and the quartermaster was brought over by the waiter to join them, as part of the 'Jonas Smith' party. There was additional security. They had agreed an exchange of chatty sentences, in sequence, the usual cloak and dagger stuff that does happen, not just in spy stories.

"Can we order you a lunch?" asked Sean.

"That would be very nice," said the quartermaster, in a very strong, possibly Russian, accent.

They ordered three portions of fish and chips and three draught beers. They exchanged a few pleasantries and then the quartermaster said:

"A friend of mine tells me that you would like to buy some ingredients for a recipe that you are cooking up. I think I have most of the ingredients you need, but there is competition for these ingredients, and someone else has approached me for most of what I have. Are you open to sharing the goods with someone else?"

Sean and Robert were both a bit lost at this moment. What did the guy mean, sharing? The look on both their faces amused the quartermaster.

"I think I may need to take you somewhere to explain what I mean," said the quartermaster.

"Don't look so concerned. I think this could be very much to your benefit. If you agree to what I'm asking, I might even be able to let you have most of the ingredients free of charge. I'm going to ask you to trust me. When we finish this delicious meal, I would like you to come with me back to my car and let me take you to meet someone. No need to be alarmed. I can assure you this is all to your advantage."

Robert and Sean looked at each other. Robert's sixth sense was not triggering any alarm bells, he looked at Sean, and indicated, by a nod of the head, that it was alright by him.

"That sounds very nice," said Sean. "We look forward to it."

There was, of course, no surveillance in the restaurant, but they were being very cautious in case anything they said might be overheard.

"We have our bikes here." said Robert. "They're locked up at the railings outside."

"I'll bring you back afterwards," said the quartermaster. "It shouldn't take long. There are just a couple of people I want you to meet, and, if everything works out, I will arrange for the ingredients to be delivered to you in the next couple of days."

They finished their meals and chatted about inconsequential things. The quartermaster recognised that Robert was American, so they chatted a bit about the eccentric behaviour of the present US government, and about the rise of China as a Super-Power. Then they talked bicycles. It would have been impossible for anyone to think that this was anything other than a group of colleagues, meeting for a business lunch.

Robert and Sean left their cycles chained to the railings by the river and walked with Igor, that was the quartermaster's name, back to the car park. Igor was driving a very new BMW sports utility vehicle, it had less than three thousand miles on the clock. It had blacked out windows.

"Get in the back please and put the hoods on," said Igor. "I'm afraid I cannot let you know where the goods are stored, nor where we are meeting our colleague."

There was some anxiety on the part of Robert and Sean, but they did as they were asked, and not being used to this sort of thing, they did not bother to count the left and right turns, estimate the speed of travel, count the junctions and the roundabouts, or in any other way try to work out where they had been driven. They did not even try to measure the time the journey took, although they were aware it was of the order of half an hour.

When the vehicle stopped, Igor told them that they could remove their hoods and they found themselves sitting in the back of the car in a farmyard. The farm itself was perched on top of a hill. The farmhouse was a whitewashed building with a thatched roof. The farmyard was bounded on one side by the main farmhouse and its associated outbuildings, on a second side by a very large poultry shed, with quite a high roof, on the third side by a high roofed wooden barn, painted with black preservative; the fourth side was open to the fields, and had an excellent view of the access road, running down to the public road. The access road, effectively a long private driveway, led up to the yard. From the public road, it passed through open pasture, where little pig shelters were scattered across the hillside, and lots of pink pigs, with black patches, were rooting around in the pasture, which was now more mud than grass. The door of the barn was open, and they could see that the walls of the barn were hung with pitchforks, and similar manual tools, and that, inside the barn, there were vehicles of various descriptions. It was clearly being used as a combination garage and workshop. There were large food stores for the poultry and the pigs, these were situated along the lateral road which went out between the end of the barn and the farmhouse, perpendicular to the access driveway. This was clearly a working farm and, like many of the farms in the East of England, was producing eggs, chicken, and pork, for the home market.

A friendly border collie bounced up to them as they got out of the vehicle. The dog tried to round them up until Igor barked a command at it and it slipped away, a little chastened, to its kennel near the pig pens.

"Come on," said Igor. "Let's go and meet the bosses."

Igor ushered them into a large room, a typical farm kitchen. Low exposed wooden beams greeted them. Robert, who was quite a tall man, had to watch his head on the entrance lintel but, once inside, there was more headroom and no one, not even the tall man waiting inside, 6ft 6 inches at least in American money, or 198 cm in European, had to bend their heads. The tall man signalled to them to sit down around the table and, in an Eastern European language of some sort, asked the woman waiting by the stove to bring them some coffee.

"Would you like a coffee?" he said, with the same strong accent as Igor. "My name is Viktor. Welcome to my little hideaway."

"Would you like cream and sugar?" he asked them.

Sean had cream and two sugars, a long-standing habit from his youth; Robert, smelling that the coffee was good, had his black and with no sugar.

Viktor took a cigarette out of a very expensive looking gold cigarette case. It looked like an expensive handmade cigarette, like the old Balkan Sobranie cigarettes that used to be on general sale from specialist tobacconists. It looked like them because it was one, handmade, and specially imported by Viktor. Sobranie Black Russian, the top of the Sobranie totem pole.

Robert looked at Viktor's hands. They were beautifully manicured, they had long, elegant fingers, they were adorned with a single gold signet ring, with a spread-eagle symbol on the face. He caught a glimpse of the watch on Viktor's wrist. It was not for telling time. It was for saying I'm f***ing rich and I could buy you a million times over.

Viktor lit his cigarette with a gold lighter, as ostentatious as the cigarette case and the watch. He inhaled deeply, and then let the smoke out in a perfect smoke ring, through which he immediately blew a second tiny ring to make the shape of an archery target.

"I'm wondering," he said, "if we have the same target in mind."

They watched the rings disperse.

Robert, not a smoker himself, found the aroma from the cigarette not unpleasant. He took another sip of the excellent coffee.

"What do you mean?" he asked.

Viktor pointed at Sean slightly dismissively. "Mr O'Connor there wants to make a huge explosion to destroy a few scientists who are conducting research he doesn't like. Is that correct?"

Sean began to bristle a bit.

"It's not so fucking trivial. Those bastards are multiple murderers. They kill unborn babies. Do you approve of that?"

Viktor ignored Sean and went on.

"Unlike Mr O'Connor's targets," Viktor addressed himself to Robert, "my potential target kills born babies, not just unborn babies, and he kills their mothers, and fathers, and anyone else who gets in the way. Compared with that I think your objective is very, how do the British say, very small beer."

Sean sucked in his breath and paused. There was something a bit menacing about this man Viktor. Sean had the good sense to keep quiet.

"I would not give you the Semtex and the electronic detonators," (Robert's ears pricked up), "Just to blow up a few scientists, but if you can do it in such a way as to take out my target too, then you can have what you want, and a million dollars each."

"Well, who the fuck do you want us to take out?" asked Sean, somewhat petulantly.

"Mr O'Connor. No need to swear. Surely you can use English better than that. If I can, you can."

Sean was getting very agitated by now. Robert, by contrast, was getting calmer and calmer and more intensely focussed on what Viktor was saying. Viktor was almost on the point of ending the conversation, he was wondering whether Sean might be a little too volatile and too much of a risk to go into partnership with, then Robert spoke.

"Viktor," he said. "Don't mind us. We do know what we're doing. It's just that we are passionate about our cause. I've watched Sean in action, and I've already trusted him with my life. I'm wanted for very serious crimes in America and Sean is helping me stay under the radar. I can see that you're worried but, believe me, we can do this job and, if you tell us who your target is, maybe we can take him or her out too? I'm the bomb maker, not Sean, and he's the one with the contacts that are going to enable us to do what we need to do."

Viktor waited silently, watching them both as he finished his first cigarette. He liked this Robert guy, he still had doubts about Sean, but he recognised that Sean was not very experienced in this sort of thing, and would probably play second fiddle to Robert, in the grand scheme of things. Should he kill them, or should he work with them?

"Could I have another cup of your outstanding coffee please?" asked Robert.

That made Viktor's mind up for him. This guy, Robert, was a cool customer. He could do the job. And if it didn't work what had he got to lose. Only a few kilos of Semtex and some fancy electronic detonators. If it did work…

"'Tasha, another coffee please for Mr Jones, and one for me. How about you Mr O'Connor, more cream and sugar with yours?" There was heavy sarcasm in that last utterance, but Sean was too bemused to notice it. He was out of his depth compared with the other two negotiators.

"OK," said Viktor. "I want you to kill Stanislowsky."

"What?" asked Robert.

"You heard me. I want you to kill Stanislowsky."

"Do you mean the oil mogul from the former Soviet bloc?" asked Robert.

"That is exactly who I mean," said Viktor.

"So how does that fit in with what we are planning?" asked Robert.

"Stanislowsky is coming to that conference you are planning to blow up. They are going to announce his gift of thirty million dollars to the university, and he's going to come and listen to his son give a presentation. We have been monitoring his son through one of our agents who is acting as his bodyguard. Stanislowsky thinks the guy works for him, but he actually works for us. If you can take the son out too, that would be a bonus. We think his mother and sister will also be joining the boy to hear him give his talk. In fact, if you take out the son and the rest of the family, we will give you a double bonus."

Robert drank his coffee slowly and thought about the proposition. Sean thought about the one or two million dollars.

Robert was thinking. Viktor noticed that, and thought it was a very good sign. Finally, after Viktor had started, and almost finished, another cigarette, Robert asked:

"Do you have any more information yet about the programme for the conference? We'll need that to get our timings right. I'll plan the event so that we have some flexibility about timing, but nearer the day we will need precision. Those electronic detonators will give us the flexibility we need. We won't need to know the precise timing until a few seconds before the event, because a simple phone call will blow the crap out of the place."

Viktor began to like what he was hearing. A flexible plan, capable of being implemented at the very last second.

"We'll try to give you as much notice as we can, certainly more than a few seconds. As soon as our man guarding Alexis, that's the boy's name, knows what is happening, we'll let you know. I have your telephone number. I will not contact you again unless there's a significant change of plan. If you need to contact me, you can do so through Igor, but I would prefer that you don't do so unless it's essential. We believe that the British Special Branch and Intelligence services have noticed the arrival of several of our group in this country and, like you, Robert, we're trying to stay under the radar. We gave them the slip at St Pancras and Kings Cross railway stations. They currently have no idea where we are, and we want to keep it that way.

"I don't know how good your security in your pro-life group is, but I suggest you two remain the only two who know about this bomb. I suggest you two do all the work on it. You have time. I do not want to know how you are going to do this. I'll give you more than enough Semtex, and more than enough detonators. They will be couriered to you tomorrow morning. Make sure that one of you is there to sign for the parcel. It will be labelled for the attention of Sean O'Connor only. I don't want anyone else accidentally trying to see what's in the package. And remember to use gloves when you handle anything connected with this venture, especially if it's likely to survive the blast. Good luck."

Viktor sat back and lit another cigarette. Robert and Sean finished their coffees and Igor signalled them to go. They said goodbye to Viktor and 'Tasha, the woman who had served them coffee, and went back to the car.

"Hoods on," said Igor.

By 3.30pm, they were back at the bicycles and cycling towards Cambridge.

"Fucking arrogant shit," said Sean.

"Cool it Sean," said Robert. "He was riling you to see if he could trust you. I think we were very close to getting our selves buried somewhere on that pig farm, either buried or eaten by the bloody pigs. You just don't know how happy I am to be back on our bikes. I need to stop for a minute. I need a pee. So much coffee. I didn't want another cup, but I had to do something to stop Viktor thinking about terminating us."

They both stopped just after the next swing gate on the path and peed in the hedge either side.

"You are fucking joking?" asked Sean.

"I wish I was," said Robert. "I've seen the look on Viktor's face before, on the faces of some of the guys in prison, when some of the big boys were deciding whether to put a contract on one of the smaller fish. The little fish either ends up dead, or he gets lucky, and the big boys decide he can be useful to them. Either way it's decision time and I noticed that the contracts usually happened when the big boys had too much time to think. Distraction favoured the small fish, and make no mistake, to Viktor we are small fish. Everything about him was so big time."

He zipped up his fly and the pair of them got back on the bikes. Sean suddenly stopped again, went over to the side of the path, and vomited. It had just occurred to him how close to death he had come.

"It's over now," said Robert. "We're safe, at least until after the bomb explodes. I think we need to ask the big boys to give us half the money in advance, and we need to arrange to disappear as soon as the bomb goes off. If you want to realise your assets, sell your shop, before the bomb that might just be smart. I can help you with getting the money abroad. I reckon we could go to Canada. You can do a visa waiver to get into the States, and then I have contacts who will get us both into Canada, after I deal with a bit of unfinished business in California. If we stick around, Viktor will have us killed. Big fish don't feed little fish, they feed on them."

Sean thought about it. He had no real permanent ties here in England. His dad had died of a heart attack when he was in his late 60s and Sean's mum had died of ovarian cancer not long after his father. There was nothing to keep Sean in England. Thinking about it, he did not really like his life there. He enjoyed cycling and he enjoyed the outdoors. Canada sounded perfect.

The colour was coming back to Sean's face.

"OK," he said. "I guess we're forewarned. Let's do it. It would be great if you could help me sort it out."

Chapter 23

When Sarah and Martha had reported to Jeff Glover that there had been a couple of men on bicycles who had stared at them rather too intently on the tow path near the flyover, it all seemed a bit trivial. None of them made too much of it, but the policemen asked the river wardens to keep an eye open for anything suspicious along the riverbank near the lock and the flyover. Jeff was inclined to put it down to a state of paranoia induced by the news from America of the rape of Theresa, Jerry was not so sure.

"Those two girls have been through enough not to get spooked easily," said Jerry. "I'm a day off tomorrow. I might just walk that path to Ely. The girls said that the men looked as if they had ridden that towpath, they had a lot of mud on their bikes. The walk should take about four or five hours. I might see something. Do you fancy coming along? I'll buy you a beer at the inn by the river when we get to Ely, and, if the Fish and Duck Marina is open, I'll buy you a beer before we get there. I'll also get you a train ride back! Five hours to walk and twenty-two minutes to get back, brutal."

"Do I have a choice?" asked Jeff. "I guess I do, but I can't leave it to you to spot anything interesting, you're so bloody desk-bound these days."

They agreed to meet the next day and make the walk along the riverbank to Ely. The first part of the walk, alongside the part of the Cam that the university and the city use for rowing, was simply a case of covering the ground. Nothing could happen here easily without anyone seeing it. There were sculls and eights on outings all along the river, and the coaches of the eights, cycling in their green wellington boots, shouting at the crews through their megaphones.

"Bloody Hooray Henrys," said Jeff.

"Come off it, Jeff," said Jerry. "For every Hooray Henry out here, there are half a dozen likeable young kids who just want to exercise."

At that exact moment an obviously novice crew of young ladies passed them. They were all far too tiny to be serious rowers but were having an uproarious time of it as they struggled, womanfully, to make the boat, using oars which looked far too big for them, move through the water without capsizing. Even Jeff had to admit that it looked like a group of youngsters having fun, and he admitted that the 'Hooray' bit was far from the mark.

It took them an hour to get to Baits Bite, about 3 and a half miles from their start point at Parkside Police Station.

Downriver from the Lock there was a nice straight stretch of river that some crews sometimes used for practice, especially some of the university crews. On this morning, nothing was happening there.

The walk was relatively uneventful nearly as far as Dimmock's Cote and the Newmarket Road, another good two and a half hours of walking, and they were beginning to wonder if this was not a wild goose chase, but as you approach Dimmock's Cote you start to get a view of the Cathedral, and it is impressive on a clear day like the one they were experiencing. It was probably some sort of sixth sense that led Jerry to start to take more of an interest in the off-trail surroundings as they walked on the right of some typical dark peat fen fields, clearly planted with young vegetables, and followed the path into the little coppice where Sean and Robert had exploded their device earlier that week. Maybe the wind had changed to a north easterly and was blowing some of the scent of the explosion in their direction. Maybe they thought that there was a bit more treading down of the undergrowth near the path. There had been some heavy rain the day before Sean and Robert had made their expedition and going off the path had certainly churned things up. Jerry and Jeff went off trail for the first time, almost like trackers following the trodden and broken cow parsley, long grass, and nettles.

The 4ft area of burnt undergrowth stood out clearly in front of them. Right by the riverbank. There was the smell of fireworks, there were a few little pieces of wire. It wasn't much but Jerry called it in, giving the location with his Sat Nav. He wanted the forensic boys to see if they could get anything useful. It was another long shot.

"I wonder if the two girls might recognise either of the two men they saw?" asked Jerry. "I wonder if this burnt area is kids having a campfire, or something more serious?"

"The bits of wire are a bit odd," said Jeff.

"I agree," said Jerry, "and those bits of metal there, the sort of cogwheel bits, look as if they could have come from a small clock or something."

"We haven't got a picture of Sean O'Connor. I doubt we currently have a picture of either of the two men, O'Connor doesn't have any criminal record."

"Let's get a picture of O'Connor and also let's get the police artists to do some mock ups on Robert Jackson pictures, different hair colours, beards, facial hair, you know the sort of smart stuff they do," said Jeff.

"No need to spook O'Connor," said Jerry, "we'll get the guys to take a photo without his knowing."

The two of them sat down to drink a coffee from the flask Jerry was carrying in his small backpack. They were waiting for the forensic boys. Given the proximity to the Dimmock's Cote Rd it didn't take that long for the team to arrive. Jerry and Jeff left them to it, and decided to finish their walk, it was, after all, their day off.

The train journey back to Cambridge was a pleasant sit down, they skipped the beer at Ely as it was getting a bit late by the time they reached journey's end, so they caught the first train they could.

"I reckon there is definitely a bomb going to be involved in something happening very soon. I reckon it's very likely to relate to that blasted stem cell conference and I reckon the pro-lifers are involved somehow. I really want to know who those two men were that the girls saw on their run."

They lapsed into silence. A five hour plus walk along the riverbank, for relatively desk bound detectives, is tiring. Jeff was almost asleep before they reached Waterbeach. He was woken by the train stopping, briefly. Jerry noticed Jeff open his eyes.

"Come and have supper with Marianne and me," said Jerry. "Marianne is up visiting for a few days, and she always cooks in the evenings. It seems to be her French habit."

Jeff didn't need any second invitation. Marianne was a superb cook, and her regular trips to visit her family in France always ensured that the wine with the food would be a little special too. It had been a very good day for the two policemen.

The weekend passed uneventfully for everyone, but Robert and Sean talked about how they were going to engineer the introduction of Robert into the business, without upsetting the old guy who had worked for Sean for so very long. In the end, they decided that Sean would describe Robert as a relative, who had come from America, and was looking for something to do while he sought a permanent job elsewhere. From the introduction onwards, Robert would keep himself to himself, he would not help in the shop, but work away in the outbuilding, a former mews stable, at the back of the shop. The outbuilding had an alternative way out onto the service road at the back of the row of shops and was, as far as they could tell, not covered by CCTV. This would minimise the profile of Robert during the time when he would be preparing the bomb, under the pretext of repairing bikes. He would, also, be repairing bikes.

They discussed whether it would be sensible for Robert to move in with Sean over the shop, but the flat in Gwydir Street was working well for Robert, and they both recognised that some down time from the bomb project was important.

Robert arranged to call at the shop at lunchtime on the Monday, to be introduced to Ravinder, the assistant, and begin setting up the workshop for the task in hand.

The plainclothes detective tasked with visiting the cycle shop and getting a photograph of Sean went to the shop on the Monday morning and managed to get a very good photograph of Sean, and of Ravinder. It was fortunate for Robert and Sean that Robert did not arrive until lunchtime, or the adventure might have been over before it had begun.

Sarah and Martha were asked by Jeff to call in at the police station at Parkside, at their convenience, so, later that day, they were given a set of photographs to look at, including the one of Sean taken that morning. Both young women picked out Sean as one of the two men they had seen that day by the A14 bridge over the river.

"Thank you both," said Jerry. "He runs the bike shop in Mill Road, and he was once trying to be a professional cyclist, so there's probably nothing in this, but he's also very involved in pro-life, in fact he seems to be the Secretary or Chair of the movement in Cambridge. If you see him around anywhere unusual, please call us immediately on this number."

Jerry gave them both his card with the direct contact number.

"We're going to try to find out who he was with that day, but it might well be completely innocent, of course."

That afternoon, around 3pm, Jerry and Jeff went to the cycle shop in Mill Road.

Robert had just settled down in the back room, he had walked out of the shop just moments before Jerry and Jeff arrived.

"Mr O'Connor," said Jerry, "I'm Detective Inspector Gregory, and this is my Colleague Sergeant Glover. Can we talk somewhere privately?"

Sean looked a little startled, but probably no more startled than anyone else would when confronted by a couple of policemen that visited them unexpectedly.

"Sure," said Sean, "come through to my office. Can I get you a tea or something?"

"No thank you," said Jeff. "This shouldn't take very long anyway."

"How can I help you?" asked Sean.

"Well, there are two things really," said Jerry. "The first one is just a question about where you were last week on Wednesday."

"I don't know why you would want to know but I expect I was here in the shop," said Sean, his face colouring a little.

'*I don't think he should play poker,*' thought Jeff.

"Are you sure? We have a couple of young ladies who said you were out on the towpath near the A14 flyover."

"Oh! wait a minute. That's right. I think last Wednesday was when I cycled along the tow path to Ely, and back. I was trying to be a pro cyclist once, but I expect you clever guys know that already. You probably know, from the fact I'm here, that I didn't quite make it, but I made enough to buy this business. I like to go for longer rides sometimes but the path to Ely, it's quite fun you know. Bit of fresh air and a few muddy bits. I recommend it if you have a decent cross-country bike. I can sell you one if you like." Sean gave them a grin.

Jeff chipped in with the obvious question, "Would you mind telling us if you went alone or if someone came with you, and, if so, who it was?"

"Do you know, I offered to cycle with a customer from the shop," said Sean, "I don't know his full name, just called him Geoff. He was keen to go so I said OK; he was a bit older than me, and I think he just wanted me along to make sure he didn't get lost; mind you, how you can get lost on the riverbank for God's sake? But it was money, and business is business."

"Have you got a record of the transaction?" asked Jerry.

Sean went very pink in the face.

"I took cash. I must admit I didn't put it through the books. I guess that makes me a tax evasion criminal?"

'*Clever bugger,*' thought Jerry. '*He could be telling the truth but somehow I don't buy it.*'

"Well, if he comes in the shop again, please could you get his name and contact us?"

Another business card was handed out.

Jerry put on his very serious face and stared at Sean. Sean began to be a bit more uncomfortable.

"The second thing is a bit more worrying for us," said Jerry. "You probably know that there is a big stem cell conference in Cambridge this summer and we have heard rumours that the pro-life group, I think you are the Cambridge Chair of pro-life, are planning a protest. Is that correct?"

Sean was immediately more aggressive; he went onto the offensive.

"Inspector, I'm not aware that peaceful protest is illegal in this country. If we organise a protest march against the use of aborted foetuses, killed by doctors, then that is surely within our constitutional rights?"

"It is," said Jerry. "As long as it stays peaceful. But we've heard rumours, from Special Branch in London, that rent a crowd is getting involved and there are likely to be agitators coming in from all over the place to make a big event of the protest. Is there any truth in those rumours?"

"I swear on my mother's grave," said Sean, "I know nothing about agitators coming to join the protest. As far as I'm aware it's local. We have quite a following, especially among the young. There's a big Catholic population here as you know, and lots of them follow the church's teaching."

"I'm glad to know that the rumours have not reached you," said Jerry. "I'm sure the chief constable will want to know the planned route of any marches, and the sites of any gatherings that you are likely to convene."

It was not that warm in the office, and Sean was sweating buckets by the time the questioning ended.

"Just one more thing," said Jerry. "Have you had any new members lately? Anyone from America?"

The 'tell' was there again. The colouring of the features, the slight fidgeting with the fingers.

"Not that I recall," said Sean. "I tend to remain a bit separate from the members during meetings and people come and go all the time. I'll let you know if anyone new does join us."

'*Lying toad*,' thought Jerry.

Just at that moment a courier van drew up outside in the street and a parcel was delivered to the store.

Ravinder knocked on the office door and reported to Sean that there was a parcel that only Sean could sign for. Sean excused himself and went to collect it.

He brought it back into the office and put it on the shelf behind the two detectives.

Sean was sweating profusely again, and Jerry and Jeff were left wondering why that was.

On the way back to the police station, they talked about the interview. Neither of them believed Sean, about the peaceful parade, about not knowing his cycling companion, about not remembering who had recently joined his group. The problem for them was that they did not have enough evidence of anything to be able to get a search warrant or to become more aggressive in their questioning. They were going to have to play a waiting game, and, meanwhile, they were still going to have to chase the Semtex and consider every other high profile and contentious event as a potential bomb disaster.

As soon as the policeman had left Sean went out to the garage to see Robert.

"We need to be bloody careful," said Sean. "I don't think those policemen believed me that I didn't know the person I cycled with or that I didn't know that someone had recently joined our group. Thank goodness you decided to stop coming. I think you're right that there is a mole in our group. Not quite sure how we deal with that. You got any ideas?"

Robert paused and thought for a minute.

"As long as I stay out of sight, I think we're still OK. I would make sure the security on the site is even stronger. A few more padlocks and bolts wouldn't do any harm, and an extra lock for the garage, that Ravinder doesn't have a key for, would be very helpful. I think we mustn't be seen out together either. I'm sure they will put facial recognition cameras onto you, watching your movements wherever you go, and if they find me with you, they might just get a still from the CCTV. I think they knew you had cycled along the riverbank, and I wouldn't be surprised if they had found our test explosion site. They can't get anything from that, nothing useful anyway.

"What to do about the mole? We must use it to misdirect. Think about the alternative sites for a bomb that would make sense during this conference. We need the programme in detail, a list of speakers and venues. I think registration for the conference is still open and I think Mr Robert Jones, an American Gynaecologist, living and working in Britain, needs to register for the conference to make sure we remain fully up to date with the programme. These conferences aren't too fussy about who attends, as long as they pay the registration fee.

"I'm well set up in here, thanks. Just need to get the Semtex and the detonators now. And then a lot of fertiliser."

Sean looked at Robert.

"The Semtex has arrived," he said. "Came while I was talking to the two cops. I had to go and sign for it. I'll bring it through here after Ravinder goes home tonight. Meanwhile there are a couple of bikes, and a bloody lawnmower, that need repairing. I suppose you'd better get on with it or Ravinder will wonder what the Hell is going on."

Robert was already wondering when and if he might have to take Ravinder out of the equation. He might have to do it at the very last minute, just before the bomb, and just before he and Sean got the train to Heathrow.

Chapter 24

DI Gregory contacted Special Branch and the chief constable and requested surveillance on Sean's Cycle Emporium but neither the local police nor Special Branch could spare men for a stakeout in Mill Road. The evidence was not sufficient that this was the main threat to security. There were other conferences going on that summer. A meeting of the Anglo-Irish group, a meeting of the Political Historians about recent tribal conflicts in Africa, a meeting of the Palestinian Society, the list was long, not quite endless, but long enough. There was a compromise, DI Gregory got permission to set up a camera for 24-hour surveillance of the front of the cycle shop, to see who came and went. They were hoping for the American to appear. It revealed what the policemen thought was a surprisingly high footfall, but Cambridge is one of the cycle capitals of the world, so perhaps that should not have been surprising after all. Unfortunately, they did not have a camera covering the back of the shop, budgets are tight.

Arrangements for the conference were going ahead rapidly. The delegates, including Mr Robert Jones, the American obstetrician, received their conference pack, with the schedules and accommodation details. Mr Jones had not requested accommodation, but all the other details were complete. He knew who would be presenting papers, and at what times; he knew when, and where, all the plenary sessions were to be held; he knew about the social programme. He could now plan his attack.

The students, who were due to present their research at a poster session during the conference, were putting the finishing touches to their work. There was lots of lab time, and, with lab time and keeping fit for various sporting events, all five of the students were busy. James was still very busy in the lab and had also been roped in as an examiner for the finalists in Plant Science, the Part II students, who were specialising in Plant Science in their third and final year.

In the background were preparations for the visit of the friends and family members who were planning to take advantage of the presence of the gang of five in Cambridge that summer. It is always difficult, unless you book early, to find hotel accommodation in Cambridge during the tourist season.

The whole group had managed to find a very large farmhouse, with an annexe, in the village of Fulbourn, near to Cambridge. They had booked it as an Airbnb. There were separate parts of the accommodation for the parents and for the youngsters, although everyone knew that the youngsters were likely to spend a lot of the holiday sofa surfing with their friends. They were going to need hire cars; the bus route did not go near enough to the farmhouse to allow them to use public transport. Martha and Sarah, always very polite and well-liked by the college staff, managed to get permission for three vehicles to park in the car park at the college hostel near the station. They were also allowed to park in the college grounds outside working hours. Given the state of car parking and traffic congestion in Cambridge, that concession was important.

Thus, the social side of late June and early July was successfully set up. The academic work was being completed and the poster preparations were well under way.

At the end of the Academic year, Sarah and Jonny were staying on in Cambridge for the second year of their PhD Programmes. James' fellowship would continue, so James would also be staying on. Ceci, and Martha were going back to the University of San Francisco to complete their medical degrees. There was a fair amount of angst. James and Martha were trying to avoid thinking about the impending separation, they had been together for more than four years. They put all thoughts about it on hold for the duration of the term and agreed not to talk about it again until the end of July.

In late May, the four Americans, James and Alexis were sitting in Savino's coffee shop enjoying one of Sarah Savino's homemade amaretti and drinking the excellent coffee. Alexis' bodyguard was at a nearby table, watchful as ever.

Alexis suddenly announced: "My father is coming to Cambridge for the conference. I so want you all to meet him. I think the university's going to hold a special reception for him because he's giving a lot of money to the university for the Stem Cell research centre and for Plant Sciences. I shall make sure you are all invited. It should be a good event."

There was a general buzz of appreciation around the table. Martha spoke up first: "That's very kind of you. We have a lot of friends and family coming over for the conference, and for a holiday, before we all go back to our regular career paths, and we would like you to meet them too. Sarah and I both have little brothers, about 2 metres tall, each, and we would like you to meet them, and our parents. Jonny has a sister, Iris, and she's coming too. We're off to Europe after that, who knows when we're going to be over here again? In Ceci and my cases, we're doing medicine, so it could well be eight years or more before we can get away to Europe again, and we so want to see Paris, and Brussels and Berlin, and Vienna, and Rome, and Amsterdam and, well, everywhere we can get to in just under two months."

Alexis looked a little sad.

"Maybe I can meet you for some of it? I find it hard to make good friends, because of all the security around me and because I never know when people like me or like my father's money. I've just been so happy meeting you all. I would be very grateful if, over the summer, I could see you all."

Sarah said, "I'm sure I speak for everyone when I say that we've really liked getting to know you and we would love for you to come along when and where you can. I'll write out our itinerary and you just let us know when and where you would like to meet up with us."

There were nods of the head, smiles and general murmurs of approbation.

"Any idea where the reception for your father is being held?" asked Jonny. "I wonder if we'll get to see a bit of the university that students rarely get invited to?"

"I'm not supposed to tell you," said Alexis. "But I suppose it won't do any harm with you lot. But please don't tell anyone else as there may be a security issue. I think the reception is going to be in the Senate House at 5.30pm, just after the closing ceremony of the conference."

"That sounds great," said Jonny. "Is your dad going to the Stanford Dinner too?"

"Yes, the Master invited him."

"There was muttering all round and it turned out that everyone was going to the Stanford Dinner and that all the relatives of everyone round the table, including Alexis's mother and sister, would be at this annual event."

Nobody looked at Alexis's bodyguard. Nobody wondered why he was grinning from ear to ear before he composed his features and went back to looking attentive but disinterested.

Suddenly Sarah jumped to her feet.

"Come on Jonny," she said, "we have a time trial to prepare for. It's only a week away. Race you to Bury St Edmund's and back."

Viktor, at his farmhouse in the countryside north of Ely, looked incredibly content with life. He now had another option for wiping out that dangerous man, Stanislowsky; conference and post-conference options. As soon as the coffee session at Savino's had ended, Vasily, Alexis's bodyguard, had called Viktor with the new information about the reception for Stanislowsky. Viktor thought to himself how wise he had been to send such a substantial amount of explosive, and the extra detonators, to the pathetic little duo who were going to do the bombing for them. The O'Connor man was clearly out of his depth, the other man, Jones, or whatever he called himself, was more intelligent, and much harder, and could be relied on. Thinking about that reminded Viktor that he ought to get the message to Vasily that immediately after the bomb went off, he wanted O'Connor and Jones terminated. There was no point in leaving loose ends around.

Robert was sitting in the garage-cum-workshop when the message came through from Viktor that there was to be a second bomb, and it was to be in the Senate House, and it was to explode at some time after 5.30pm when the reception for Stanislowsky was in full swing. The package from Viktor had contained some very sophisticated, tiny, surveillance cameras, as well as the necessary bomb making items. There were half a dozen of these cameras, all Wi-Fi accessible. Robert had a very high-quality laptop on which he could monitor them. He was thinking where to place the cameras to best effect. He needed to make sure they gave him optimum timing for his explosions. One overlooking the platform in the Babbage Lecture Theatre was an obvious location, one overlooking the stage of the Senate House, the area where the vice-chancellors chair was always placed, facing the body of the room, for graduation ceremonies; that was a second obvious location. He knew where he was going to place a third camera but that still left three more that he could place. He would have another look at the detailed itinerary and plan where they would go.

Robert thought about the bomb types. The one associated with the Babbage would have to be a very large explosive device, placed somehow under the stage itself. He would have to work out how to keep it from being discovered. The first thing that was important was to try and stop the Special Branch from thinking that the conference was going to be targeted. That was about two things, security, and misdirection. He was going to have some fun with misdirection. It would be good practice for the real thing, working out how to get what would be effectively dummy bombs into key places. What he learnt from that should help with the real thing. He had a list of the controversial meetings happening in the next few weeks, and several of them would have little surprises.

Security had already been taken care of. Only Sean and he knew what the target was and only he knew precisely where and when things were going to happen. He was not even going to brief Sean fully until the very last minute. To be perfectly blunt he was thinking of taking Sean out after the explosion. He would prefer to travel alone, and not have to wet nurse Sean all the way to Canada. For the Senate House bomb and the lecture theatre, he would need Sean's help, for the rest, maybe not.

He thought the bomb that Viktor had instructed him to make for the Senate House would have to be essentially anti-personnel. It would have to kill by shrapnel dispersal rather than the blast effect alone. It would have to be incorporated in some way into the structure of the lectern, or the stage, from which the speeches would be made, or placed under the seats around the sides of the Senate House. It might even have to be an array of smaller devices, linked together to a single explosive trigger. A reconnaissance was in order.

Then…well, he had his own ideas.

Chapter 25

Lectures in the Babbage Lecture Theatre stopped well before the end of May and the maintenance department of the university, Estate Management, moved in to do the annual maintenance work on the audio-visual system, the fabric of the building, and everything else that needs to be done in a huge 500-seater lecture theatre. There were lots of contractors wandering around, and not everyone knew everyone else. It was a simple matter for Robert to find suitable clothing, a hard hat, boots, overalls, to blend in with the others working there. To say he found suitable clothing was a slight mis-speak; he stole it, bit by bit, from Estate Management teams working on other sites.

Under the stage at the front of the lecture theatre was a huge crawl space. It was not used extensively for storage, there were some items left under there in loose canvas sacks, or in large cardboard boxes. Most of the space was vacant, and there was cabling, for the lectern and the various controls servicing the theatre audio-visual functions. The stage floor was supported by beams, about 15cm in square cross-section. One beam passed directly under the lectern, the stage was about 10-metres deep and the beams were spaced about a metre and a half apart, a total of six cross beams in all, plus the beam attached to the rear wall, and the one attached at the front of the apron, to which the vertical panel, hiding the under stage from the audience, was also fixed. Robert knew what he was going to do. The attachment of small cameras to the wall of the theatre, overlooking the stage, was a trivial matter. He was not going to want these back, so with a bit of superglue, the tiny cameras, invisible against the background of the wall, were permanently placed. The battery charge in the cameras was said to be at least 48 hours of monitoring and up to eight weeks of stand-by. Robert turned it off as soon as he placed it. The conference was comfortably less than eight weeks away. Reactivation around lunchtime on the day of the event would be easy. A quick test when he got back to the cycle shop, and then all was ready for the big day.

Inspection of the Senate House was relatively simple. Robert did not even need to make special arrangements. He simply walked in and looked around when some of the extensive, publicly accessible, activity associated with the end of the university year, graduation, congregations, debates, was going on. It was a simple matter to get a gown and mortar board and wander in with everyone else. Where the bombs would go was simple, when the bombs would go in there, less so. Again, Robert placed a camera at a suitable vantage point. He chose to use the gallery to give himself a better view, and this camera was camouflaged in a wood coloration, just under the top rim of the gallery rail.

Most of Robert's time over the next few weeks was spent on developing ways to ensure that the explosives he was planning to use would be non-detectable by conventional methods. It was all about sealing the explosives into containers, which would prevent any leakage of detectable traces of explosive into the atmosphere, but would allow signals from remote triggering devices, essentially a mobile phone, to get through and initiate the big bang. Semtex contains volatile trace elements which sniffer dogs, and handheld chromatographs, can detect. Robert wanted to make sure that his bombs would not be detected by either of these means. Robert communicated with Viktor on this and a second couriered package, containing a hand-held state of the art chromatograph, for detection of both organic and inorganic explosives, arrived within a day or so.

Robert knew that he had to be able to seal the container without blowing himself up. Soldering tight a metal box would not work; he, Sean, and half Mill Road, would end up spread over a considerable area. In the end, he settled for using epoxy resins, a very thick layer of epoxy resins, and found the gas permeability low enough that the handheld device was unable to detect the explosives within either a wooden, or a metal, container. Where he intended to put the devices he was making, there would be plenty of epoxy resin in the fabric of the surrounding wooden structures.

He went with wooden containers for his explosives, simply because wood does not block the signal transmission he needed for the remote detonation.

Over the next few weeks anyone looking into the workshop would have thought that Robert was making a set of four coffins for a half metre-long stick man. 15cm square in cross section and just under half a metre long, they were tightly sealed with only the lid left unfastened. In addition, he was making a couple of curved containers, which he was planning to use to replace some sections of the black step that edged the stage at the front of the Senate House. These he planned to pack with all the nasty pieces of scrap metal and stone detritus that he could find around the garage, or purchase in the local hardware shop, and then make sure there was enough explosive to turn it into a shrapnel scattering lethal weapon.

Sean, meanwhile, had been acquiring the fertiliser and the other ingredients to pack the rest of the explosive punch when the Semtex triggered the initial explosion. It all came together in good time, and Sean and Robert began packing the devices carefully and sealing them closed, with the triggering devices *in situ.*

Robert, meanwhile, was also repairing bicycles, including the bicycles for the University cycling team and the triathlon team. Ironically, he repaired and serviced both Sarah's and Jonny's bikes in the two weeks leading up to the Varsity match. He almost exploded with anger when he saw them both wheeling their bicycles into the back yard to await attention. He nearly lost it when Martha, Ceci, and James, also brought in bicycles for repair. Then he remembered what his main purpose was, and he calmed down, and got on with his preparations. Sean told Robert about the usual schedule for the repair and servicing of the university team cycles.

"We do them before the university time trial, which is in late May or early June, and then again for the local cycle club's time trial, called the Viking-50, which is a little later than that."

Robert looked up and noted the dates of each of these events. The exact dates were important to him.

The first of these two big races for Jonny and Sarah took place during the first week of June. They had lots of pasta for supper the night before and both had a good night's sleep.

The following morning was almost perfect for the time trial. The bicycles were collected from the basement under the conference centre and loaded onto the club trailers. The rendezvous for the trial was out at Hardwick. Oxford, Cambridge and five other universities turned up with their teams of four men and four women. Each of the universities provided stewards for the race and they were duly despatched, in various support vehicles, to man the crucial points along the route. This route was a two lap out and back route mainly along the A428 road.

At 10 am, the first rider went off. The men's race was first, and the twenty-eight riders went at 1-minute intervals, as per standard time trial practice. The women's race started at 10:45 am and again the riders were set off at 1-minute intervals.

The winning times were all round about the hour mark, the men just under and the women just over.

In common with all serious time trial events, the bicycle, and the competitors, were weighed on completion of the course. There is a minimum weight of 6.8kg for trial bikes and none of the bikes failed the minimum weight test. The Cambridge bikes weighed in at 7.2kg each, all very much the same, as they were identical machines, sponsored by a generous alumna. Jonny and Sarah were the first Cambridge cyclists home in their respective races, Jonny was third overall in the men's event and Sarah second in the women's race; but the Varsity match was decided on the placings of the first three riders from the two universities, and Cambridge won comfortably in both races.

A generous sponsorship for the time trial allowed all the participants to return to St Joseph's for a buffet lunch, and a presentation ceremony. The Cambridge bicycles were put back in 'the cage', everyone showered and changed, and the presentation meeting was started at about 3pm. This meeting served as the Annual General Meeting for the British Universities and Colleges Cycle Clubs so there was routine business first. Then came the presentations.

The friends and relatives of the teams were admitted to the presentations after the finish of the formal business of the AGM. Jonny and Sarah had no relatives present for this event, but all the friends turned up, as well as several other students from St Joe's.

Late that afternoon, the captain of the cycling team drove the club trailer to Sean's Cycle Emporium for all the bicycles to be serviced prior to the next big event, the 50-mile time trial called the Viking 50, to be held in early July, on the weekend of the stem cell conference. This event was intended, by both Jonny and Sarah, to be a final fun outing for the season before they went off with the others on the 'Grand Tour'.

In some ways, the hardest site for Robert to access to place a bomb was the lecture theatre. The roof was much too high for comfortable access, the building itself was well covered outside by CCTV, and the custodian was on site all night. Robert decided that he needed some way to do the work in the theatre during the daytime. Encouraged by his success with the reconnaissance operation, he decided to rely on the idea that nobody would challenge someone, in University Estate Management clothes, someone looking purposeful, going into the theatre to 'complete the check and repair of the audio-visual system'. He packed his wooden beam sections in cardboard boxes and labelled them with a false logo and name for an electrical company. He packed his saws and glue and other items into his tool bag and was ready to begin to place the first bomb under the theatre stage.

He created a Cambridge University Estate Management transfer for the cycle shop van and loaded the four beam sections and his tools into the van. He telephoned the site security and told them he was coming to complete the audio-visual work on the lecture theatre, they just accepted his word for it. He said it would take most of the day and asked whether he might have a key to the side door at the stage end of the theatre, leading out into the internal roadway of the New Museum Site. The custodian told him just to call and pick it up when he got there. It was very simple.

Robert took Sean with him. He needed a pair of hands to help, especially with inserting the beam sections.

They spent about four hours under the stage. Each beam section took about twenty minutes to cut out. Inserting the beam section replacements, anchoring them in place with superglue, thin metal plates, and screws, took another twenty minutes. Cleaning up and making the joins as invisible as possible took another ten minutes for each beam. With the access time, removing the front panels, and the exit time replacing them, four hours was a good shift. There was no messing around with the explosives. Robert checked for traces of explosive with his hand-held detector and was satisfied that there were none. A swift exit from the site, handing back the keys to the custodian and bidding her a cheery goodbye, and all was done. Robert and Sean went back to the cycle shop, removed the logo transfer, and burnt it. They drove up to the recycling centre in Milton. They left the remains of the beams that they had removed, in the wood skip at the centre, and, well pleased with themselves, drove back to the cycle shop and sat down in the garage for a sandwich and a beer.

"One down, one to go?" asked Sean.

Robert just nodded. No need to tell Sean what else he had in mind.

Placing the second bomb was a much greater adventure. It required some intelligence gathering and a lot of planning. The intelligence gathering was about the routes used by the Cambridge Night Climbers. Sean's shop probably had more of the university's adventurous and active students through its doors than almost any other shop in Cambridge. Robert and Sean decided that they needed to find a night climber or two, if they could, to give them some intel on how to get onto the Senate House roof. Sean put up some posters and photographs, including a very famous photograph of a car on top of the Senate House roof. Some engineering students in 1958 had managed to hoist an Austin Seven, without its engine, onto the Senate House roof. It had taken some days for the authorities to get it down again and they had to cut it into pieces to achieve that. Robert and Sean had no intention of trying to repeat the event but thought it might lead to useful conversations, they were correct.

About three days after they put the posters up a young woman from Gonville and Caius, a hot bed of Cambridge climbing and the college from which the engineers had hoisted the car, engaged Sean in conversation. She was very open about her night climbing activities and answered very straightforwardly when Sean asked her if she had ever been on the Senate House roof.

"We often go up there for a coffee and to watch the stars," she said.

Sean told her he was planning to write something about this for the Parish Magazine. It had tickled his imagination. He asked her how they got there, and she told him two different routes from within the college. She also told him how to climb into the college from the street. They were laughing and giggling as she talked about it. It was all a poke in the eye for authority and Sean played her along.

"I wouldn't mind you showing me where the climbs are," said Sean. "Tell you what, if you show me the climbs, I'll service your bike for free and I'll even throw in a new bike lock, better than that rubbish one you have there."

The deal was struck.

The girl kept her promise and showed Sean the way into Caius, over one of the many ancient walls and through a former coal cellar into the main courtyard. She also showed him the two routes onto the roof. Sean snapped away with his phone camera.

"We prefer this one," she said. "If you look up, you can see that there is a flat bit on our side and a flat bit on the other side. Just out of sight from the ground is a plank, just long enough to bridge the gap to the Senate House. We simply walk over that. I would tell you where we keep our stove and kettle and cups on the other side, but I think the team would kill me if you nicked them."

Sean laughed.

"You've done more than enough for me," he said. "Thank you. I didn't believe all that stuff in the papers, but now I do. I shall be able to tell my friends

I have really seen how the night climbers do things. Now can I offer you a coffee?"

The pair of them went off along King's Parade to 51 Trumpington Street, and the famous Fitzbillies' cake shop. They both had a coffee and one of the Chelsea buns for which the shop has always been rightly famous.

A cheery goodbye and a very satisfied Sean headed back to the cycle shop.

Robert sent Sean out to buy several lengths of climbing rope, some pulleys and hooks, and several items of cordless cutting and drilling equipment. They ordered a collapsible tripod, which was fitted with a hoist and winch, that could lift 500kg. These items are used for mountain and cliff rescue and are lightweight as well as sturdy. Robert had long decided that the best route into the Senate House would be through the roof at night.

The two of them thought more about the plan, once they had the photographs printed out, and Sean was able to debrief Robert. They knew they had to complete the exercise in one go, leaving anything on the roof would risk the night climbers going up there and finding the stuff, on one of their regular trips to look at the stars.

"If it's cloudy and wet, the little bastards won't be climbing over for a cup of tea," said Sean.

"OK, let's get everything ready to go and make our move on the first cloudy and rainy night within a week or so of the conference. We have a slight problem getting the stuff down there because cars aren't really allowed on King's Parade, as far as I can see," said Robert.

For Jerry and Jeff, these were very anxious times. The large consignment of Semtex, which Special Branch had been warned about, had shown no signs of surfacing in the area. The site on the riverbank where they had uncovered the explosion had shown no trace of anything other than fireworks explosives and very simple wires, and a slightly damaged clockwork trigger mechanism, the sort of thing that any well-read amateur could set up. Nevertheless, Jerry and Jeff both thought this was significant. Most kids playing around with explosions do not set up time switch detonators, surely this had to be significant.

The Americans, meanwhile, were preparing for the various athletic events in which they would be taking part towards the end of June, and the beginning of July, as well as working hard on their Master's theses. Sarah and Jonny in particular were cycling, running, and swimming every day, just to keep fit and sane. In preparation for the Viking-50 cycle race, they were concentrating mainly on the cycling. It was due to take place on the day after the main conference. Jonny and Sarah were timing their cycle rides and were both alarmed to find that their timing was consistently slower than usual, but they put that down to a lack of serious training during the intense periods of laboratory and library work that had preceded their first year viva's for continuance to a PhD. They just started to train harder, but they also arranged an additional service of their bikes at Sean's Emporium.

The family and friends were all planning to be there for the day of the cycling event, they would be arriving in the United Kingdom shortly before the conference. The day after the race was the evening of the Stanford Dinner in St Joseph's, the evening when the scholarship connection between St Joe's and Stanford was marked by the invitation of all those who had shared in the exchange arrangements, either way, between the two institutions. Current students could invite guests, and, between them, the Americans had managed to invite all their parents, siblings, and friends, who had made the trip to be with them in England. Dr Robert Simms, Jonny's father, was a Stanford Medical School alumnus and so he was invited to give a short address in the conference centre, on the subject of 'Medical ethics and the conflict with religious belief'. It was controversial, but the Stanford Dinner always chose a controversial topic for its annual address. Because Ceci had invited Alexis, the Master of St Joseph's had invited Stanislowsky Senior to accompany his son to the dinner. Alexis's bodyguard had reported this to Viktor earlier in the month.

Jerry and Jeff noted the Stanford Dinner and recognised that the subject of the address was controversial, but they thought little more about it. This was an annual event, and likely to be relatively low key. They were concentrating on the much more high-profile events going on around that time, and in advance of the conference itself.

Surveillance of the cycle shop had shown a big increase in activity during late May and mid-June. It was mainly students coming in and selling their machines to 'Sean's Cycle Emporium', before graduating and leaving Cambridge for good. Sean was building up a stock of bicycles, for sale at the beginning of the next year, when freshers from less cycle friendly parts of the world might need something on which to get around the city. It kept Sean and Robert occupied.

Ravinder was kept very busy receiving bicycles and putting them into storage after Robert and Sean had serviced them. He was a little curious about Robert;

he engaged him in conversation about where he came from and how he had come to be here in Cambridge. He tried to be friendly and sociable, but Robert handled him politely and made excuses whenever Ravinder started to suggest further social interaction. Over a few weeks Ravinder just came to accept that there was a highly reserved, probably neurodiverse, American working on bike repairs in the outbuildings.

Sean had arrangements with some of the colleges that he would place bikes in their bike sheds for storage and the porters at those colleges would sell the bikes on to the next crop of freshers for a commission. It meant that Sean had a much bigger turnover than he could have managed with the storage facilities he had on site in Mill Road. It created real good will between himself and the porters and they sent students needing repairs or servicing to the Mill Road shop. It was good business.

It was usual for Sean himself, and occasionally Ravinder, to take a batch of bicycles to a college and give the pricing list to the porters, but on one Friday, when the shop was incredibly busy, Ravinder called in sick. Sean felt that there was no option but to ask Robert to deliver a batch of cycles to St Joseph's. He thought Robert would be annoyed about that, but instead Robert seemed strangely excited by the thought of going into St Joe's. Sean knew nothing about the rape, nothing about the relationship between Robert and Sarah, nothing at all about the past criminal or social history of his partner in crime. Robert, with dark glasses, a hugely shaggy and unkempt mass of facial hair, and his black hair tied in a ponytail, under a Red Sox baseball cap, was confident that he was unrecognisable. He was proved right.

He loaded his special consignment of bicycles onto the shop bike trailer and drove to the college. Sean's cousin, Donald, was expecting Robert, and opened the automatic gates to the conference centre car park to let the truck and trailer into the delivery space. The two men lifted the cycles one at a time into the storage cage in the centre of the underground car park.

"Whose bikes are these?" asked Robert, even though he already knew. He had serviced them not long ago. They belonged to Jonny, Sarah, and Martha, among others.

"Oh, you mean those identical flash jobs painted light blue?" asked Donald.

"Yeah," said Robert.

"They belong to the University Cycle and Triathlon Club students. We have quite a few of the team here, and so the whole team uses this facility, because it's safe. Those bikes are a bit expensive to risk getting them nicked."

"Interesting," said Robert. "Are any of them any good at cycling?"

"You might be interested in this," said Donald. "We have a couple of Americans this year who are bloody good at it. Nice thing is they are staying on to do a Ph.D. so we will have them for at least two more years."

"That's great," said Robert, thinking, meanwhile, '*and maybe you won't.*'

"Would you like a coffee while we do the paperwork?" asked Donald.

"Sure," said Robert, "but I just have to make a phone call, so can I come over to the lodge when I'm ready?" Robert got out his mobile phone. He tried to call Sean but, from where he was standing, he was unable to get a mobile phone signal. He spent some time wandering around the basement of the building, mapping out in his head the signal strength in different parts of the basement car park.

The misdirection began very shortly after this.

Chapter 26

The first Semtex bomb that Jerry and Jeff found was under a car parked in the grounds of St Alfred's, right next to the Master's Lodge, where the Cabinet Secretary, an Old Member of the College, was staying with the Master before taking part in a debate at the Cambridge Union. It was routine for Special Branch to send in sniffer dogs, and take with them hand-held detectors, as part of their protective function for high level civil servants and politicians. The bomb was picked up by the sniffer dogs and the bomb squad defused it safely.

Analysis of the device showed it to be relatively simple. A clockwork timer, which had been set for midnight, a quantity of Semtex, and some fertiliser explosive to augment the explosion. It was quite a powerful bomb. Had it gone off it would have destroyed the car and probably demolished a large part of the lodge. It was so naïve that it was almost a parody. The wires were simply cut from a standard electrical plug cable. The clockwork mechanism might have been the same as the one they had found pieces of, on the riverbank north of Dimmock's Cote.

It didn't feel right. Jerry thought it was far too simple a bomb for someone to waste that much Semtex on, and it was not booby trapped at all. This was not one of the big boys. Jerry and Jeff were sure of that.

The second Semtex bomb was found a few days later at the Senate House, under the vice chancellor's throne. This again was easily detected by sniffer dogs. It looked as if it were set to go off in the middle of the degree ceremony for St Joseph's, when the Master of St Joseph's, Lord Fairfield, would have been sitting on the throne conferring degrees. It was a much smaller device, but it was also more sophisticated. It was booby trapped with a movement sensitive trigger as well as a clockwork trigger. It was easy enough for the experts to defuse, and there were partial prints on some of the timing pieces. One of these matched a print in the police database. This got everyone excited for a moment, until it turned out to be the print of a man working in a local hardware store, who's print had been left on record after a robbery at the place he was working in. They questioned him, but it was clear he had no knowledge of the bomb. Going through the hardware shop records they did find an entry in the sales register of someone buying eight clocks of the sort used in the timing devices found so far, but it was an over-the-counter purchase, a cash transaction, so there was no record of the identity of the purchaser. The record was also more than a month ago and the shop had CCTV internally, but had a rather limited storage system, and the records for the day of the transaction had already been wiped.

"We have less than 5% of the Semtex we think is in this area," said Jerry. "We have two amateurish attempts at bomb making. We have a shed load of explosives still out there."

"You know that riverside explosion, was the timing device one of these eight clocks?" asked Jeff.

"Good thought," said Jerry. "Let's ask forensics."

The third Semtex bomb was found in the car park of a public house in one of the villages, very close to the American Air Force base at Mildenhall. It was big. It would have been enough to flatten the pub, and everything else for about twenty metres radius around the bomb. It was virtually the whole boot of the car packed with fertiliser bomb and half a kilo of Semtex. This bomb had booby trap devices, and the detonator was an electronic detonator, of a very recent and sophisticated type. A search of the area showed a surveillance camera focussed on the car park, which would have recorded the comings and goings of all the customers. This felt much more like the real deal. The device had been discovered following a tip-off from someone with a heavily disguised voice. The language analysts had suggested that the sentence structure and the vocabulary was typical of an American, and the obvious conclusion was that this was aimed at American Service personnel.

An interview with the landlord revealed that the base commander of Mildenhall often called in for a drink at the pub. It was an obvious deduction that he was to have been the target. There was no clue to which group, or person, was targeting him.

There was no DNA evidence, no fingerprints, nothing that could obviously link this bomb with anyone.

"These bombs all seem to be linked to politics," said Jerry. "Why don't I buy that?"

"Well. Each one of these bombs seems to have been targeted at an individual," said Jeff.

"Exactly," said Jerry, "and individuals are usually targeted by hit men. You don't blow up half a field, a pub, and a terrace of houses, to take out one man. You can do it with a drone, or with an assassin's bullet, or something else much more personal. Even a smaller car bomb would make more sense. I think someone's testing us, teasing us, even taunting us. I still think that a conference or an event is much more likely to be the Semtex target. Let's get that list of conferences and events in the area and have another think."

The sniffer dogs and the local police forces were very active over the next few weeks. There were a couple of big concerts at football stadia in the area, Norwich, Ipswich, and Peterborough, all hosted one of the major British bands on tour. There was a meeting of the Royal Society of Engineers at Cambridge, with accommodation based at one of the colleges. There were other events.

Every time the sniffer dogs went out there and, every time, they drew a blank. But there were no explosions and no incidents to trouble the peace of these social and academic happenings.

Just as Jerry had suspected, the word came back from forensics that the few pieces of the timing mechanism they had picked up by the riverbank could have come from the batch of eight identical clocks that had been purchased from the hardware store.

Jerry began to think again about Sean and his bicycle shop. The hardware store from which the clocks had come was in the same arcade as the cycle shop.

"I think we might just pay another courtesy call on Sean O'Connor tomorrow," said Jerry.

Chapter 27

That night was cloudy, and rain was promised. Not heavy rain, but just the miserable sort of misty rain, that makes everything slippery, and makes those walking in it feel miserable, without getting them soaked.

Robert went home and had his supper as usual, but he returned to the cycle shop as soon as it got dark. It was after 10pm, the middle of summer is very light in the evenings in England, and this was the middle of summer.

Robert and Sean dressed in dark clothing, a pair of relatively tight-fitting jogging pants, a long-sleeved polo neck shirt and dark running gloves. They put black balaclavas into their pockets, along with some black face paint, for application later that night.

Robert had a black backpack containing the light weight but highly durable, collapsible tripod rescue winch, that he had asked Sean to purchase earlier that spring. It could handle 500kg, which was more than enough for the use they had in mind. Neither Robert nor Sean was overweight and 500kg load would deal with anything they were planning. Robert's backpack also contained tools, some black fast drying paint, some instant white plaster, some thin Perspex sheets, and some wood filler.

It was not unusual to see people walking around Cambridge with heavy back packs, lots of tourists were travelling through the city at this time of year, and there was no reason why Robert and Sean should stand out from the crowd. To all intents and purposes, they looked as if they were, albeit slightly elderly, tourists.

In Sean's backpack were three gently curved sealed boxes, cross section about 25cm by 15cm, the height and width of the black step that surrounds the staging at the front of the Senate House, the staging on which sit the vice-chancellor's throne and the lectern used for addressing the congregation. The curved sections were about half a metre long. They contained the explosives and the shrapnel which was intended to cause the devastation during the reception for Stanislowsky.

The two of them drove together to the parking spaces along Queen's Road. They put on their back packs and walked along Queen's Road, turned right into Garret Hostel Lane, crossed the river, and then turned right again, along Trinity Lane, towards Senate House Passage.

Sean found the spot in Senate House Passage where it was easy to climb into Caius College. The girl had shown him exactly how to do it. The ascent of the wall and the drop into the courtyard took only a few seconds. Through the coal cellar and into Main Court, and then they followed the route the girl had shown Sean, to the roof top of the Caius Building. They found the plank that Sean had been told about. They carefully put it in place, bridging the gap to the Senate House roof. They put on their balaclavas and blacked their faces. They were almost invisible against the outline of the building and the darkness of the sky.

Once on the roof of the Senate House, they drew the plank over behind them and hid it beneath the parapet surrounding the roof. There was no need to risk attracting attention should anyone walking along the passage decide to look up.

They knew exactly where to make a hole in the roof without damaging the ornamental plaster. They removed several slates and stacked them carefully for replacement later. They then attached some of those self-adhesive coat pegs to the plaster board and the battens that were revealed underneath the slates. Sean hung onto them, while Robert carefully cut a hole just large enough for himself to drop through. The coat pegs were used to lift the board out of its hole, and there below them was the floor of the Senate House.

Robert took the rescue hoist tripod out of his backpack, opened it out and set it up over the hole they had just cut. He set up the pulley, the hoist, and the winch, and fixed the 25-metre steel cable in place. They put a cover over the tripod, to try to keep the rain from falling into the Senate House and leaving water marks on the floor.

Using the winch Sean lowered Robert to the Senate House floor, by the cable to which a harness was attached. Robert had his tools with him and began to cut out the section of the steps on either side of, and right in front of, the vice chancellor's throne. He measured as precisely as he could.

When he had cut his three sections, he put the wood in a pile by his backpack and signalled to Sean to lower him the replacement sections. Sean lowered his whole backpack to save time. Robert put the three sections in place, they fitted perfectly. He put a thin smear of wood filler at each of the joins and smoothed it. He then applied a single coat of fast drying matt black paint to each of the joins and the rest of the step. It did not take long, and it meant that the whole of the step looked the same as the joined sections.

Robert put the bits of wood into Sean's backpack and took out a small handheld vacuum cleaner to suck up the saw dust, and the little bits of plaster that had fallen when they had made the hole in the roof. He risked a quick scan with the flashlight on his phone, and, when he was satisfied that he had cleared up sufficiently, he put everything into Sean's backpack and Sean hoisted it back up to the roof.

Sean lowered the harness again and winched Robert back up. It was quite slow work, but the whole visit to the Senate House floor had taken less than an hour.

Sealing the ceiling hole in the plaster was a slightly trickier proposition, but they solved it by super gluing four strips of thin transparent Perspex to the ceiling side of the edges of the hole they had made and leaving it to dry. That made a frame onto which they could drop the square plaster section they had removed to make the hole. They then put a very thin layer of plaster along the sides of the hole and lowered the cut-out section back into place. The plaster nicely filled the tiny space between the cut edges of the hole and the replaced piece of ceiling. It was still necessary to make sure that the weight of the square piece of ceiling was adequately supported, but that was achieved with a combination of super glue, nails, screws, and wooden strips attached to the laths.

The pair repacked the hoist into the second backpack, replaced the slates carefully, and retraced their footsteps back to the roof of Gonville and Caius.

"Bloody good thing we took the planks with us," said Sean. "While you were in there a copper walked down Senate House Passage and he shone a light up here. I nearly wet my pants."

Robert laughed.

The night was still pitch black and the rain had suddenly become very heavy.

"Damn good thing it didn't do this when we had the hole in that damn roof," said Robert.

They wiped the black camouflage paint off their faces, removed their balaclavas and, once again, became slightly elderly tourists, ready to wander over to the backs and collect their vehicle. Back through the coal cellar, over the wall and then a short, very damp, walk to the car.

They dropped everything back at the cycle shop, and Robert jumped on his bicycle, and returned to his flat. He crept in very quietly in order not to disturb any of the neighbours. The morning alarm clock sounded far too early! Robert woke with the alarm clock but made a more leisurely than usual breakfast and left the flat a little later than usual. It was that which saved him. He pedalled on his bicycle towards the service road at the rear of the Mill Road shops and noticed some burly gentlemen, obviously policemen, standing in the road behind the outbuildings where the cycle repairs took place. He continued down the road, not glancing at the men as he passed them and turned left at the end of it along one of the roads that ran perpendicularly from Mill Road.

The next morning was a busy one for all concerned. The visiting Americans were arriving at Heathrow, and Martha and James were preparing a welcome party at James's flat, using the garden behind the terraced house as an overspill, and setting up a barbecue there, under an open sided gazebo, in case the rains came. The written theses, and the first-year continuance examinations, had all been handed in or taken, and Sarah and Jonny were beginning the final phase of their preparation for the 'Viking 50' time trial. The entire American Contingent, all based in the Bay area, were arriving on the Virgin Atlantic overnight flight from San Francisco. Nobody was slumming it in the knees-up-your-nose class, all were flying Upper Class. It was, perhaps, a sensible arrangement. Young Vincent was now nearly 2 metres tall and Tim, Sarah's younger brother, was not far behind at about 1.92 metres. Lukey felt dwarfed at only a tad over 1.85 metres. Only Iris, Jonny's younger sister, was tiny. Martha had arranged two large airport taxis to collect the three families and the friends.

Amid growing excitement Sarah and Jonny went to the bike store under the conference centre to collect their time trial bikes which, ironically, Robert had serviced again earlier in the month.

They had a bit more of a fight than usual to get their bikes out of the 'rabbit hutch', the name they had given to the wire caged bike store at the centre of the underground car park.

"Who put all these goddam extra bikes in here?" asked Jonny.

Sarah just grinned and told him to stop being so grumpy.

They headed out along a route that they used regularly. Much of the route was along relatively well made-up roads, but some of the roads were less well maintained, and it was always important to watch not only the traffic, but also the state of the road itself. Pothole repair had not yet been completed after what had been a particularly harsh winter. The pair of them were glad to have gone out to check the state of the roads and make a note of where they needed to be particularly careful about road position, not too near the edge of the causeway.

They timed themselves. They were still a bit slower than they might have liked, but they knew that they were still probably a lot faster than many others in the race, so just accepted the idea that the hard study had made them less fit than before.

Chapter 28

The two taxis arrived at about 2pm. They had dropped off the luggage at the Airbnb in Fulbourn, where everyone was officially staying, and the airport taxis then dropped them all off at the conference centre car park. It was an incredibly joyous reunion. Jonny and Sarah had made it back in good time to shower and join the welcome party.

Inevitably there was a need for Theresa and Martha to go somewhere private and talk about their rapes. As they talked it became apparent to them that Robert Jackson had been the rapist on each occasion. It was not an easy conversation. There is nothing about the outcome of rape that stops anyone wishing that it had not happened. But these two young women were both, in their different ways, very resilient and quite special, and they had, with the help of their friends, handled the aftermath. There was no guarantee that it would not come back to haunt them at a later date, but for the time being they had it under control.

"They haven't found him yet," said Theresa. "The bastard. Sky and Lukey have been great with me. Lukey has kept on saying that sex and gender don't define anyone; that it is who you are, and what you do to show who you are, that matters. He's incredibly supportive of my career. He keeps saying he's going to make a lot of money in a dotcom start-up so that he can support me to do what I'm great at. He also says that he wants us to get married, but that it must be my choice, if, and when, it happens. I'll be honest with you, Martha, I stopped doing the saving sex for marriage bit. It hardly seemed relevant after being raped and, in a way, I sort of wanted to make love to Lukey, or, rather, have him make love to me, so that I could de-Satanize sex. It was kind of nice to find out that I didn't regret it!"

They chatted a bit more and then re-joined the others. By this time, Alexis had arrived and was being introduced to all the visitors. The Martha antennae went into Jane Austen mode, and she realised two things, Ceci and Vincent were a little bit pleased to see each other, and Alexis and Sky were sneaking surreptitious glances at each other at every opportunity. Even Sarah's brother Tim was paying a lot of attention to Jonny's little sister, Iris. Iris was maybe not so little any more, she had just finished her fresher year at college.

The designated drivers went to the car rental centre and picked up their vehicles. They made plans for the evening, for the barbecue, and the parents, including Jonny's mum and dad, went off to the Airbnb for a nap. Even with flat beds and upper class quiet, overnight flights don't always give you the best rest and travelling West to East is, as Lukey described it, the pits.

The younger members of the party were too excited to waste the afternoon. Lukey had done a course on nineteenth and twentieth century poetry at Stanford and he kept quoting 'Grantchester' so they all decided to take a punt upriver to Grantchester and have afternoon tea in the Orchard.

They all had a turn at punting and, given their youth and their great sense of balance, the round trip was made without any mishap. They punted Cambridge style, standing on the platform at the back of the boat.

A short walk to the church at Grantchester disappointed Lukey.

"Who fixed the damn clock?" asked Lukey.

They dropped the punt back at the Mill Pond and walked along the backs. Ceci had inherited the parental passion for the Chinese poet, Xu Zhimo, so she took the party along the backs to King's College bridge and quoted large chunks, first in Mandarin and then in English, of his poem written on leaving Cambridge in 1928. They walked through the college grounds out onto King's Parade and then along Trumpington Street to Fitzbillies', where Chelsea buns, pre-ordered to prevent disappointment, were awaiting collection.

"You guys will need a run tomorrow after eating these," said Alexis.

"They can't do it, unless they go very early," said Ceci. "We have our tennis match against Oxford tomorrow, at Fenner's, and you're all coming to watch. It starts at 11 am. So, if you want a run, it's early morning. I have the match so I won't be joining you."

The whole group, all still quite fit, decided that a run to Baits Bite Lock would be a great pre-breakfast experience and remind all of them of the runs that they used to take together back in their college days. A quick telephone call to the parents meant that the younger members of the party had some of their luggage brought back in that evening. There were spare rooms in college, and spare beds, that enabled them all to stay together in college after the evening barbecue.

180

That evening at the barbecue Martha's mum and dad asked her about James. It was an inevitable question, and they were probably a bit surprised at her answer.

"I know we like each other, and I think we love each other, but we're both still too young to define ourselves by our relationship. I have my medicine to pursue, and James is still chasing his dream of helping to power the world with green electricity. I think we can handle separation for a few more years. I could live with him, but I don't know whether I could live without him. I think he feels the same. Remember how Jonny and I were once so close, and then along came Sarah, and I realised I loved Jonny, but not enough to commit for life, and not in a sexual way."

****

While this day was passing so pleasantly for the Americans, Jerry and Jeff were very busy chasing up the new thought about the bombers. Their day had begun with a visit to Sean's Cycle Emporium.

The two detectives came armed with a search warrant. They sent some of the squad round to the back of the shop, to make sure that nobody escaped with any incriminating material, then they went in through the front entrance of the Emporium.

They questioned Sean about his activities and plans concerning the upcoming conference and Sean was quite open about the 'peaceful protests' that the pro-life group had planned.

The search revealed nothing obvious. They found tools you would expect in this sort of minor repairs workshop. They found all those items that the two would be bombers had taken with them on their ventures the night before. They found the tripod hoist. Although the equipment was in the workshop, it was damp. Jeff noticed that and was a bit puzzled.

"What do you use that for?" asked Jeff.

"I only just bought it," said Sean. "I'm thinking of doing up an old Triumph Stag my mate told me about. I always wanted one of them. They rust really badly but I thought I could repair the body with modern materials, and I wanted this hoist to lift the engine out safely."

"Expensive?"

"Nah, just a few hundred quid. Only just took it out of the box but I reckon it will do."

"Why is it wet?" asked Jeff.

"I unpacked it and set it up when it arrived yesterday afternoon and I got distracted in the shop and forgot to put it away," said Sean.

They found the handheld device that Robert had used to ensure his explosive devices were undetectable.

"What do you want that for?" asked Jerry.

"I haven't used it for ages," said Sean. "But sometimes I do a little bit of welding in here and I wanted to check that there were no organic fumes before I started setting sparks off. Acetylene for welding can be a bugger you know."

Unbelievable, or, rather, just believable, bullshit.

There were no timing devices. There was cable, and wire, and wood, and metal strips, and bits of Perspex, and black paint, nothing at all to suggest bombs.

Nevertheless, Jerry and Jeff got the forensics team to run their own explosives detection devices over the place. There was one small area on one of the benches that gave a hint of a trace of something, but the profusion of organic substances, oils, paints, glues, and plastics, meant that it was a bit of a forlorn hope that they would find clear evidence of Semtex. Had they put the sniffer dogs, or the detector, on Robert's flat, it would have gone off the scale. Robert had made the basic devices at the cycle shop but packed them and sealed them in his flat.

The poster of the car on the Senate House roof intrigued Jeff.

"What's that doing there?" he asked.

"I dunno really," said Sean, showing a little of the discomfort that the detectives had noticed in their previous interview with him.

"I sort of like it because I remember one of my friends telling me he used to catch the bus outside Great St Mary's church to get to school, and one morning he looked up and saw this Austin Seven on the roof. Apparently, it took the authorities ages to get it down but the students put it up there in one night."

They had a bit of a conversation about it and Jeff said: "I don't think your little hoist would get an Austin Seven up there. I reckon it weighs near a 1000kg. What does your hoist do?"

"Well," said Sean. "It would lift the engine, I guess. I hope so, or I've wasted my money."

"Mind if we have a quick chat with your assistant?" asked Jeff.

"Not at all," said Sean.

Ravinder came into Sean's office holding his early morning break cup of coffee. He offered a cup to the two detectives and there was a pause while he went out and made them their drinks.

When he came back in, the three of them sat down and began to talk.

"Do you know about your boss and his anti-abortion stance?" asked Jeff.

"Of course I do," said Ravinder. "He feels very passionately about it. I think it *is* partly due to his Catholic upbringing, but I think there might be something else there as well. I never asked him, but I think abortion might have come in somewhere in his private life. But I think that's his business."

"Do you think he would be involved in any violent demonstrations?" Jeff asked him.

"Sean is quite driven you know, and he does have a bit of a bad temper at times, but I don't have any reason to believe he would be involved in a violent demonstration. Besides which a lot of the people who see him about the pro-life stuff are definitely not violent types."

"Has anything unusual happened around the shop in the past few weeks?" asked Jeff.

"Not really. We have had a lot of extra repair and servicing work, but we always get that around this time of the year, with students getting their bikes serviced before they go home and the university team getting their bikes ready for the big time-trial in a couple of days. The boss sometimes takes on a student helper, someone who knows his or her way around bikes. He took someone on this year too."

Jerry's ears pricked up.

"That person still working here?"

"Yes. He's late in this morning. Not really like him. I hardly ever see him. He just sits out the back in the workshop and repairs anything we take out to him."

"A student?"

"No, older than what we usually employ. And he's American I think, or Canadian, judging by his accent. Very hairy!"

"Thanks Ravinder. You've been very helpful. Here's my card. If anything else odd happens, please let us know. Thanks for the coffee."

The detectives went out into the shop and found Sean at the counter.

"I understand you've taken on a temporary worker for the last few weeks," said Jerry.

"That's right, Inspector," said Sean. "I met him at the pro-life meeting, and he was short of some paid work while he waits to finish up some research he's doing in the university. He sits out the back there and patches up any items that come in for repair or service. Good worker."

"Will he be in today?"

"He should be here by now, not like him to oversleep. Not like some of the students I've employed in the past."

"When he comes in, will you call me, please? We would like a word with him," said Jerry.

"OK," said Sean.

The detectives left the shop and stood outside for a moment or two.

"I still reckon Sean O'Connor for something more than a peaceful protest," said Jerry. "That comment about meeting the American at a prolife meeting is a bit of a contradiction. Think it would be a good idea to put a watch on this place for the next four or five days, at least until the conference is over."

"Want someone watching the back of the shop?" asked Jeff.

"Too right, mate," said Jerry. "Someone could easily get in and out there without being seen. There are no surveillance cameras there."

"We could put one," said Jeff. "We would probably need to run it past the Commissioner, but I'm sure it would be justified on this occasion."

"Let's get onto it fast." said Jerry. "Just one camera eyeing the back of the property should do it."

It was a good idea, just too late. Robert and Sean were already completely spooked by the visit, and Robert had seen the cops outside the back of the property. He was never coming back. Everything was in place. There was no more need for his presence at Sean's Cycle Emporium.

As soon as the policemen left the shop Sean called Robert on his mobile, using the land line. It was a very short telephone call. They simply agreed to get new pay-as-you-go phones for all future communication. Sean was going to tell Ravinder that Robert had left the county and moved to London. He was going to call one of his previous student helpers to come and replace Robert in the workshop.

Chapter 29

It was now Friday. The grey skies, and rain, of earlier in the week had cleared away, but there had been a short sharp shower in the early hours of the morning, and the tennis match was planning to start, a little later than usual, at 11:30 am, because the lines needed repainting. The courts were immaculate. The match referee was a famous referee from Wimbledon, well known for a previously televised spat with an American tennis player. He had no trouble controlling the youthful contestants in this annual event.

It was pleasant in the summer sunshine to sit on the benches behind the courts against the old 'Cambridge White' brick wall and watch young and talented tennis players competing. The level of talent was high this year. Several players were taking part who had previously been highly ranked junior national and international competitors but who, for a variety of reasons, had chosen an academic career, rather than chasing the pipe dream of tennis fame and success. Ceci was one of these; tiny, and pound for pound, quite the most exquisite player present.

The first round of ladies' matches had completed, and the men were just going on, when a slightly scruffy individual, with a big beard, dark glasses and very dark hair came through the gate from Gresham Road and wheeled his bicycle over to the far end of the row of benches. He sat to watch the next round of men's matches and then the second round of the ladies. It was Robert.

No one recognised Robert, there was no reason why they should. No one took any notice of his presence, there was no reason why they should. Spectators often entered the ground to watch Varsity cricket, the tennis and cricket shared the same large sports field. It was simply assumed that the gentleman sitting watching the tennis had happened on it by chance and was sitting enjoying the afternoon sunshine.

Robert was relishing viewing his two rape victims, knowing that they had no idea who he was, and remembering the lustful pleasure of the two events. Behind the beard, he was almost smirking with the pleasure of it all. He changed his plans for after the bombing. Before he left England, he was determined to have one more rape victim. He spent the next hour, between politely applauding points, trying to decide whether it would be a repeat performance, with Martha or Theresa, or a new victim such as Sky, or Ceci, or, and the thought began to excite him greatly, even his own daughter Sarah. Yes, that was it, he would rape Sarah to pay her back for starting him on this route to depravity. If it hadn't been for her involvement in athletics, the sickness of mind dictating his behaviour might never have developed. She deserved to be raped.

Blissfully ignorant of the depraved thinking going on near the courts the entire American party watched the matches to their conclusion. The slightly strange man left midway through the second round of ladies' matches, but nobody remarked on that. James was not present at the event; he was busy working on the completion of some experiments that he was due to demonstrate to the Royal Society, as one of their invited speakers. The molecular biological conversion of photon energy to electrical energy was making great progress. That evening they all went to the University Arms Hotel for dinner in Parker's Tavern.

Robert, meanwhile, went home via the mobile phone shop. He decided that it was time to become a hermit. It was now Friday evening, the conference proper began on Sunday, with the opening ceremony, and lasted until Wednesday. The University Time Trial took place on the Thursday, the Stanford Dinner took place on Friday. He had airline tickets for himself and Sean, booked in their new aliases, for the Saturday afternoon flight next week, the day after the Stanford dinner. It was time to complete his planning. The first thing he did was to book an online grocery delivery to tide him over until he left on the night of the following Friday. He then called Sean and exchanged the new mobile numbers. He gave Sean detailed instructions about packing, and where to meet him on the Saturday morning very early. He arranged for Sean to put all his false documentation into a folder and post it, for 'collection on arrival', to one of the hotels. He just did not want anyone finding that documentation because it would be a link to Robert's own travel plans. He booked Sean and himself, separately, into a hotel near the station.

On the Saturday morning, Jonny and Sarah had a morning training ride, the Viking-50 was happening the next week, and the others simply had a leisurely breakfast and then went to watch the climax of the tournament. Ceci had always quite understood that not everyone was going to watch both full days of the tennis. Everyone had watched on the Friday but, on the Saturday, all the older members of the party went to London. They took the tour bus around the main London sights and visited the London Eye, they had booked tickets well in advance, Buckingham Palace, Trafalgar Square, and the Tower of London.

Robert spent some of the Saturday in St Joseph's College walking round the college and looking at the names on the boards at the bottom of the staircases. He identified exactly where Martha, Ceci, and Sarah lived. He also noted where the college's CCTV cameras were and identified the easiest way to climb into and out of the college. It was actually a very easy route. There were several external walls that were easily scalable, and at least two stretches of the external wall were covered, neither by the city CCTV, nor the college's own internal CCTV systems. He knew that Sky, and Theresa, and 'that black kid' were using a room somewhere in college, but he had no way of finding out where, other than following them home from some event or other. That option seemed unnecessarily risky. Attacking one of the other three would be perfectly fine. Perhaps he would toss a coin to decide.

Jerry and Jeff were working that weekend. They knew something was going to happen with the demonstration, the conference opened on the Sunday, and they had liaised with the university security about extra police presence and extra surveillance, for the weekend before, and the duration of the conference. They were just sitting having a morning cup of coffee when the telephone rang. It was the private number on Jerry's business card.

"DI Gregory here," said Jerry.

"Good morning, Inspector. This is Ravinder. I thought you might like to know that the new American has not been into the shop since you called on us that second time, and Sean told me that the American had left the county and gone to London."

"Thank you. Did Sean give you any explanation?" asked Jerry.

"Not at all," said Ravinder. "He just said the man had gone to London, and he immediately called up one of the students we have used before. The student is coming in on Monday to start work on the repairs. Sean didn't seem very surprised. I think he must have known it was going to happen."

"Are you in the shop?" asked Jerry, who had put the conversation on speaker phone as soon as he had answered it.

"Indeed," said Ravinder.

"Is Sean there?" asked Jerry.

"He is indeed here," said Ravinder. "He went out earlier to the Post Office, but he's back now."

"I think we ought to come and visit you again. Can we get another cup of coffee from you?"

"It would be my pleasure Sir. I will put the filter machine on now," said Ravinder.

Jerry and Jeff were both caffeine addicts. It went with the job.

Jerry ended the call and turned to Jeff.

"That is bloody suspicious."

"Yeah. I reckon he must've seen us, one or more of those big buggers we sent round the back."

"I wonder if we missed something," said Jerry. "Have we still got that warrant? We did make it multiple entry, didn't we?"

"Thank God we did!" said Jeff. "I think we argued that we might need to go in again, near to the time of the planned demonstration, and that things might be moved in and out of the building."

Knowing that the American had disappeared; knowing that Kesandu had fingered an American stranger as an unusual visitor to the pro-life meetings; knowing that Sean had forgotten to mention this on their first interview with him; it all suggested that a focus on Sean's shop could have growing significance. This time Jerry and Jeff were going to go over the workshop area with a very fine-tooth comb.

What had they got so far? They had electrical cable, and wire, and wood, and metal strips, and bits of Perspex, and black paint. They had no trace of Semtex; they had nothing to suggest timing devices. There was a garden shed as well as the workshop at the back of the property and, perhaps foolishly, they had not bothered to look there on the previous occasion. They were probably too focussed on the workshop. This time they would not make that mistake. They were also lucky in that Cambridge waste disposal and recycling collected the recycling bins fortnightly, and there had been no collection in that part of Mill Road for nearly two weeks. Nothing of significance had been found in the big blue skip at the shop but they had not examined the bins of neighbouring properties, and someone clever enough to know about hiding their tracks might well have disposed of items in someone else's bins.

The search this time was much more interesting. The garden shed contained a half empty 25kg sack of ammonium nitrate. That was interesting, but in a neighbour's waste bin they found two more empty 25kg bags that had contained the fertiliser. They also found some large packets of sugar and several empty packets in the neighbours recycle bin. These were all standard bomb making ingredients and there had been no trace of either of these ingredients in the bombs that the sniffer dogs had found earlier in the month. It was beginning to look as if other bombs were out there, and, as if Sean's American 'helper' might have been involved in making them.

It seemed unrealistic to imagine that the helper could have made these bombs without the collusion of his 'boss'. Sean must know something about it. Could they find anything else with which to apply some leverage in the questioning that was undoubtedly going to follow this search?

They sifted through all the paper disposed of in each of the bins in the street. There were measurements and calculations of weight and volume. There were also some shredded pages, in the bin behind the shop. Jerry thought these might be important and set a team to trying to fit the several shredded pages together. Fortunately, the shredder was a simple one-cut strip maker and not one that chopped in two dimensions. They also found a photograph of the University Estate Management Van. They scanned the bins for Semtex with the chromatograph and found traces of Semtex on a brown paper wrapper, addressed to Sean O'Connor. There were fingerprints on the wrapper. They anticipated that Sean's would be one set, but there were at least three other sets, and one of the team was given the task of identifying the owners of those other prints.

Sean came into the shop a little later in the morning, and was immediately asked to come, with Jerry and Jeff, to the station for questioning. They put him in an interview room, offered him a cup of coffee, and left him alone with his thoughts. Robert, ever wary, had finished his walk around St Joe's and had been watching the shop from a distance. He had seen the police taking Sean away. He went home to brood over his laptop. He checked the surveillance cameras, briefly, and thought about how he was going to handle the new situation. It was clear that the police were now focussing their attention on the shop. Robert had no doubt that Sean would eventually crack and tell them that bombs had been made. It might mean that they found the ones Sean knew about. It was a good thing that he had not told Sean about his other plans.

"So, what do we know?" asked Jerry, more a rhetorical question than anything else.

"Kesandu tipped us off that this lot are planning something dangerous, there was an American involved and he's disappeared off the face of the earth, there are bomb ingredients in the shed and empty packets of them in the dustbins. I wonder how the shredding material is coming together."

"I think we have to assume that this lot are planning an attack on the conference," said Jeff.

"I agree," said Jerry. "Let's look at the conference programme and let's get the team in here to think this through together."

The search team, the regular Special Branch squad, forensics, everyone who had been involved in surveillance and investigation, crowded into the conference room. The itinerary was projected onto the interactive white board; Jerry asked the obvious question.

"Where and when would you bomb if you wanted to make sure of the most damage?"

There was only one answer.

"The Babbage, opening or closing ceremony." It was almost a general chorus.

"Did we search the Babbage yet?" asked Jeff. "I don't think we did. We searched the Senate House and we found that bomb under the lectern, but nothing was happening in the Babbage until this conference."

"Okay," said Jerry. "Now we search the Babbage. It might be a timing device there, like those rather crude ones we found on the other three bombs. It's only Saturday now and we have until tomorrow for the opening ceremony, and Wednesday for the closing ceremony. I think daily searches of the Babbage would be in order, and checking the New Museum Site CCTV, and the Downing Street, and Free School Lane cameras."

"Anyone see anything else odd about this list?"

Jerry put up the list of items found in the outbuildings of the cycle shop.

Detective Sergeant Jenny Taylor picked up on something immediately.

"Why is there a hoist and winch, Sir?"

"He said he wanted it for lifting an engine out of an old Triumph Stag."

"Then why has it got 25 metres of cable attached to it?"

"Probably came like that," said Jerry. "I could ask him."

"The stem cell stuff isn't limited to the conference Sir," said Jenny. "What about the ceremony the next day in the Senate House? Aren't they giving Stanislowsky a reception and isn't Dr Simms giving a talk there?"

"That's right, Sergeant. But we found the bomb in the Senate House a few days ago."

"I was watching the first episode of a rerun of 'Spooks'," said Jenny, "I love that series, and I think there were 20 bombs in that episode, or something like that."

"Are we sure we found everything? Do we know if it was *the bomb* or just *a bomb*?" asked Jenny.

Jerry thought about the comment. He felt a bit embarrassed. They had been so pleased with themselves for finding the three explosive devices, Senate House, Master's Lodge at St Alfred's, and the pub near Mildenhall, that they had lost sight of the possibility that there might be several other bombs in the same buildings. Come to think of it, you could argue that they had been *meant* to find the bombs. The sniffer dogs had easily found the two in the university, and the third bomb, the one at the pub, had been a tip-off. Jerry caught his breath as he thought about what Jenny Taylor had just said, "Good thinking. We should do another search of the Senate House and we search the Babbage."

Jerry called the bomb squad and asked them to search the Senate House again, and, in addition, to go and search the Babbage Lecture Theatre. The dogs, and the detection devices headed off to do as they were asked.

"Let's just run through the photographs of the shop and the outbuildings, in case anyone notices something we ought to think about?"

They were about to do this when one of the team working on reassembling the strips of shredded note paper came into the room.

"Sir, you need to see this," said Detective Constable Jessica Harper.

Jerry took the reassembled sheet of paper. It was a sketch of a tripod, like the one they had seen in the outbuildings, and there were some calculations. There was a cable hanging down from the tripod with a caricature of a man hanging from it, wearing a backpack. There were some weights written down. There was a length also, twenty-one metres, four metres less than the cable length they had found.

"We are working on some other calculations Sir," said Constable Harper. "They seem to be calculations of volume and weight for two different sizes of wooden container. There is a bit written down that says something like 5kg is equal to nearly 3 litres. Sergeant Jacobs says that's about right for Semtex Sir."

Jerry let out a low whistle.

"There must be some bombs out there," he said. "But where the bloody hell are they? And why is there a picture of the hoist. Is there a bomb in a roof somewhere?"

"The picture could be about hoisting something up or lowering something down," said Sergeant Taylor. "There's a man dangling from the tripod so somebody must be on the roof working the hoist. They had to get onto the roof to put the hoist there. I reckon this could be getting onto the roof and lowering someone into the building to plant a bomb. A bomb in the roof could also discharge upwards and would not be anything like as effective as one at ground level. The bomb is probably meant to be in that backpack."

There was a general murmur of approval for the suggestion.

"Twenty-five metres," said Jerry. "Let's get the plans of all the buildings where the conference is taking place. Start with the Babbage and the Senate House."

He broke off to call the search teams and warn them about the possibility of the bomb being at roof level, then he decided it was time for a coffee. He said as much to Jeff.

"Let's have the slide show," said Jeff, "and coffees all round."

The slide show was conducted at a sedate pace, giving everyone time to look at the detail in each picture. First the front of the shop was shown, then the series of photographs of the outbuildings, including the discovery of the various items. Towards the end there were some interiors of the shop. By this time, coffee had been consumed and some members of the group were losing interest. Not Jenny Taylor.

"Can you just blow that up for us Sir? The photograph behind the till."

The slide show was stopped, and the photograph was cropped and enlarged.

"Is that our roof, Sir?" asked Jenny.

She had picked up on the photograph of the Austin Seven on the Senate House roof.

"Bloody Hell," said Jerry. "I think you're right Sergeant." There was a pause.

"What's the height of the Senate House?" asked Jerry.

"The Elevation is less than 25 metres to the apex of the roof," said the Sergeant with the building plans.

"Well," said Jerry. "Who has a head for heights? Someone Google Austin Seven on Senate House roof!"

They got the story from the web.

"I reckon the tripod could have been used instead of the A-frame." said Jeff. "Mr O'Connor has some tricky questions to answer."

Jerry was looking at the plans provided by the University Estate Management. It triggered a thought. Hadn't they found a photograph of the University Estate Management van among the bits of rubbish in the waste bins? Could Sean and his American accomplice have masqueraded as Estate Management? Never mind that this was the weekend. The conference started on Sunday and time was getting short. They needed information about the maintenance schedule of Estate Management, especially around the buildings being used by the conference.

While Jeff followed up on the maintenance schedule, Jerry took Sergeant Taylor with him to interview Sean.

By this time, Sean was really sweating. He sensed that this interrogation was going to be a much more serious and searching inquisition than the rather tentative questioning he had endured previously. He was weighing up his options. Thus far, he had not physically damaged anyone. He could be charged with conspiracy to commit a terrorist act, but it would attract a far lighter sentence than if the two bombs went off and killed lots of people. On the other hand, he could deny all knowledge of the bomb making and suggest that the American had planned and executed all this without his knowledge. He was trying to weigh up how feasible it would be to try the second approach. It might be worth a try.

The usual formalities about the interview procedure were followed. Sean was told that the interview would be recorded, he was cautioned and then the interview proper began.

"Good morning, Sean," said Jerry Gregory. "Where have you planted the bombs?"

There was no point in messing about.

"What bombs? I don't know anything about any bombs."

"Really?" asked Jerry. "I suppose you don't know anything about Semtex and ammonium nitrate either?"

"No," said Sean, thinking that the less he said the better it would be.

"Where is your American helper?" asked Jerry.

"I don't know. He stopped coming in a couple of days ago. I've had to advertise for a new helper to deal with all the bike servicing and repairs. I was always a bit suspicious of him. He was a bit too good to be true. I think he just wanted somewhere to work in peace. He used to work late a lot and I don't know what he was doing. He always got the work for me done on time, but I reckon he was doing something else himself, using my equipment."

Jerry smiled. Sean had been right about saying nothing and now he was beginning to talk. Jerry could tell that Sean was rattled and he needed to put more and more pressure on him. Sean was going to crack, and soon.

At that pre-arranged moment, there was a knock on the door and one of the team stuck his head round it.

"Can I have a quick word please sir?"

Jerry went out quickly having turned off the recording.

He came back into the room a few moments later; he restarted the recorder and the proceedings.

"Can you explain why there are traces of Semtex on a parcel wrapper addressed to you?"

Sean thought. He was not yet ready to give up the pretence of ignorance.

"The American, his name is Robert by the way, ordered something and, because he didn't have a permanent address, he asked me if it could be addressed to me at the shop. I had no idea what was in it. There were quite a few parcels like that."

"Why don't I believe you?" asked Jerry. "Come on Sean. Tell us the truth. If a bomb goes off and anyone gets hurt, you could be charged with murder."

"I've told you," said Sean. "I had nothing to do with this. If there was any bomb making going on, it was Robert all by himself when I was not looking. I just got him to do my bike repairs."

Jenny Taylor took a gamble.

"Then what were you doing on the Senate House roof?"

Sean went white. All the colour drained from his features.

"I was never on the Senate House roof," he said.

"I'm asking you again," said Jenny. "What were you doing on the Senate House roof?"

Sean's conviction, that the people involved in stem cell research and abortion were worthy of death, was beginning to crumble in the face of his likely imprisonment for almost the rest of his life. It was one thing to plant bombs and get away with it, quite another to plant bombs and be caught. It had been a bit of an adventure really, planning it all and living the excitement, but it was now all going very sour on him. He decided to cut his losses and admit to the bomb in the Senate House.

"Bombing the Senate House," said Sean.

There was an immediate reaction from Jerry. He leapt to his feet and stared hard at Sean.

"I want a written statement from you on everything you know about the bomb, and the bomb maker. You can go back as far as the first time you met the guy, and I want it all."

Jerry left Sergeant Taylor to witness the statement taking. He called the search team and told them that, for certain, there was a bomb in the Senate House and that they had missed it on the previous sweep.

"Thank you, Sir," said the head of the bomb squad. "We'll get some other equipment, not just the tracker dogs and chromatograph. We'll find it this time, Sir."

Jeff Glover joined Julie Taylor, as a second witness to the statement. Sean started to talk, but very slowly. He started from the beginning. Jeff wrote it down, long hand, as Sean gave his account. He told them about the practice bomb by the riverbank. It merely confirmed what they already knew. He then started to talk about the second trip to Ely, to meet the quartermaster, and then about the meeting with Viktor's gang of thugs. He confirmed that they were given the Semtex and detonators by Viktor. He was about to mention that Viktor wanted them to make sure that they killed Stanislowsky, that that was the deal, when, at that very moment, there was a loud explosion from somewhere in the centre of the town. The interrogation was put on hold while the detectives went to find out what was going on.

The search team had gone off to the Senate House. The sniffer dogs and the hand-held devices had crawled all over the building and, again, not found the shrapnel bombs. That was when they sent for the other scanners.

Robert, sitting in his flat in Gwydir Street, had switched on the surveillance cameras; he had been doing that, very briefly, two or three times a day. He saw the search team in the Senate House and continued to watch them on his laptop. The surveillance camera, focussed on the throne and the front of the stage, showed him that they were not making any progress in finding the three sections of bomb. Sniffer dogs and the hand-held devices got them nowhere. He was

195

about to switch off the cameras, and make a cup of coffee, when he noticed that some new equipment was being brought into the building.

His smug expression changed when the team brought in the ultrasound and laser detection devices, used for finding hidden objects behind light opaque materials. They evacuated the building and only the two technicians handling the devices remained there.

They scanned the roof. Nothing important showed up. They scanned the walls. Nothing showed up. They scanned the floors, and then they scanned the stage. Robert noticed them focussing their attention on the three sections of the staging where he had inserted the bombs. He got out his mobile phone and sent the detonation signal. The two technicians were killed instantly. The stage, the lectern, and the rows of chairs were splintered almost to matchwood. The walls were pock marked with bits of metal and stone that made up the shrapnel in the devices that Robert and Sean had planted. The windows and doors were all blown out. The roof fabric over the stage area disintegrated.

Chapter 30

Jerry called the station and spoke to Jeff, who had just left the interrogation room.

"Evans and Reilly have been killed. There was an explosive device in the Senate House stage. It must have been remotely triggered. I reckon the bomber saw them getting close, he must have a surveillance camera somewhere, and just decided to blow it for the hell of it. It wasn't on a timer. The timer bombs must have been diversion tactics. The bombs were not detectable by sniffers or the machine. They were talking all the time during the search and they said that they thought that, using the laser and ultrasound devices, they had found three foreign objects under sections of the staging. I think that's what made the bomber set off the bombs. That changes everything. We need electronic signal jammers, lots of them, for everywhere that the conference is taking place. This bomb was meant for the presentation to Stanislowsky. It wasn't just targeting the conference, I think this bomb was targeting Stanislowsky. I think we have a bigger problem than just the pro-lifers. I reckon there must be some big boys behind this. That might explain how they got hold of the Semtex and the detonators."

Jeff was clearly deeply shocked. It came through in his tone of voice, but he was also very professional.

"That fits with what O'Connor just told us. They met a guy in a pub in Ely and he took them in a car to a remote farmhouse somewhere about thirty minutes' drive from there. It was occupied by a gang of Eastern Europeans headed up by a man called Viktor, and Viktor provided them with the Semtex and electronic remote-control detonators. He'd just told us that when the bomb went off. I think we need to try to get some more details about the farm from O'Connor. It might help us find the gang behind the supply of the Semtex."

"I bet there are other bombs," said Jerry. "Get back into that interview room now. We all heard the explosion. Sean must have heard the explosion. I bet he can hear all the bloody sirens going now, especially from the fire station next door. We need to find this American, and we need to see if we can find out who the people who gave them the Semtex were, where they are, and what the deal was."

"Do you think the American has a criminal record in the States?" asked Jeff.

"Could be, definitely, could be. He doesn't play like an amateur. The prints on the writing paper, can we check with the FBI to see if they have anything on file?"

"I'll get onto it right away," said Jeff.

Jerry thought for another minute then rang Jeff back.

"The point of contact between them will be the wrapping paper for the Semtex parcel. They might have slipped up and there might be fingerprints from the gang members on the parcel paper. They probably wouldn't have thought it would survive to get into our hands! Get the prints on it to Special Branch HQ and to Interpol? The security services, MI6 especially, might know who they belong to as well. When I get back to the station, we can see whether we can work out where that farmhouse is. See if he can tell you anything about it. We might just be able to find these bastards before they do any more damage. I bet they made Stanislowsky the main target. And while you're at it make sure you tell Mr O'Connor just how deep he's in it. Might shake him up to give us something more," said Jerry.

Jeff went back into the interrogation room.

"I thought you should know that a bomb just went off and killed a couple of police technicians. It was the one in the Senate House. I think you'd better tell us if there are any more. Your American friend clearly saw the team about to find the bomb, and blew it up. I think you need to start talking. Are there any more bombs?"

Sean was shaking now with fear. He looked completely defeated.

"The other bomb is in the Babbage Lecture Theatre," he said. "I don't think you're going to find it without me. It's under the stage and there's a surveillance camera watching it; actually, there are two cameras. The bomb's supposed to be detonated at the final plenary session of the conference when all the bigwigs are on stage."

Sean started to cry and to mumble: "I'm so sorry. I just sort of got caught up in this. I didn't really think it through. I hate the abortionists and…"

"Just shut up," said Jeff. "Spare me the bleeding heart. You just caused the death of two of my mates, and you were planning to kill a lot more innocent people. You make me sick. Did you think you were playing cowboys and Indians, like some bloody kids in the sixties? Where is this fucking bomb?"

"I'll take you there. Like I said it's in the Babbage."

Jeff called Jerry and arranged to meet him at the Babbage Lecture Theatre. Jeff handcuffed Sean and shoved him in the back of a police car. Jeff and Sergeant Jenny Taylor got into the car. Jenny was driving.

"We need a signal blocker for mobile phones and radio," said Jenny. "The American bastard obviously triggered the bomb remotely, and anything we do in the Babbage is going to be visible to him, and he'll probably take out a lot more of us, if he thinks we're getting close to his bomb."

"You're right Jenny," said Jeff. He got on the radio and asked switchboard to patch him through to the bomb squad. He requested electronic jamming equipment to be taken immediately to the New Museums site. He also wanted bug and camera detection devices. He didn't trust this American bastard not to have gone behind Sean's back and put other devices into the theatre.

On the way, Sean explained where the surveillance cameras were situated. They were watching only the stage and the front of the theatre. Entry from the back would be unobserved.

The team met up in the courtyard outside the theatre. Sean began to explain what he knew Robert to have done.

"He made these wooden sections which he packed with explosives; then he fitted them under the stage at the front. He said they were set to go off at a certain time. 3.15pm on the last day of the conference." said Sean.

"I think that is bullshit," said Jenny. "I don't think he trusted you. Was there anything else in that parcel you were sent other than the Semtex?"

"Well, there were about eight or ten of these little transistor things, and those surveillance cameras; they were very tiny," said Sean.

"Describe the transistor things to me," ordered Jenny.

Sean did his best, and it was good enough for Jenny to say, immediately, that they were electronic detonators, activated by mobile phone signals.

"He really took you for a mug. He was just using you," said Jeff. "My bet is he was going to kill you before he left."

"No, he wasn't," said Sean. "He got me a false passport and papers and he was going to take both of us to Canada. We have a flight booked for next weekend, after the conference is over."

"I bet he didn't book anything," said Jenny. "I bet he never even bought the tickets."

"He did," said Sean. "He showed them to me. He got me to send him all the papers in case you guys came round to the shop. I posted them to a hotel he was going to stay at and he was going to collect me in the morning and we were going to Heathrow."

"Which hotel was that Mr O'Connor?" asked Jeff, a bit sarcastically. He thought he might as well continue winding O'Connor up since that approach seemed to be yielding a lot of dividends.

"The new Novotel near the station," said Sean.

"What name was he using?" asked Jeff.

Sean told him and, over the radio, Jeff arranged for a squad car to go and pick up the package. Not surprisingly it had only information relevant to Sean. The hotel booking was made using a credit card that had been stolen and cloned. No way of getting back to the elusive American from that source.

Further pursuit of that line was put on hold while they tried to deal with the second bomb in the Babbage. The electronic scramblers to block mobile phone signals were put in place all round the building and switched on. All radio frequencies were also blocked. Not knowing exactly how the American planned to detonate the packages, they were trying to cover all the bases.

The first thing they did, acting on the information from O'Connor, was to start at the back of the auditorium and move forward, scanning every bench and all the walls and ceilings for cameras and bugs. They found both the cameras that Robert had inserted in the wall fabric, and they had a debate about how to deal with them. The field of vision of one of the cameras included the large clock on the left-hand side of the stage, looking from the auditorium. That had to go. The other camera was a simpler proposition. A photograph was taken from the exact position of the camera and printed out on high quality paper, and then placed in front of the lens. They took a risk that the American would not be looking at the camera at the exact moment they made the change, but they blocked the signal for a second or two while they made the switch. They also arranged with Radio Cambridge to put out a brief announcement that the explosion in the Senate House had been caused by a mains gas leak and had damaged electrical cables supplying some of the university buildings and some domestic customers in town. It was hoped that normal supply could be resumed as soon as possible. Engineers were working on it.

Robert, sitting in his flat, was watching the cameras in the Babbage. He was on high alert and he was ready to detonate the bombs as soon as anyone went into the theatre. It didn't matter to him. These bombs were just a means to an end. They had got him the explosives and the other equipment; he had the money in advance that Viktor had paid him. Killing a few policemen was neither here nor there to him. He saw both cameras go down, but he had heard the radio announcement, so he thought nothing of it. One of the cameras came back. That was fine. As far as he could tell nothing was happening in the Babbage, Sean had clearly kept his head and not told them anything yet. Maybe he could complete that element of the contract. It depended on Sean keeping his mouth shut. Perhaps, Robert had underestimated the character of Sean, and the level of hatred he had for the abortionists. He could see that the clever cops could have put two and two together and identified the Senate House as a target. Leaving that picture of the bloody car on the roof, that would have been enough, with the other things like the tripod hoist, to get them thinking.

For the moment, Robert switched off the surveillance cameras and went off to make himself a cup of coffee. He thought the Babbage devices were probably safe, at least for now. They would be too busy dealing with the aftermath of the Senate House explosion to think about further searches.

The experience in the Senate House had taught the bomb squad that they were not going to find the Semtex by using sniffer dogs or gas chromatographs. They went under the stage with the ultrasound and laser probes and identified the sections that had been inserted in the stage support beams. These were carefully removed. They thought it unlikely that there would be trembler mechanisms, any heavy thump on the stage might have triggered an explosion prematurely. They did think the devices might be booby trapped. There was no point in trying to dismantle the bombs *in situ* so they were taken away, with great tenderness and loving care, by the bomb squad, to a hangar at Marshall's Airport, where they could be examined carefully behind blast walls and away from civilian danger.

There was a corporate sigh of relief from everyone concerned once the four bomb sections had been taken away. They were not booby trapped so the squad managed to dismantle them quite quickly and hand the electronic triggers back to the Special Branch detectives. The electronic blocking devices were switched off and the cameras were restored to normal function. An announcement over

Cambridge Radio gave the all-clear to the citizens of Cambridge that their electrical supplies had been restored.

"We must let the bastard think he's still in play," said Jerry. "We don't want him hiding away even more than he already is. Can someone interrogate these trigger devices to see that they are still active, without setting them off?"

"These really modern ones, you can," said the head of the bomb squad.

"Well put the bloody things back then," said Jerry.

"What range do those camera transmitters have?" asked Sergeant Taylor.

One of the technicians came up with the reply that the maximum range was probably 3 to 4 miles.

"The bastard is somewhere in Cambridge then. I suppose we could have guessed that because O'Connor said he came to work on a bike," Jeff paused. "I wish we knew where he is."

Chapter 31

During the search for and removal of the bombs Sergeant Jenny Taylor had been busy over the radio. She reasoned that the one possibility of making a link to the American was to see if the tickets had genuinely been booked. Sean had said he had seen them, so they did probably exist. One would have been in Sean's false passport name. Jenny Taylor contacted all the airlines to check what double bookings, one way or return, had been made with Sean's false identity as one of the booked passengers.

They were moving fast. The information came back very quickly. A double booking had been made for a flight to Montreal on the Sunday morning. The airline provided the passport details of the second passenger, who had paid by credit card, the same cloned credit card that had been used for the hotel booking. There was a passport number and further details. There was a passport photo of the second passenger. That photograph was sent to the FBI, Interpol, and everyone else they could think of.

By the time the search had been completed, they had a facial match. The hair colour was wrong, but the features were right. The answer came, not from the FBI, but from the California Police Department. It gave the information that Jerry and Jeff were suspecting, but hoping not, to receive. The American with the false passport was Robert Jackson, the convicted rapist. The partial prints they had from some of the material they had recovered from the bins at the back of Mill Road were Jackson's.

"I guess that guy will have more aliases than the devil himself," said Jerry.

"Oh shit," said Jeff. "Those girls at St Joseph's. One of them was Jackson's daughter and one of them was his first rape victim."

"I remember that," said Jerry. "He's escalated to killing now. I think we need to be very careful with those girls. Until we catch Jackson, I think we need a 24-hour guard on them."

"I could do that Sir," said Sergeant Taylor. "Let me go round to the college and see where they live, and do you want me to talk to them and warn them?"

"Too bloody right I do. It can't possibly be a coincidence that the guy is here in Cambridge. Thanks Jen. Go find out what we need and then get back to me. We'll be at the station as soon as I've gone round to see the families of the two technicians that got killed. Oh my god, I hate this bit of the job."

Jerry started sighing quite heavily. This was not going to be easy. He couldn't help feeling he had messed up a bit. He ought to have thought about a trigger device, but he was so busy hunting the bomb and thinking they still had time. I guess, if he hadn't seen them looking, they would have had time, but they had the method of detonation wrong. That clever bastard had misdirected them with the timing device on the riverside bomb, and the two other university bombs they had found. It got Jerry thinking. Was he missing something still? But his mind wouldn't give him an answer.

Sergeant Jenny Taylor went round to St Joseph's immediately. She called at the porters' lodge and found Donald O'Connor, Sean's cousin, on duty.

"What was with the explosion Sergeant?" asked Donald.

"I'm afraid I can't tell you," said Jenny.

"Okay, how can I help you?"

"I need to see the senior tutor please," said Jenny. "And I need to talk to two of your students, Sarah McElroy and Martha McArthy."

"Well, they aren't here now, any of them. Martha is watching one of the other girls playing tennis and Sarah has taken her bike out, with her boyfriend, for a training run. They have a big time-trial on Thursday."

"It's really urgent," said Jenny.

"I have their mobile numbers. I can get the senior tutor. He will come in as quickly as he can."

"Please call him. It is very urgent."

Jenny sat in the office at the back of the porters' lodge and had a rather good cup of coffee. The head porter, Donna, liked good coffee and had insisted that the college got the porters a decent coffee machine. The senior tutor, Adrian Armstrong, had billed it to the welfare account. Donna had pointed out that the porters were often the first welfare stop for students in distress. She also pointed out that good coffee for porters on night duty was a necessary welfare feature too.

Adrian came in within about fifteen minutes. He had clearly just jumped on his bike and pedalled as fast as he could. He was undoing his cycle helmet and taking it off as he came through the archway to the back office of the Lodge.

"Hi. I'm Adrian Armstrong. I'm the senior tutor here."

"Good afternoon, Sir," said Jenny Taylor. "I'm Detective Sergeant Jenny Taylor. I'm with Special Branch."

"I thought I knew everyone in Special Branch," said Adrian. "Since we elected Lord Fairfield to the Mastership, and built that conference centre, you lot have virtually camped on our doorstep."

Adrian smiled and stuck out his hand to shake Jenny Taylor's.

"I'm fairly new to Special Branch here," said Jenny. "I was previously in London."

"Well, nice to have you here," said Adrian. "How can we help?"

Jenny explained what had happened; that there was an American rapist who was involved in a bombing campaign in Cambridge and had just caused an explosion that had killed two officers.

"How does that relate to us here at St Joe's?" asked Adrian.

"I'm going to tell you in strict confidence, but I think you absolutely do need to know. The rapist is Sarah McElroy's father, and his first rape victim was Martha McArthy," said Jenny.

Adrian looked deeply shocked.

"My God," he said, and he sat down. Quite inappropriately, in shock, he said, "Would you like another coffee, Sergeant?"

Jenny replied that a coffee would be very nice. She was not that bothered about another coffee herself, but she knew that Adrian needed time to recover his composure.

"Don, can you get us coffees please?"

There was a pause while Adrian collected his thoughts. Jenny was good at pauses. Important in conducting interviews. Then Adrian spoke as Don, the porter on duty, put the coffees in front of them.

"So you probably think he might be after these two girls, do you?"

"We fear that he might be. You recall that we came to see the girls a few weeks ago after one of their friends had been raped in California."

Adrian nodded his head.

"I gather you were to ask the porters to watch out for strangers with American accents hanging around the college."

"That's right Sergeant," said Adrian.

"Has there been anyone?" asked the Sergeant.

"Not that I'm aware. Let me just ask Don."

Don didn't even think about the American who had brought the bikes from his cousin's shop. He had not been hanging around the college, he had just been making a delivery.

Adrian came back into the room.

"There really doesn't appear to have been anything unusual," he said.

"Would you mind taking me to see the girls' accommodation please?" asked Jenny.

Adrian got the master key from the porters' cupboard and they walked over to the Cumberland Building, the old wing on which the Stanford Scholars lived.

Ceci, Sarah, and Martha had rooms on the second floor of the staircase. Ceci and Sarah were sharing a set. Martha had sole occupancy of the Stanford Room.

"Is there a spare room on this staircase at all?" asked Jenny.

"In fact, there is," said Adrian. "Many of the students have already left after graduation, so one of the rooms on the ground floor is vacant."

"Can we go into one of the rooms please?" asked Jenny.

"We can go into the empty one if you like; the rooms are pretty much identical, except mirror image across the staircase."

He unlocked the door, and they went in. There was a main sitting room, there were two bedrooms, studies off the main sitting room and there was one of those self-contained pods, with a lavatory and shower, in the corner nearest to the staircase.

In common with many buildings of that era, the windows were small, and the amount of natural light was rather limited. Rather than this being a disadvantage, under the present circumstances, it was a source of relief to Jenny.

"It looks as if the only reasonable access to these rooms is from the staircase. How does the fire escape system work?"

Adrian explained the kick panels and crawl spaces, through to the rooms on the adjacent staircases.

"Fire escaping is a noisy business then!" said Jenny.

"Yes," said Adrian.

"I do need to talk to your girls, all three of them. We know they are friends and linked to Stanford," said Jenny.

206

"You can find Martha and Ceci at Fenner's," said Adrian. "Ceci is playing in the Varsity tennis match and Martha's watching her. I think all their families are there too, including Sarah's, and there are some other American friends with them. If you like, I'll text Sarah and ask her to go to Fenner's when she gets back. Her training cycling sessions usually take about four hours and she must have been out almost that long now."

They locked the empty room and went back via the area known as The Meadow, the large open space with the pond and the rough grass tennis courts, and the volleyball court, and the croquet hoops. Jenny looked around. Lots of boundary walls, easy access from the city.

She had a lot to think about as Adrian showed her a short cut to the area of Cambridge known as Parker's Piece. She walked across it, avoiding the cricket matches and the impromptu soccer games, and went into Gresham Road. Fenner's tennis courts were just down that road on the left. One thing she had noticed was that, although Martha had a set of rooms to herself, there was a spare bedroom in that set, and Jenny was thinking that it might be a good idea for her to ask Adrian Armstrong if she might sleep there, until Robert Jackson was apprehended.

Fenner's was, as always, looking immaculate, the beautiful smooth green grass of the tennis courts was set in contrast to the clear white markings of the court and the pristine outfits of the players. White and light blue, white and dark blue, and then lots of colourful prints and the inevitable linen jackets among the spectators. There were a few Panama hats and wide brimmed hats among the audience.

Cecilia Tan stood out among the players, the only light blue lady player with striking East Asian features, and, Jenny thought, probably the best player there. Sitting watching her court was by far the largest contingent of spectators, several youngsters and one rather bulky and tough looking male, it was Vasily, Alexis's bodyguard.

Jenny waited patiently until the match finished and then moved over to the group.

"Good afternoon, everyone," she said, "I really need to talk to all of you as a group and I would prefer not to be overheard. We need to be out of earshot of everyone else so can we go to the far end near the hardcourts please? Cecilia, do you need to shower first or can we talk immediately?"

"I'm fine to talk now," said Ceci.

They went to the far end of the run of seven courts and Jenny started to explain why she was there.

"I'm sure you heard the loud explosion earlier today."

They all nodded their heads.

"It was a gas explosion wasn't it? At least that's what student radio said," said Martha.

Jenny looked grave.

"I wish it had been," she said. "It was a bomb, in the Senate House, and it killed two of our policemen."

The announcement was greeted with a stunned silence.

"There is something else," said Jenny.

"We believe the bomber may be an American and that all of you may know him. We think the bomber is probably Sarah's father Robert Jackson."

You could hear a pin drop.

Theresa and Martha went almost into shock. They both sat down, they looked at each other. Everyone else was silent and scared for each other.

Eventually Martha spoke.

"May I ask why you think that?"

Jenny explained about the history and the forensics.

"Why did he do it?" asked Theresa. "What was he targeting?"

"We think he was targeting the stem cell conference."

Theresa interrupted.

"That makes some sense. Robert Jackson was a fanatic pro-lifer."

"Yes," said Jenny. "But he was also given some highly sophisticated bomb making equipment and we think there may have been a secondary motive. Is one of you Alexis Stanislowsky?"

Alexis indicated who he was.

"We think he may have been hired to kill your father and the bomb making equipment was a gift from a dissident group, from your own country, to enable Robert Jackson to complete that task, as well as his own anti-abortion and stem cell mission."

The bodyguard was taking note.

Jenny continued.

"We managed to find where the bomb was located, but we think Jackson decided, probably in a flare up of his violent temper, to blow the bomb as soon as he saw we were getting close. Fortunately, we discovered that there was a second bomb, but we have managed to find and defuse that, without Jackson knowing. We think he still believes he can set that bomb off."

"It isn't a coincidence that he's in Cambridge, is it?" asked Martha.

"We don't think it is," said Jenny. "We think he came here for a different reason. We think he came here for revenge on Sarah and Martha for putting him in prison, and this other stuff going on was just a lucky break for him. We think it distracted him from his main purpose which was revenge on the two girls. It probably bought us some time, or he would have attacked one or other of you, Martha, several days ago."

"What about my father?" asked Alexis.

"We think he will try to kill your father and complete his contract before he leaves the country," said Jenny.

"Well," said Alexis; "I have my bodyguard here, so I suppose I feel fairly safe myself."

Alexis looked in the direction of his bodyguard, who smiled back at him.

There was something about that smile that alerted Jenny Taylor's sense of danger. Was she becoming paranoid, that smile looked too false?

Jenny said, "I just wanted to alert you all to the potential danger and ask you to be especially on guard. I'll talk to Sarah as soon as she gets back from her training ride, and to, what is his name, Jonny?"

They nodded.

"I'll talk to Jonny too. Meanwhile, Martha, would you object if I asked your senior tutor to let me sleep in your spare bedroom until we catch Jackson?"

"I think I would be very grateful to have you there," said Martha.

"Hey," said Jenny. "You all look so gloomy. Can we cheer you up, and can I take a photograph of all of you, for the album? Especially you, Ceci, I think I might see you at Wimbledon one day."

They all stood against the background of the Victorian wall behind the courts, and Jenny casually asked the bodyguard to be in the photograph too.

"No dark glasses anyone, I want to see the faces, and please smile, let me know I've not totally ruined your day."

"Well, we've just stuffed Oxford," said Ceci, trying to lighten the mood. "I reckon I can manage a smile."

Jenny took her photograph and then she took her leave.

"Please be vigilant. I think Robert Jackson will remain hidden until he's tried to explode his second bomb, and I think that will not be until later this week when the plenary session takes place in the Babbage. Until then, I think you can pretty much get on with life as normal but keep your eyes open, and try not to spend too much time alone, stick together as much as you can. I'll see you this evening Martha. If Sarah comes here, please send her and Jonny to the police station and get them to ask for me, Jenny Taylor. You can tell them what it's about but be discrete please. You can also tell your families about the situation; I'm sure they need to know too. Don't worry too much, I think we have your back. I've asked the senior tutor to send Sarah and Jonny over to the station if they go back to college first."

As she walked back to the station, Jenny sent the photograph she had just taken to Special Branch headquarters and to Jerry and Jeff. The text accompanying it said: "Please see if the burly gentleman on the back row right of this photograph is known to Special Branch or to MI6. There is something not quite right about him."

Chapter 32

Robert Jackson, meanwhile, was planning his exit strategy. He had to assume that Canada and his Canadian travel identity were 'out', but he had never intended to use that route, or that identity, anyway. It was just for dealing with Sean, who he would kill before leaving. He had his other identity ready, and his ticket booked. It was more how he was going to take revenge on Sarah that he was working on, although almost everything was in place for that too.

Adrian Armstrong agreed to an extra police presence in college for the duration of the conference. The presence of the delegates was an important consideration in his agreeing to that. He also agreed to Sergeant Taylor staying with Martha in the Stanford Set. He had helped Martha, through his role as the Senior Treasurer of the ADC Theatre Club, to get a block of tickets for the Footlights' Tour Show, and he now called in a further favour to get an extra seat for Jenny Taylor.

Sarah and Jonny went over to the police station late that afternoon and were updated by Jenny Taylor and Jeff Glover on the situation regarding Sarah's father.

"We think you can go about your normal business, provided that you're vigilant," said Jeff.

"What about the time trials?" asked Jonny. "Is it safe for us to keep training and do the race?"

"Well, you are out of doors, and you are with lots of other people, and I don't expect Robert Jackson is going to risk anything, not until he's tried his second bomb anyway."

The older generation returned in the late afternoon and they were quickly brought up to date by Martha and the others. They were obviously very concerned, especially Sarah's mother, but they were reassured by the obvious police presence, by the briefing they got from Jenny Taylor, and by the fact that

Alexis's bodyguard and Jenny Taylor were accompanying them on their evening entertainments.

That evening, at dinner in Hall, Jenny Taylor was present with the other younger members of the group. Ceci and her one allowed guest, Vinnie, had gone to the presentation dinner for the Varsity match teams. It was held in the Long Gallery at St Joseph's. The menus were identical and very good. Pan fried scallop with hazelnut butter, lamb cooked three ways, and a delicious and fun pudding in the form of a vanilla ice cream tennis ball and chocolate tennis racket, on a bed of lime jelly.

When the fruit and chocolates were being passed with the port, Jenny started to tell the girls about the finding of the 'practice' bomb on the route to Ely. She had just started to speak when Martha suddenly said, "Could it have been the other one of the two we saw when we were out under the A14 flyover. The other one of the two who stared at us?"

Jenny was immediately all attention.

"Can you give us a description?"

Between them the two girls did their best. The one thing they did know was that the second man had very dark hair, quite unlike Robert Jackson, and a very bushy beard.

"He was about the same build and height as my father," said Sarah.

Jenny arranged for them to go the next day to the station to work with a police artist to see if they could get a decent likeness. It was a long shot, but it could be helpful.

After the dinner, the whole party, including the older generation, met up at the ADC theatre and went to the 11pm showing of the Footlights' Review. The ADC Bar stays open until very late on these occasions and, apart from Sarah and Jonny, who were still in training, the rest of the gang had, perhaps, a little too much to drink.

The night passed uneventfully. Jenny slept surprisingly well, given how concerned she was about the safety of her charges. She had set electronic warning devices in various places, without telling the occupants of the staircase. Nothing disturbed the peace. Martha and Jenny had a light breakfast of cereal, toast and coffee in Martha's room and Sarah, Jonny and Ceci joined them. So did Vinnie, which caused Martha to raise at least one eyebrow!

Martha and Sarah, as arranged, went over to the police station, and did their best with the artist. The result was more accurate than they realised at the time.

They looked at photographs of Sarah's father, suitably aged by special software, and they became convinced, as did the police, that the man they had seen that day under the flyover was Robert Jackson.

That Sunday morning a message arrived at the police station from MI6. They had identified Alexis's bodyguard as Vasily Protiov, a former member of the secret police in Alexis's home country.

"Is he pro- or anti-Stanislowsky, do we know?" asked Jeff.

"I don't bloody care," said Jerry Gregory. "Jenny sent the picture because she felt there was something wrong about him and she has a great instinct for danger. We treat him as hostile from now on and we insist on a Special Branch bodyguard for Alexis. In fact, I suggest we get Alexis out of St Alfred's and put him somewhere we consider to be a safe house."

"What about Alexis's girlfriend, the American punk lady?" asked Jeff.

"I think we move her into the safe house with him. We can give them escorts during the day, but it's more at night that I think there is a risk."

Vasily Protiov was 'talked to' by Special Branch detectives. They searched him and found him to be carrying a concealed firearm. He was arrested and immediately put in the cells at Parkside Police Station.

"My father hired Vasily to protect me," said Alexis. "I think he ought to be told what has happened."

The older members of the team, including Jonny's father, were at the opening ceremony of the conference.

They had to run the gauntlet of abuse thrown at them by a group of about a hundred and fifty pro-lifers, including Kesandu, still under cover, who were placarding at the entrance to the New Museums site. They had marched from Parker's Piece, down Regent Street and St Andrew's Street to the Market Square, where their speaker, a well-known American Pro-lifer, had harangued everyone about the evils of abortion and stem cell harvesting from aborted foetuses. They had then gone down Corn Exchange Street to Downing Street and laid siege to the archway from Downing Street into the New Museums site. It had only been placards and verbal abuse. Several of the protesters had come up from London by train. Most passers-by saw it as a slight diversion on a Sunday afternoon.

Robert Jackson watched the opening ceremony on the two surveillance cameras, which were now working properly again after the disturbance which he believed had been caused the day before by the explosion. He tested the integrity of the detonator devices and, satisfied that all was well, he opened a packet containing carrot cake, and had his tea.

It was an interesting conversation between Anton Stanislowsky, Alexis's father, and D.I. Gregory. Stanislowsky was convinced that Vasily was on his side but accepted the wisdom of changing the bodyguard duties to Special Branch during this period of heightened concern. He gladly accepted further protection himself for the duration of the conference and through the reception to mark his generous donations. This reception had now been moved from the Senate House and was to take place immediately after the closing ceremony of the conference, in the Babbage Lecture Theatre. The Senate House was going to be out of action for some weeks as the internal damage was repaired. Much of the seating, the staging and the roof structure had been destroyed and the rest of it was being checked and replaced. Fortunately, the structural integrity of the building itself had not been affected, but it was going to take some months to restore the building to its former glory.

"I will make you some more enquiries about Vasily," said Anton Stanislowsky. "I will let you know definitely whether he is a threat to me and my son. I have good contacts at home. It had not occurred to me to mistrust the man. He has been useful to me before this. I wonder if he has been purchased. No, that's not how you say it, you say 'bought'?"

"That would be helpful," said Jerry. "Meanwhile we would like to assign the bodyguards to you and your son until we've resolved the issue with our bomber. There may also be other intended assassination or kidnap attempts."

"I, and my son, would be most grateful for your help."

At this point, Jerry Gregory felt that he was doing all he could do to keep the potential targets safe. He was not sure how he was going to handle the immediate aftermath of the conference. Given the range of transmission of the cameras, Jackson, for, surely, he was the bomber, would know that there had not been the loud explosion that the triggering of the electronic detonators should have set off. Would he then try to flee Cambridge? How would he travel? Would he try to get at the girls before he left? All good questions and all without obvious answers.

Despite the continuing protest by the pro-lifers, whose numbers had dwindled during the week as many returned to their jobs in London, the conference itself went well. Police presence at the picket points ensured safe passage for those going in and out of the conference venues, and it seemed as if the protesters themselves began to lose momentum. There was some heckling during one of the keynote presentations, until the heckler was removed by a couple of burly Special Branch policemen in the audience. Otherwise, all went smoothly.

Those presenting their posters at the poster session in the large classroom in the Physiological Laboratory, often used on these occasions by National and International groups, received more than polite interest. Martha was grilled for about twenty minutes by the Professor of Ob-Gyn from UC San Francisco. He finished his grilling by saying:

"Ms McArthy, I understand you will be coming to join us on the medical course at UCSF. I'm delighted. Please call and see me as soon as you return. I've a proposition to put to you to enable you to continue with your research interests during your clinical study. It's very selfish of me to ask this of you, but I've always managed to surround myself with outstanding people and I view this piece of work, for a Master's Thesis, as outstanding."

He moved on to the piece of work done by Ceci. He had a similar conversation.

Not surprisingly both posters were accepted for publication, and the editorial board of the Journal for Stem Cell research asked Ceci and Martha to prepare a full paper for publication. The work that they had done was far more than the volume normally done in a single year by a Master's candidate, the studies complemented each other, and between them they had enough material to produce a full peer reviewed paper in that leading journal.

There were two very happy young ladies at the end of the session, and one or two very proud parents and friends. Martha was delighted when Dr Simms came over to her, quietly, during a short break in the poster session. He gave her a big hug and whispered his own quiet congratulations and praise.

"I'm in awe," he said.

Alexis Stanislowsky also received praise for his paper, and it too was accepted for publication. His father made quite a fuss of him. It was clear that they were very fond of each other and that Anton Stanislowsky was proud of, and respectful of, his son's achievements.

James was giving a special invited lecture on the plant stem cell material, and the whole group went along to hear him present his work. The paper he was presenting was already accepted for publication in *Nature*, and, as such, attracted almost all the important names in the field. He had several job-offers during the brief drinks reception after the talk. Stanford University is only a few miles down the peninsula from UC San Francisco and the University of California, Berkeley, is only a bridge span across the Bay. When you are in love with someone about to spend the next few years of their life in the Bay Area, you can be forgiven for accepting a full professorship that lets you remain near them, especially if it does not mean compromising your career and your passion for the work that you do. With offers from both these institutions, James had a decision to make.

The visitors, apart from dutiful attendance at the presentations by their hosts, spent the rest of the time exploring Cambridge and its surroundings. The youngsters took one day to walk to Ely and marvelled at the sight of the 'ship of the fens' towering over the flat landscape, visible from just north of Dimmock's Cote. They enjoyed a leisurely lunch at the very same pub where Sean and Robert had met the members of Viktor's group, and they caught the train back to Cambridge in the early afternoon. They had no idea about the irony of this trip.

The other things were all the touristy things like punting, again; this time they went on the lower river around the backs. They visited colleges and museums and, for a little more exercise, hired cycles and cycled out to the winery at Chilford Hall, using the Roman road as part of their journey. Afternoon tea, with wine tasting, completed that afternoon's entertainment.

Meanwhile, Sarah and Jonny were training hard. They still could not understand why their times were slower than usual, but they were too distracted by events around them to make it a major concern.

Sergeant Jenny Taylor, meanwhile, was having a very pleasant spell of duty. A very intelligent young woman she enjoyed the conversation with her charges, which went on basically from 'morn 'til night'. She remained glued to Martha and Ceci. A member of the motorcycle section of Cambridgeshire police was deputed to shadow Sarah and Jonny on their training runs.

"Feels like the Tour De France," said Jonny.

Robert, meanwhile, had used his Amazon Prime account to purchase another Bear Grylls knife. You never knew when it might come in handy to assist in a rape. He thought that the police might be a bit busy after the bomb went off in the lecture theatre, and he might have a chance to attack one or other, or even both, of the girls at St Joseph's. If not, he would wait a night or so and try again on the Friday, just before he left for the airport. He was getting bored with his isolation, so he did venture out for a walk from Gwydir Street, out to the Cambridge Airport and round through Cherry Hinton and back along Hill's

Road. He was careful to dress relatively smartly and not to draw attention to himself.

The concluding session of the conference began, as scheduled, at 2:30 pm on the Wednesday. The dignitaries duly took their places on the stage. As a registered delegate of the conference, Robert Jackson had been informed that the presentation to mark Stanislowsky's generous donation had been tacked onto the end of the closing ceremony. Robert was almost drooling with pleasure. He could kill all those goddam abortionists and stem cell users and he could get Stanislowsky at the same time. It would mean a million dollars more in his bank account, and he no longer needed to share any of it with Sean O'Connor.

Robert waited and waited for the right moment. It came when the vice-chancellor, having made his speech about the wonderful generosity of Anton Stanislowsky, called Stanislowsky forward to join him at the lectern and to shake his hand.

Robert allowed himself a triumphal exclamation and sent the electronic signal to the four detonators in the four large bombs under the stage. He glued his eyes upon the computer showing, in split screen mode, the images from both concealed cameras.

Nothing appeared to happen.

In the theatre itself, there was a muffled popping sound, from a well-padded box just outside the theatre door to the left of the stage, as you observed from the auditorium.

Robert was puzzled. He sent the signal again. This time nothing was heard in the theatre and, again, nothing was seen to change in the auditorium.

He started to rant and rave in the privacy of his flat.

"*They found the fucking bombs,*" he said to himself. "*Sean must have cracked and told them.*" He thought a lot more expletives before he calmed down enough to be rational again.

"*I still have the other plan that Sean knows nothing about. I need to go and check that everything is still in place.*"

Robert was giving up on the conference plans, there was nothing left to do there. One bomb had exploded, killing the wrong targets, and the other had been found and defused. His hope now was that the forces of law and order would be satisfied that they had aborted any attempt on the pro-lifers and Stanislowsky.

217

It would, indeed, have been very easy for the Special Branch team, and for everyone concerned, to think that all the immediate danger was now past. There were a few matters though that were worrying Jerry and the team.

The first of these matters was that, although the threat to the stem cell conference delegates was probably over, Stanislowsky, who was still around Cambridge, had been under threat, and presumably, was still in danger. Jerry wanted to know what, if anything, the interrogation of Vasily Protiov had revealed. He also wanted to remind himself of the itinerary for the rest of Stanislowsky's visit.

There were private meetings arranged for Stanislowsky and his lawyer, within the Old Schools, with various of the pro-Vice-Chancellors for research and teaching, to work out the details of the donations. These meetings could be possible targets. There was the Stanford Dinner, to which Stanislowsky had been invited. That involved the lecture and reception in the conference centre at St Joseph's.

There was more searching of premises and grounds to be done.

The bomb squad was sent in to do a thorough job of surveying the Old Schools Buildings, including the Syndicate Room, the Council Room, the Pro-Vice-Chancellors' and the Chancellor's offices, and the cloisters at the back of Senate House Lawn. They were smart enough now to know that Robert, if he had been making bombs for either of these locations, would have made them odour proof. They would need the ultrasound and laser probes to look everywhere. A painstaking search found nothing of note. As a precaution they would put signal jamming in place during the meetings in the Old Schools. They were also advising Stanislowsky and his son to wear bullet proof vests for all the official occasions. The vests would not protect against a head shot but they might buy time if the assassin tried a body shot. There was some grumbling, it was rather hot at this period, and, as always in Cambridge, quite humid.

They also arranged for a search of the conference centre at St Joseph's. They had quite a bit of experience there. Lord Fairfield had kept them busy at the conference centre, over the years of his Mastership.

The clinching evidence that persuaded both the Stanislowskys to wear the body armour was the information from the interrogation. Vasily Protiov confirmed that he had been employed by a man called Viktor Rubinsky, to spy on Alexis, and to report any useful information about Stanislowsky Senior's movements. Rubinsky was well known to be a hard-line communist, who was against the liberal reforms for which Stanislowsky stood. He was also one of the men that Special Branch had noticed arriving at Heathrow several weeks earlier, one of those who had disappeared on their way through the underground complex at St Pancras and Kings Cross.

Sean O'Connor, meanwhile, had been informed about the second bomb, and how it had been defused. He had been asked about the trip to Ely to meet the hard-liners who had provided the Semtex. He had given very little away. Special Branch had sent photographs of the group of foreign nationals who had arrived with Viktor, and Jerry had shown them to Sean. Sean had been told that the police would seek to have his sentence reduced, if he were to cooperate in helping them to find the source of the explosives, and so prevent further terrorist acts. He looked at the photographs and identified several of them as people he had seen during the visit to the farmhouse.

Sean told them as much as he could about the layout of the farm, the arrangements of the buildings, the view to the road, and the nature of the farming enterprise, with the pigs and poultry. They sent the police helicopter, with a cameraman on board, to take aerial photographs of all the likely farms within a forty-minute drive of Ely. It was not a trivial task, but it was not an impossible one either.

The other thing that they did was to re-examine the packaging for the parcel that had carried the Semtex. The delivery by courier had several bits of information written on it and they could still identify the tracking number. Many couriers record the weight of any packages that they distribute, and this company was no exception. A quick telephone call to the courier showed that the package had weighed just under 10kg. They had found 4kg of Semtex in the four unexploded bombs in the Babbage lecture theatre. The forensics team had suggested that about another 1kg of Semtex had been involved in the Senate House bombs. The detonators between them could not have weighed more than another 500 grams, so what had weighed the other 4 or so kilogrammes? It had to be more Semtex, and where the hell was it now?

Further interrogation of Sean O'Connor made it very clear that he knew only that Robert Jackson had made the bombs already discovered. He did confirm that the parcel had contained more than just 5kg of material, but he had no idea where that material was now.

They had more luck with the identification of the farm. There was one farm on the outskirts of Somersham, a village to the west of Ely, which was immediately identifiable from its layout. Arrangements were made for a visit to the farm as soon as possible.

They were too late. Immediately on his arrest Vasily had pressed a pre-arranged quick dial number which warned the team at the farmyard. On his visit there with Jackson, Sean had noted the clear lines of sight to the road and the ease of escape from the farm if hostile forces were approaching.

The armed response squad were sent, with members of Special Branch, to talk to the occupants, but they arrived at the farm in time to see the buildings blow up, one by one, apart from the food and grain stores, the chicken houses, and the other buildings where livestock, and food for the animals, were housed. Tracks suggested that the occupants had escaped across country in four-wheel drive all-terrain vehicles. The vehicles were later found abandoned, and burnt out, in a field just outside Ely, near to the station Car Park. CCTV footage later confirmed that eight men, who made sure their faces were not registered by the cameras, had boarded a train for Stansted Airport, via Cambridge, about an hour after the buildings blew up.

Anton Stanislowsky's sources in his home country had confirmed that a hard-line group, led by a man called Viktor Rubinsky, had been active in opposing Stanislowsky's liberalisation movement. They were believed to have killed more than one of the members of Stanislowsky's opposition party. Stanislowsky's sources sent some photographs to Special Branch. The photographs were of the same men who Sean had previously identified as the ones he had seen at the farm.

Jerry took the set of photographs, the aerial photos of the farm, and the report from Stanislowsky's contacts, into a further interview with Vasily.

"We know who you are," said Jerry.

"We know that you're part of a gang headed up by this man."

He showed Vasily the photograph of Viktor Rubinsky.

"We know that you're here to kill Stanislowsky."

Jerry paused to let his words sink in.

"*We* know that you're here, but we made very sure that nobody else knows that you're here. I'm sorry to have to tell you that we could make you disappear permanently. What you read in the papers about British Fair Play is a bit exaggerated. I *will* have you killed, just like that, if you do not cooperate with me. Is that clear?"

Jerry was bluffing, but he knew that interrogation techniques and civil rights abuses in Vasily's home country would encourage Vasily to believe that this was not a bluff. He was counting on Vasily accepting his words at face value.

Jerry paused again. He started drumming his fingers on the table between himself and Vasily. He yawned, he rubbed his face and his eyes with his hands. He leant back and stretched. Then he sat forward suddenly.

"What did you tell Viktor about Stanislowsky's movements?"

"I didn't have to tell him anything," said Vasily. "It was all obvious from the conference schedule and the announcements in the University Reporter."

Most liars, like amateur poker players, have a tell. With Vasily, it was a habit of pulling the lobe of his right ear. That was useful. Jerry knew there was something else.

"You did tell him something. I want to know what it was."

Vasily answered very rudely, in his native tongue. The interview was being recorded and, subsequently, Jerry discovered that he had been given impossible instructions, to mate with himself, in that somewhat guttural and impenetrable language.

Jerry decided to give Vasily one more night in the cells, but he arranged for it to be in a cell, next to an empty cell in which a recording of a very noisy drunk was played on a looped tape all night long, to make sure that there was no sleep. They also arranged for the lights to be turned on intermittently as fictitious new prisoners were brought noisily along the corridor.

Jerry himself went off home to sleep the sleep of the just.

With the conference behind them, the whole group of Americans began to relax, and to turn their attention to the Time Trial taking place the next day.

On the Wednesday evening before supper, they all went down to the basement car park in the conference centre and looked at the collection of bicycles there. The entire Cambridge time trial team had their bicycles in that store. All around the cage were other undergraduate bicycles in the racks, many scattered all over the place, many in stages of disintegration and disrepair. In a month or so, the porters would come down and sort out the serviceable from the unserviceable. They had a list of the numbers painted on the frames of the ordinary bicycles in the shelter. They would not touch the bicycles of those returning to study the following year, but the abandoned bicycles were fair game. They would send the unserviceable bikes to the scrap metal merchants and the serviceable ones to Sean's Cycle Emporium, for Sean to repair and sell.

Just as the group were leaving 'the cage' one of the gardeners came in and placed a huge bag of something quite heavy into the garden store cupboard next to the bicycle racks. He was muttering very dark sentiments about the head gardener.

"What's the matter?" asked Jonny.

"Gerry Bugg, you know him, the head gardener. He sent me down to the stores to get something and I took this bag up, and he swore at me, and told me we never use this stuff, and to get some of that blooming *Grow Organic* stinky stuff. Anyway, I'm going home now, and it can wait until tomorrow."

"Never mind," said Jonny. "You can spread your stinky stuff while we cycle our way round the countryside. I just hope they aren't out spraying that slurry rubbish on the fields tomorrow. It's going to be hotter than hell, and that slurry stuff they spray stinks something terrible."

The gardener laughed, said good evening, and trotted off to his car to drive home for his evening meal.

Sarah and Jonny both had an early night after a good pasta meal. Time trials, this was just over 50 miles, are quite draining on muscle glycogen. Making sure the muscles are loaded with glycogen, just as with marathon runners, is a good move, and pasta is still one of the best ways to do that.

The other Americans, and James, trotted off to The Chop House for a very English style evening meal. There was a sense of 'after the Lord Mayor's Show', although they were aware that Sarah and Jonny still had unfinished business. The two medics were a little sad to think that their time in Cambridge was coming to an end, but this was counter-balanced by the excitement engendered by reconnecting with their college chums and knowing that they would all soon be together again in the Bay Area, and the friendships were strengthening, rather than weakening, with time. The partnerships, Martha with James, Sarah with Jonny, Sky with Alexis, Ceci with Vincent, Theresa with Lukey, were all serious, but not all consuming. Tim and Iris were just beginning to think about seeing more of each other when they returned to normal life.

Everyone had something important to do with their life before they could even think about permanence in their relationships. The principle of unripe time is one of procrastination, elegantly described by Francis Cornford in his Microcosmographia Academica. For the moment, procrastination was not unwise but, just as Cornford talked about the medlar being a fruit which could rot from the inside before there was evidence of decay on the outside, so too might some of these relationships lose their vitality without any of the parties, involved or observing, recognising the weakening of the bonds. Only time would tell which of these signal pairings had a future. For the moment, they were as they were, comfortable perhaps, or were they exciting? Which of them would finally utter that brilliant line from 'Sleepless in Seattle', 'marriage is hard enough without bringing such low expectations into it'?

At around midnight, Robert went out of his flat and walked to St Joseph's. He took great care to keep a low profile and he made very sure that he avoided as many CCTV cameras as he could. He used the backstreets between Gwydir Street and East Road and then again from East Road to Elm Street. He walked across the grass areas over Parker's Piece and then, avoiding having his features picked up, made his way to the outside walls of St Joseph's. He climbed in, well clear of CCTV surveillance, and wandered round the deserted college grounds looking at the residential block where he knew Sarah, Ceci, and Martha lived.

The lights were on in Martha's room and, having climbed one of the trees on 'The Meadow', he could see, through the window, a dark-haired woman he did not recognise, talking to Martha as they sat in two comfortable looking armchairs. Through another window he could see Ceci and Sarah, also sitting in those comfortable looking armchairs, drinking something, steaming slightly, from college mugs. Robert had previously ascertained that Martha lived in a single occupancy set, so he was a little surprised, but he concluded that this was another American visitor who was staying temporarily in the set with Martha, probably, he hoped so anyway, just for a night or so before the woman went off to Europe for the American version of the 'Grand Tour'. A revenge rape might still be on the cards, it would just need a careful recce before execution.

Robert resolved to come back again tomorrow. He had intended to do so anyway. He had a few final preparations to make.

Chapter 33

The following morning was almost perfect for the time trial. The bicycles were collected from the basement under the conference centre and loaded onto the two club trailers. The rendezvous for the trial was out at Hardwick. All the local clubs, and the university team, provided stewards for the event. These stewards were duly despatched in various support vehicles to man the crucial points along the route. This route is a four lap out and back route mainly along the A428 road.

At 10 am, the first rider went off. The men's race was first, and the forty-eight riders went at 1-minute intervals, as per standard time trial practice. The women's race started at 1 pm, and again the riders were set off at 1-minute intervals.

The winning time was about one hour and forty five minutes for the men and about ten minutes more for the women.

In common with all serious time trial events, the bicycle and the competitors were weighed.

Jonny and Sarah were the first Cambridge cyclists home in their respective races, Jonny was third overall and Sarah second. Given that they were competing against very experienced club racers, as well as a few students, they were very pleased with the outcome. James picked up the results sheet, with all the data on it. Weights, times, calculated speed, split times for the laps, all the data were there.

The Cambridge bicycles were put back in 'The Cage', everyone showered and changed, and then Sarah and Jonny joined their friends, to let their hair down on the first 'out of training' afternoon and evening that they had had for quite a few weeks.

"I want a steak tonight," said Jonny. "Pasta and carbs are all very well but there's nothing like a good steak!"

"Or you could save it for the Stanford Dinner tomorrow night," said Martha. "They usually have seven courses and I bet a substantial bit of meat is part of one of the courses."

"Nah," said Jonny. "I want steak tonight. I reckon that French place, Chez Pierre, is going to do a very good steak-frites. I bet the wine is good too, and Sarah and I missed out last night while you lot were getting a bit smashed."

The same morning as the time trial was the second morning in a row where Vasily was woken from a very disturbed sleep. A team of detectives had kept him awake most of a second night. He was hot and sweaty, they had turned off the ventilation in his holding cell, he stunk of garlic and sweat.

They dragged him into the interview room. The lights were bright and harsh, the room was almost unbearably hot.

"What information did you give Viktor that he could not have obtained any other way?"

"Nothing."

"What information did you give Viktor that he could not have obtained any other way?"

This time, Jerry picked up a hammer and started to bang it on the table.

"In your country, do you break the knuckles first or do you smash the kneecaps?" Jerry leant forward and leered in Vasily's face as he said it.

"I pressed a button on the phone and warned him when you arrested me," said Vasily.

"I didn't ask you that," said Jerry. "What information did you give Viktor that he could not have obtained any other way?"

This time, Jerry smashed the hammer down and made a big hole in the desk, only an inch or so from Vasily's hand.

"I'm leaving this room now," said Jerry. "You have ten minutes to make up your mind to tell us what you told Viktor. Then I'm giving up and sending in MI6. They don't play by any rules."

At this moment, the door opened and a very large and brutal-looking man stuck his head round the door.

"Can I work him over now, Chief?"

"Not yet. He has ten more minutes to make up his mind to talk to us."

"Can I just give him a taster?"

"Well, maybe just a taster."

The brute entered the room, picked Vasily up by the hair and hit him hard, once, in the stomach. Vasily collapsed on the floor.

"Thanks Chief. Do I have to hide the bruises, or can I hit him anywhere I want?"

"If he doesn't talk, he isn't coming out of here, so you can hit him where you like."

Jerry walked out of the room leaving the brute sitting there cracking his knuckles with an annoying sort of regularity.

They got nothing more out of Vasily on the Thursday. The brute tapped him about a bit a few times, but Vasily was saying nothing.

****

The Friday morning followed the third night on which Vasily had been sleep-deprived, Jerry called the team together for a tactical meeting. Jenny Taylor was not present; she was still on protective duty with the girls.

"We lost Ankit and Jason in the bomb at the Senate House, but we did manage to prevent the bomb at the Babbage going off, so that has to be a plus, but we're no nearer finding Jackson, or the Viktor Rubinsky gang, and I think that all our targets are still at risk. The meetings in the Old Schools also went off without incident. I think we were wise to have the precaution of signal jamming but are we going to wander around with Stanislowsky, and jam signals everywhere he goes? Would that be overkill? No pun intended."

Jeff agreed with Jerry.

"They are all still at risk. With all those guys still on the loose, I wonder if we now ought to think more about firearms, and sniper, or small arms based, assassination, especially for Stanislowsky, and, maybe, his son."

"I'm going to ask for some extra help on the case. Experienced bodyguards, and a few snipers to place at strategic points," said Jerry.

"We've got the itinerary for the Americans, and for Stanislowsky, until they leave on Sunday. Let's have a look and see if there's any obvious vulnerability."

They scanned the PowerPoint slide that had the rest of Stanislowsky's calendar on it. The speech before the Stanford dinner stood out as a significant event, because it was a point at which every one of the possible targets was in the same relatively small space, along with the President of Stanford, the Vice-

Chancellor of Cambridge, and only Jerry and a small number of 'need-to-knows' knew this, one of the royal princes.

"Where's the dinner being held?" asked one of the team.

"In the Long Gallery above the cloisters," said Jeff.

"Where's the speech happening beforehand?"

"In the lecture theatre in the conference centre," said Jeff.

"Can we see the plans for these spaces?" asked the same keen voice.

They looked at the plans for the conference centre and for the Long Gallery and cloisters.

"Not much opportunity for a long range shot when they're in the conference centre," said Jerry. "They're really only going to be in the theatre and the reception area, and these have good blackout blinds, and tiny external windows to the street. There are some large windows in the reception area, overlooking the gardens. The nearest high buildings are the college buildings on the street next to the bus station. In line of sight beyond that, there is absolutely nothing high enough to provide a sniper with a shot."

"Gallery is a bit different sir," said one of the women. "Lots of windows onto the main courtyard, but I guess we could deal with that by putting people on the roofs around the Front Court?"

"I guess we could, and we should," said Jerry. "We'll also need guards on the roof of the high building next to the bus station. I know it seems a lot of effort to protect one man, but Stanislowsky is probably the next President of his country, if they can get rid of the undemocratic regime currently in power. I think the Foreign Office would give him a very high priority. He's one of the few friendly politicians in the area, and the area is of high strategic importance."

"I think the dinner is our high-risk event," said Jeff.

"What about the car park in the conference centre basement?" asked the keen one. "Can we request the college to stop anyone parking there? It wouldn't take much to crash through those wooden gates from the street and ram a car bomb into the car park, but it would be equally possible, and a bit more subtle, to move a car bomb in, during routine daily business."

"Good points. I'll phone the senior tutor now and ask him to make sure that all the cars are removed from the building before 5 pm."

"How about jamming radio signals during the talk and the dinner?" asked Jeff.

"Could be difficult. I think they're supposed to be broadcasting the speech to an adjacent building. There's been considerable interest and there's a big overspill. And there are some significant dignitaries there who need to be in constant touch with their governments. I guess we need to just make sure we have cleared the building and we need to run our search again, using the laser and ultrasound."

"We could ask the audio-visual boys to make the link to the adjacent building using hard wiring, they have a fibre optic network. The link doesn't have to be wireless," said Jeff. "I think we should do that, and plan to jam during the reception and lecture. Surely the people who need to be in constant touch can leave a lackey outside with a working phone."

Jamming was agreed and clearing the cars from the building car park was also agreed.

"What about all those bloody bikes?" asked Jeff.

"Except for the university team bikes they look as if they have been there for ages," said Jerry. "Just run the sniffer dogs through and check for bombs."

The Special Branch reinforcements were despatched to trail and protect the significant dignitaries. HRH brought his own bodyguard with him. The car park was emptied of cars and the detail on roof duties was duly briefed. All the buildings were scanned, the panelling in the walls of the Long Gallery, the roof, and the floor, were given great attention. The conference centre was also scanned and only some garden supplies and the bicycles were left in situ. There was nothing else of note found.

Everything was put in place by about 4:30 pm; a temporary crash barrier as defence against a car bomb attack, was put just behind the gates in the forecourt of the conference centre.

Jenny Taylor and the American group were sitting having tea in the Stanford Room. Jonny had brought the results sheet with him and all of them were having a quick look. He also brought the results sheet from the Varsity match, a shorter distance of course, but the different members of the party were interested to see how the two lap splits compared between the two-lap race and the four-lap race, on the same course.

It was not the lap times that caught Sergeant Taylor's eye. It was the bicycle weights. The Cambridge cyclists in the Viking-50 four-lap race, all seemed to have bicycles about 500 grams heavier than when they had raced in the 25 kilometre, two-lap Varsity match a week or two earlier.

Jenny got out her phone and photographed the results sheet.

The Americans went off to get ready for the reception, lecture and dinner.

Jenny Taylor excused herself briefly and, with her charges safely escorted to their rooms to get ready, she called DI Gregory to catch up on events.

DI Gregory explained to Jenny Taylor what had been arranged.

"We've emptied the car park of all cars. The only thing I can see that is left in there are the bicycles, including those flash ones in that bit they call the cage."

"The Cambridge team bikes?" asked Jenny.

"Yeah," said Jerry. "Why do you ask?"

"Well, it looks as if the Cambridge team cycles used yesterday were about half a kilo heavier than when they raced on them two weeks ago. Apparently, there's a minimum weight, for safety reasons, and all competitors' bikes get weighed before every road race or time trial."

"How many bikes are we talking about?" asked Jerry.

"Eight Bikes Sir. Four ladies' and four men's."

"Four kilograms," said Jerry. "Four bloody kilograms. If you were here Jenny, I would hug you, politically incorrect though that might be. I think you may have just saved a lot of lives. I'll call you back."

Jerry slammed down the phone and immediately rang the bomb Squad.

"I know where the rest of the Semtex is. It's in the bicycle frames of the Cambridge cycle team in the basement of the conference centre in the cage. Go get it and be careful. Jam signals while you're working there and do it fast."

Chapter 34

Robert was anticipating the pleasure he would get from exploding the huge combination bomb, composed of Semtex from the eight bicycles, and the garden supplies which he had sneaked into the gardeners' store. The ammonium nitrate and other simple chemicals that are over the counter purchases had been placed in position during one of the visits he had made to deliver bicycles for Sean. He had been most careful to find a place where the Faraday Cage like skeleton of the conference centre allowed a phone signal through. That was what he had done when he had delivered some bicycles a few weeks earlier. Last night, the Thursday night, after watching the girls going to bed, he had gone down to the car park in the conference centre and arranged the bicycles, and the fertiliser, and the rest of the material, into a bomb quite capable of blowing the building to pieces. He was confident that, having just finished their time trial, the keen cyclists would not be moving their bikes again for a couple of days. The attraction of socialising with their friends would be far greater than the desire for yet another bicycle ride.

The main frames of the bicycles contained the Semtex, which he had put in there when they had dropped the cycles off at Sean's Cycle Emporium, after the Varsity match. He had sneaked back at night to do it when Sean was not there. The electronic detonators were mounted in some of the eight machines, and he had arranged alternative connections between the machines so that any one of them detonating would set off a chain reaction. He was able to use the bicycle locks and the fabric of the bicycle stands to connect the machines together as a single unit, and he was able to link them, through a hole made in the door of the gardeners' store, to the fertiliser bomb he had created inside the shed. It was hidden behind the door of the store, behind the GrowOrganic and some hessian sacks. He placed a final small quantity of Semtex, and his last detonator, on top of the fertiliser bomb.

He had decided to move a little closer to the action this time. He had booked into the hotel next to Parker's Piece and left his luggage there. He was standing on Parkers Piece, hoping to see the results of his handiwork.

The lecture began on schedule at 6 pm, and Robert sent the trigger signal at 6:15 pm, and again and again. His language was just a little bit bad. If they had managed to defuse that bomb too, there was nothing left to do but get out as quickly as he could, but he was going to have one last attack on that daughter of his, and that little teaser, Martha, who had started him on the journey, and this time he was going to finish the job. They had to die.

He had plenty of money, and back to America was where he was headed.

The assembled company in the conference centre moved serenely through the proceedings, completely unaware that a bomb big enough to take out the building and half the bus station in the street outside, had been safely defused.

They were also unaware of the activity on the roof tops around Front Court when they finally moved up into the gallery for the dinner. It seemed that Viktor's gang had decided that discretion was the better part of valour and had retreated to plan for another day. There was certainly no attempt to use the roof tops around the courtyard to fire bullets at Stanislowsky or his son.

Jerry and Jeff retreated to the police station. They alerted the surveillance teams at the bus and train stations to watch out for Jackson. The description was not great; but they had his height and build, and the various pictures from the States and from the girls' police sketches, and they reasoned that he would be travelling alone. There would not be a lot of passengers going to London on a Friday night,, but tomorrow morning there would be a huge exodus from Cambridge, of people travelling to London to sight-see, or go to the theatre, or otherwise enjoy the delights of the Capital. They also alerted the airports and ferry ports, just in case Jackson went through, and they gave the immigration officials the most up to date passport picture of Jackson, the false passport he had mocked up for Canada.

"I bet he's going to be too smart to use that picture, and he'll have changed his hair colour and facial hair by now. But this is the best we can do," said Jerry.

Jenny Taylor remained on duty. It was a pleasant duty, rewarded with an excellent dinner and some excellent conversation. Sergeant Taylor was beginning to enjoy the academic way of life.

When Jerry told Vasily that the third bomb had been defused, and there was now no more Semtex unaccounted for, Vasily finally cracked and started to talk.

Once he started there was no stopping him. He explained that he had informed Viktor about the Stanford Dinner and that Stanislowsky would be attending. He gave the names of all the members of Viktor's gang, and he explained that he, Vasily, had instructions to kill Sean O'Connor and Robert Jackson on completion of their mission to blow up Stanislowsky.

"Well," said Jerry. "That ain't going to happen now!"

The brute asked Vasily how he was supposed to find Jackson to kill him.

Vasily explained that he was supposed to meet Jackson to hand over the second tranche of the money that had been promised to O'Connor and Jackson for completion of the job. Instead of handing over the money he was supposed to kill them both.

"Where were you going to meet them?" asked the brute.

"I was going to take them out at the cycle shop, but Viktor didn't trust Jackson, he thought he was very clever, so I had a backup for him. Viktor put a tracer in the Semtex parcel, and we found out where Jackson was living. The tracer went from the shop back to this flat in Gwydir Street. I was going to go round to Jackson's flat and take him out there."

A couple of further questions, punctuated with a little more pain, and they had the exact address.

It was around midnight when they finally got the information they wanted and by the time the firearms unit got to the flat in Gwydir Street, Jackson had long gone. It took them several minutes to enter the flat. Dealing with a bomber, they were reasonably certain that he would have set some booby traps. They used fibre optic cameras to scan the interior before they attempted to open the door. Indeed, they decided not to open the door but to make a hole in the wall and enter through that. Contact and circuit break detonators are easy to set up, and with Jackson's training in San Quentin, they were confident he would have been able to set up a simple explosive trigger like that. Besides which, they were still missing about 300 grams of Semtex. This time the sniffer dogs were able to find the explosive, Jackson had not attempted to conceal it; he had not seen a need to do so. The bomb squad defused it *in situ*. The detonation would have been triggered by the opening of the door.

The forensic team moved in. There was plenty for them to find, including DNA. No difficulty at all in proving that Jackson had been there. Over the next few days there would be lots of routine police work, questioning of neighbours and examining of physical evidence, but for the moment it was a case of trying to find Jackson before he could do any serious damage to his targets.

He had smashed his computer and had mutilated the hard disc, but they took it anyway and handed it over to the experts to see if they could extract any information from the disc. It would be a very long job, even if it were possible.

Robert did not like loose ends. He still viewed Ravinder as a loose end, and he knew that Ravinder had a car. Ravinder's car, and Ravinder dead, seemed to Robert a good way of tying up at least one more loose end.

He knew where Ravinder lived because he had followed him home, what seemed now, a long time ago.

For the moment, the hotel seemed like a very safe place. He had made the booking some days ago so that it would not appear suspicious, even if the police did think to look at local hotels for recent arrivals. He had checked in as a local, using a false address in London and yet another false id and credit card to guarantee the booking. He had plans.

He put his night climbing gear into his backpack, along with his Bear Grylls knife and his duct tape, and went out, after a leisurely supper, to await the onset of darkness. He had the route into college well sorted by now, this would be his third clandestine entry in as many days. He had also decided which of the girls he was going to attack, and how he was going to manage the double occupancy of the suite of rooms. He was going to use flunitrazepam, Rohypnol, and he was going to use a very big dose of it. He had noticed that Sarah and Ceci had a habit of drinking a cup of hot milky chocolate, at least they had done so on both the nights when he had observed them. That should do it. Get the Rohypnol into the hot chocolate tin and wait for it to take effect. Those years in San Quentin had taught him a lot about breaking into rooms and these old buildings had, somehow, not been upgraded to proper electronic security. Listed buildings can sometimes continue to have antediluvial technology.

While the revellers were still at their dinner in the Long Gallery, Robert Jackson climbed over the wall, changed into his night camouflage, and hid his backpack in the shrubbery near the pond next to The Meadow. The staircase door was still unlocked at this time of night, and so it was only the inner doors that needed lock picking. He looked for the hot chocolate tin and ladled a rather excessive amount of the Rohypnol into the tin and mixed it all up. He put everything back carefully and retreated to wait his chance.

The girls came back, with Sergeant Taylor, just after midnight, at about the time that the detectives were entering Robert's flat in Gwydir Street. Robert saw Jenny Taylor taking a call on her telephone. It was, in fact, a call to inform her that Robert Jackson had evaded capture and was now on the run.

The four young women sat up talking until about 1:30 am, then Sarah and Ceci made hot chocolate. Three cups of it, and shortly after that the lights went out, in both sets of rooms.

At 2:30 am, Robert Jackson came down from the tree in The Meadow and went over to the Cumberland Building. At this time of night, the porters had done their evening rounds and had locked the staircase doors. The doors were on one of those systems where a key could lock and open from outside and, from inside, there was a simple gnarled knob that allowed anyone, without a key, to open the door immediately. Robert simply picked the lock with standard lock picking tools that he had bought online. He crept quietly up the stairs and opened the door to the set normally occupied by Sarah and Ceci.

He sat, for a moment, in one of the very comfortable old leather armchairs, savouring the thought that he was shortly to rape not one, but two, possibly even more, very beautiful young women. Sarah would be revenge, at least that was how his distorted and depraved mind saw it, but Ceci would simply be a bonus for him. And then off back to America, via Buenos Aries; not, as the police might have guessed, Canada.

He listened carefully at both bedroom doors and heard nothing but quiet breathing, with the rhythm of sleep.

'Sarah first,' he thought to himself. 'The little Chinese girl can wait.'

The little moonlight that there was showed up clearly the short hair and shorter frame of the Chinese American girl, Ceci. Robert closed the door quietly and moved back to the door behind which he believed that Sarah was sleeping a drugged sleep. He took out his duct tape, might just as well be sure that there is no noise, and his Bear Grylls knife. He opened the blade. He saw the mass of blonde hair on the pillow.

He prepared the duct tape and placed it in the palm of his hand and then slapped it firmly in place over the mouth of his victim.

"I've come for you, Sarah," he said.

Chapter 35

Things did not work out quite how Jackson had planned. He was amazed to find that his intended victim's eyes opened instantly and, rather than being passive and dazed, she immediately sprang into life. She sat up rapidly, threw off the bedclothes and leapt out of bed. She grabbed the bedside table lamp and, while Jackson stood there in shock, she smashed him over the head with it. It did not knock him unconscious, but it dazed him long enough for Martha, for it was she who had decided to spend a night sleeping in the same set as Ceci, to collect her wits and turn on the main light and rip the duct tape off her mouth.

"Not this time, Jackson," she said. "This time, I take *you* out."

Jackson had no doubt that he could handle this girl in front of him, but Martha had taken many self-defence courses and had continued to remain physically ready to deal with any attempted assault.

She smashed the fire alarm glass, just beside the light switch near the bedroom door.

"They're coming for you, Jackson," said Martha.

"You're supposed to be drugged," said Jackson, a little bewildered. "I put Rohypnol in the chocolate."

"Bad luck, Mr Jackson," said Martha. "I hate hot chocolate, except with lashings of whipped cream, and I only drink that when I'm sitting outside a cafe in California sunshine."

Deciding not to wait for the police and concerned lest Jackson should decide to use his knife, Martha continued to hang onto the table lamp.

"You look pathetic, Mr Jackson," she said. "You have blood running down your face. When you go back to prison, you're going to be everyone's plaything, especially if they hear that a mere girl beat you up, and I *will* make sure that they do. You shouldn't have raped me, and you certainly shouldn't have raped my friend. You shouldn't have raped anyone. You sick bastard, you were planning to rape your own daughter. I despise you, you little man."

Jackson's eyes became wild, and he started to advance on Martha, who remained balanced on the balls of her feet, dancing away from him and, having put down the table lamp, holding her arms in a martial arts defensive pose.

Martha was very confident she could have taken him out completely, but she never had the chance to find out. She managed to get in a few blows to his head, with her kick boxing technique, and a very hard kick to his testicles. The latter gave her enormous pleasure, as he dropped his knife and curled up in pain on the floor, just as the porters and the fire brigade arrived. One of the porters, a huge and powerful man, picked up Jackson from the floor, with one hand, and hit him hard in the stomach with the other. Jackson now had painful testicles, and a painful abdomen. Big George threw Jackson on the floor and called the porters' lodge on his radio. A few fit-looking firemen also entered the rooms.

"Get the police please, Debs," Big George said to the other night porter. "Send them up to the Stanford Set. Make it quick, I think we have an attempted rape, at least a robbery."

Martha could not help herself; she was so angry. With Jackson lying on the floor, still with his face covered in blood, she went up to him and stuck her face right in front of his.

"You deserve this, Jackson," she said.

She stepped back.

"Close your eyes," she said to everyone in the room, "I want you to be able to tell the truth when this gets to court. I want you to be able to say you didn't see anything."

They did as she asked.

"This is for Theresa," said Martha, she kicked him hard again in the testicles. There was a scream.

"This is for me." Another hard kick followed, and another scream.

"And this is for all the hurt and misery you have caused Sarah and your family." A final kick and a scream, which gave way to hysterical sobbing.

"You can open your eyes now," said Martha. "I think Mr Jackson hurt himself on the arm of the chair. Both of us are very lucky that the porters got here in time, Jackson" she said. "I think I would have killed you. You would have been dead and even though I would have claimed self-defence, I would have been a murderess. I'm glad I'm not. I think you might not be so glad. I think you might come to wish that you were dead. You killed two policemen, you've committed two known rapes, and this was an attempted rape, and of your own

236

daughter too. I think you will never see freedom again. And I'm very pleased about that."

The ambulance came quickly, and Martha told the paramedics what Jackson had said about using Rohypnol to render the other three women unconscious. The interaction of Rohypnol with alcohol is a dangerous one, greatly increasing the likelihood of serious side effects of overdose. It was clear that for all three women, the level of respiration and the blood pressure were severely depressed. They were blue-lighted to Addenbrookes and immediately put into the intensive care unit.

Nobody bothered to rush the treatment of Jackson, although he was bleeding from the gash on his head, and into his scrotum, where Martha had kicked him, or rather, as everyone present said, where he had caught himself on the arm of the chair.

A few minutes later, Jerry Gregory and Jeff Glover arrived. They had come straight from the search of Jackson's flat. Forensics moved into the student room and took the tin of chocolate for analysis. There was no doubt but that it would contain flunitrazepam, in copious amounts.

It was two days later before the three doping victims were able to leave hospital. There was a grand reunion of all the Americans. Martha was a hero. Jackson's backpack had been found by a student and handed in to the porter's lodge. The head porter had immediately recognised its significance and called the police.

The next morning, Jerry Gregory and Jeff Glover reflected on their conduct of the case. They had got away with it, but there had been a massive element of luck in it. There were still loose ends. Stanislowsky was still alive, but his potential assassins were still at liberty, and no doubt there would be further attempts on his life. If Jackson had decided to flee Cambridge immediately after the failed third bomb, then they would probably not have caught him. The escape plans and the documentation found in the backpack were clever and would have succeeded. Having been blonde originally, and dark-haired for his duration in Cambridge, Jackson was going redhead for the trip to Buenos Aries. No routine inspection by an immigration official would have picked him out as suspicious.

A couple of days later, DI Gregory discovered that his application for transfer to a DCI position in a nearby town had been approved. Jeff Glover was promoted to Inspector and Jenny Taylor was seconded for special duties. Her intelligence and intuition deserved special nurturing.

At the end of the following week, most of the young Americans began the Grand Tour. Brussels, then Paris, then a whole host of other cities and cultures. Alexis went along with them. He and Sky were now very close. Theresa went home after Paris; Lukey, the only one in paid employment, had come to the end of his holiday allowance, and Theresa went with him to keep him company. Sarah and Jonny were staying in Cambridge. They were moving into a flat together and it would be a great base, and a great magnet, for Theresa and Lukey to complete the Grand Tour on another occasion.

The trial of Jackson took place at the end of the summer. His 'accident with the chair' had caused him to rupture one testicle, which had to be removed, and it took a month before he was fit to stand trial. The trial, and conviction, were followed immediately by an extradition request. The Home Secretary took less than ten seconds to decide that the extradition was warranted. Jackson was on his way back to San Quentin. He would never be released. True to her word, Martha made sure that a letter was sent to several of the inmates welcoming Robert Jackson back to the fold. His life in San Quentin was a complete misery, no Eddie this time to protect him; and the effects of his beating by Martha, and his incarceration in the United Kingdom, had left him weak and relatively defenceless. This time, he was not put into the special wing for sexual offenders but was simply locked up with all the other prisoners. Eighteen months later, he was found hanged in his cell. The coroner for San Quentin returned an open verdict. Normal inmates do not really like rapists, especially when the rape is of younger women or even children.

That late summer and early autumn were beautiful in California. Martha and Ceci began their medical course in UCSF. Theresa and Sky went back to their courses at UC Berkeley, Lukey continued his job, with rapid progress up the career ladder. The younger siblings, Tim, Vinnie, and Iris went back to undergraduate study. James took up his permanent post at Stanford. Alexis applied for a graduate programme at Berkeley and, while awaiting the outcome of his application, moved in with Sky in an apartment in Rockridge, very near to where Lukey and Theresa were living. Only Sarah and Jonny, continuing with their Ph.D. studies at Cambridge, were missing from the ice-cream reunion, this time held in Sausalito at a sea-front restaurant.

In time, the memories of Cambridge would become blurred by wishful thinking, as so many memories do, but for now, the memories were fresh and vibrant and exciting. With Sarah and Jonny still at St Joseph's, it was inevitable that all of the group would go back for further visits. Lukey and Theresa still had a lot of Europe to see, the others had simply come to love the quiet and ancient beauty of the town and the college.

What was it that the senior tutor had said as they attended the final dinner of the academic year at St Joseph's:

"You have been with us a rather short time, but you will always be a part of us, and we will always be a part of you. We will welcome you back with open arms whenever you can visit, and we are grateful for what you have given us. We only hope that we have given you something in return that you will treasure forever."